V.L. McDermid

Val McDermid grew up in Kirkcaldy on the east coast of Scotland, then read English at Oxford. She was a journalist for sixteen years, spending the last three years as Northern Bureau Chief of a national Sunday tabloid. Now a full-time writer, she divides her time between Cheshire and Northumberland.

Union Jack is the fourth of six novels featuring journalist-sleuth Lindsay Gordon (the fifth, *Booked for Murder*, was shortlisted for the Lambda award). Val is also the author of the Kate Brannigan series and four tense psychological thrillers featuring criminal profiler Tony Hill. The first of these, *The Mermaids Singing*, was awarded the 1995 Gold Dagger Award for Best Crime Novel of the Year, while the second, *The Wire in the Blood*, lends its name to the acclaimed ITV series featuring Robson Green as Tony Hill. She has also written three stand-alone thrillers: *A Place of Execution*, *Killing the Shadows* and *The Distant Echo*.

For more information see Val's website
www.valmcdermid.com

By the same author

The Distant Echo
Killing the Shadows
A Place of Execution

TONY HILL THRILLERS
The Torment of Others
The Last Temptation
The Wire in the Blood
The Mermaids Singing

KATE BRANNIGAN NOVELS
Star Struck
Blue Genes
Clean Break
Crack Down
Kick Back
Dead Beat

LINDSAY GORDON NOVELS
Hostage to Murder
Booked for Murder
Final Edition
Common Murder
Report for Murder

NON-FICTION
A Suitable Job for a Woman

V.L. McDermid

Union Jack

HarperCollins*Publishers*

HarperCollins*Publishers*
77–85 Fulham Palace Road,
London, W6 8JB

The HarperCollins website address is:
www.harpercollins.co.uk

First published in Great Britain by
The Women's Press Ltd 1993

This paperback edition published 2004

1

ISBN: 978-0-00-787983-0

Set in Meridien by Palimpsest Book Production Limited,
Polmont, Stirlingshire

Printed and bound by Clays Ltd, St Ives plc

NOTE TO READERS

For the best part of a decade, I was an active member of the National Union of Journalists, holding a variety of posts at local and national level. During that time, I was elected as one of Manchester's representatives for several Annual Delegate Meetings. My experiences in the union provided me with the knowledge that underpins this book. But I should emphasise that neither the events nor the characters in *Union Jack* are even remotely based in fact. The truth is that, just as thousands of delegates to union conferences have told their spouses, we spent our time in earnest debate, working tirelessly to improve the lot of our members. If we looked worn out by the time we returned home, it was simply because of the energy we had expended in passionate argument. Would I lie to you?

On a more serious note, I'd like to thank the many fellow trade unionists who became friends over those years for their help, conscious and unconscious, in the preparation of this book. These include Sue Jackson and Kerttu Kinsler, Diana Muir, Scarlett MccGwire, Gina Weissand, Malcolm Pain, Eugenie Verney, Nancy Jaeger, Pauline Norris, Sally Gilbert, Colin Bourne, Tim Gopsill and Dick Oliver. Most of all, I want to thank BB, who gave me inspiration when I needed it most.

Any resemblance to real people, living or dead, is purely in the mind of the reader.

For BB:
Good things come to she who waits

PROLOGUE
Mid-Atlantic, April 1993

'I could murder some proper orange juice,' Lindsay Gordon grumbled, wrinkling her nose in disgust at the plastic cup of juice on her airline breakfast tray. She sipped suspiciously. It managed to be both sharp and sickly at the same time. 'You know, something that tastes like it once met an orange. This stuff hasn't even been shown a photograph.'

'You'd better get used to it,' Sophie Hartley said, peeling the lid back from her own cup and knocking back the liquid. She winced. 'Not that it'll be easy. Think you can survive two weeks without freshly squeezed juice?'

Lindsay shrugged. 'Who knows? If it was only the juice . . .'

Sophie snorted. 'Hark at it. This is the woman whose idea of healthy eating used to be adding a tin of baked beans to bacon, sausage, egg and chips. Listen, Gordon, you can't come the California health freak with me. I can remember

1

when the nearest thing to fruit juice in your flat was elderberry wine.'

'Huh,' Lindsay grunted. 'Don't get superior with me just because you used to eat your vegetables raw even though you could afford the gas bill. Anyway, I'm not a California health freak. It would take more than a bunch of New Age born-again hippies to change Lindsay Gordon, let me tell you. First thing I'm going to do when I get off this plane is head for a chip shop and get tore in to a fish supper.'

Sophie shook her head, smiling. 'You can't fool me, Gordon. Three years in California and you're working out, eating salad twice a day, swallowing vitamins like Smarties, even wearing jumpers made from reclaimed wool. You're a California girl now, like it or not.'

Lindsay shuddered. 'Rubbish. The odd jog up the beach, that's all, and I was doing that long before America.'

Sophie grinned affectionately at her lover, and wisely held her peace.

'Ladies and gentlemen, we are now commencing our descent into Glasgow Airport. Please return to your seats and fasten your seat-belts. Please extinguish all smoking materials . . .'

'Looking forward to it?'

Lindsay shrugged. 'Yes and no. I've been out of the game a long time. I'm not sure I even know what the issues are for trade unionists in the UK any longer.'

Sophie squeezed her hand. 'It'll be just fine.'

Lindsay smiled. 'Shouldn't it be me saying that to you, Dr Hartley? You're the one delivering a keynote paper at an international conference.'

'Play your cards right at this media conference, and you'll be a doctor soon too. Pick the right brains for your thesis, and they'll be begging you to accept a Ph.D.'

Lindsay pulled a face. 'I'm not so sure. I'm not even sure I've still got the old interview techniques. Teaching journalism's a long way away from practising it.'

'You'll be fine,' Sophie assured her. 'You'll soon adapt to being back in the old routine. After all, you'll be among friends.'

Lindsay gave a shout of laughter that turned heads three rows away. 'Among friends? At a union conference? Soph, I'd feel safer in the lion's cage half an hour before feeding time. One thing I'll never be able to forget is the aggro level of Journalists' Union conferences. You'd think we were arguing over life and death, not politics. I can't imagine that amalgamating with the broadcasting and printing unions has made the atmosphere any friendlier. It's not culture shock I'm afraid of – it's being trapped in a time warp.'

PART ONE

Blackpool, April 1984

1

'Delegates are discouraged from travelling to conference by private car, and mileage expenses will only be paid in extraordinary circumstances. This is because, firstly, the union has negotiated a bulk-rate discount with British Rail; secondly, there are limited car-parking facilities available at the hotels we are using; and thirdly, the chances are that when driving home on Friday afternoon at the end of conference you will still be over the limit from Thursday night's excesses. It is not the union's policy to encourage members to lose their licences due to drink-driving.'

from *'Advice for New Delegates'*,
a Standing Orders Sub-Committee booklet.

'This traffic's murder,' Ian Ross complained, easing the car forward another couple of feet. 'Look at it,' he added, waving his arm at the sea of hot metal that surrounded them.

Lindsay Gordon did as she was told, for once.

7

In the distance, Blackpool Tower's iron tracery stood outlined against the skyline like an Eiffel Tower souvenir on a mantelpiece. 'Only the Journalists' Union could organise a conference that involves 400 delegates travelling to the biggest holiday resort in the North of England on Easter Monday,' he remarked caustically. 'Bloody Blackpool. It's taken us an hour to travel six miles. By the time we get to the hotel, the conference will be over and it'll be time to come home. I bet you wish you'd taken the train, don't you? You could have been walking along the prom by now, eating candy-floss and wearing a kiss-me-quick hat.' Ian glanced sideways and saw the bleak look on Lindsay's face. He sighed. 'Sorry, love. I wasn't thinking.'

'It's okay. I've told you. You don't have to treat me like a piece of porcelain.' An awkward silence filled the car. Lindsay patted Ian's hand and repeated, 'It's okay.'

Ian nodded. 'Time for *The World At One*. Shall I stick the radio on?'

'Sure.' Lindsay leaned back in her seat and tried to let the radio obliterate her thoughts.

'A hundred arrests are made in Nottinghamshire and Derbyshire in the worst violence of the miners' strike so far. Police clash with miners outside several collieries, and NUM leader Arthur Scargill accuses officers of intimidation. Anti-apartheid protesters besiege the Home Office after last week's decision to grant

British citizenship to the South African runner Zola Budd. And Senator Gary Hart fights to continue his campaign against Walter Mondale for the Democratic nomination in the US Presidential race.' The announcer's voice droned on, fleshing out the day's headlines. But Lindsay's mind was already miles away.

It had been a mistake to come. She had been too easily persuaded by Ian. She wasn't ready for this. It was hard enough coping with the day to day routine of life, a routine that was manageable precisely because it was familiar, because her mind could drift off into free-fall while she gave the appearance of being in touch with what was going on around her. But to plunge into something so strange and challenging as her first national union conference was madness. It had been bad enough just reading about conference. She'd had to give up on the 'Advice for New Delegates' booklet half-way through, her head spinning with such bizarre and diverse items as 'taking a motion seriatim' and 'compositing sessions'. How on earth was she going to wrestle with the real thing with only half her brain functioning?

Ian had meant well, she knew that. He was a news sub-editor on the tabloid newspaper where Lindsay, at twenty-five, was the most junior staff reporter. When she had started to show an interest in the union, speaking up at the meetings of the *Daily Nation*'s office chapel, it was Ian who had taken the time to explain to her how their union functioned in national newspapers. He had spent the weary, slow hours of several night-shifts outlining the organisation and the internal politics that governed the union far more than the rule book.

Lindsay, who had learned about socialism and solidarity from her fisherman father as soon as she could grasp the concepts, was bemused by the schisms and hierarchies of what she had naïvely imagined would be an organisation unified by a common aim. It didn't take her long to decide that the entrenched power of the national newspaper chapels generated its own in-built conservatism, and that the real arenas for potential change within the union lay elsewhere. The radical concepts of feminism and genuinely representative democracy that were dear to her were clearly never going to find fertile soil in this sector of the industry. Here traditions had provided the hacks with a comfort zone where they could all be good old boys together, and to hell with troublesome dykes, poofs, women, jungle bunnies and cripples.

That complacency placed the *Daily Nation*'s chapel high on Lindsay's list of institutions in need of a short, sharp shock. But before she could do anything about it, she'd been overtaken by events that had rendered the Journalists' Union as significant as a speck of dust in a rainstorm. In the weeks that had followed, Ian had tried to take

10

her mind off her own problems by involving her in the JU, but she couldn't have cared less. When he'd tried to jog her out of her misery by arranging for her to be elected as one of the Fleet Street Branch's dozen delegates to the Annual Delegate Conference, she'd simply let herself be carried along with the tide.

Frances. It would all be all right if Frances was still with her. They could have laughed about these codes and rituals that made the Freemasons sound rational. Frances would have worked through the agenda with her, discussing the 246 motions. She and Frances would have snuggled up in bed together, giggling over the strange injunctions in the advice booklet. And Lindsay would have had the anticipation of nightly phone calls to keep her going through the difficulties of the days. She wouldn't be going through this state of semi-panic that seemed to grip her all the time.

But Frances wasn't ever going to be with her again. Lindsay knew that getting used to that idea was the hardest thing she'd ever have to face. No more Frances at the breakfast table, frowning over *The Times'* law reports, or, if she was due in court, taking a last-minute look through her brief for the day. No more meeting for a snatched lunchtime drink in one of the dozens of pubs between the *Daily Nation's* Fleet Street offices and the law courts. No more sitting on the press benches, watching Frances on her feet defending her client, face stern beneath the barrister's absurd

11

curly wig. No more coming home from a hard day's news reporting to sit on the side of the bath sipping dry white wine while Frances luxuriated in the suds and they swapped stories. No more Frances.

It wasn't self-pity. At least, she didn't think it was. It was the difficulty of adjusting to absence. Someone who had been there was no longer around. And it had left a Frances-shaped hole in her life that sometimes felt as if it would engulf her and drain the very life from her. That was the worst feeling of all. The pain of loss, a physical stab in the chest that sometimes made her gasp, that was bad enough. But the hollowness, that was the worst.

With a start, Lindsay realised that Ian was speaking. 'I'm sorry?' she said.

'That lot,' Ian said, gesturing with his thumb at the radio. 'Bloody coppers on their horses, acting like the Cossack army. The writing's on the wall, Lindsay. This government isn't going to stand for any sort of trade union activity, you mark my words.' When he was angry, Ian's Salford accent always reemerged from the southern patina it had acquired over ten years of working in London. The thickness of his accent was a rough guide to the level of his anger. Right now, he sounded like a refugee from *Coronation Street*.

'Before Thatcher's finished with us, she'll have the Combination Acts back on the statute book.

A few years from now, we'll all be arrested for conspiracy if we try to hold a chapel meeting,' he continued.

Lindsay sighed and reached for her cigarettes. 'It's so short-sighted,' she said. 'The government's always telling us about the wonderful economic success of the Germans, about how they don't have strikes. It never seems to occur to them that that's because the German bosses consult the workforce before they embark on anything that affects them. But this government doesn't want consultation, they want confrontation.'

'Yeah, but only on their terms. As soon as journalists try to confront them with the hard questions about what's happening in this country, they slam the shutters down. Look at the hassle they've been giving the BBC!' Ian exploded. Then, suddenly, he fell silent, mouth clamped shut, the muscles standing out against the sharp line of his jaw.

'I suppose it's keeping Laura busy,' Lindsay said uncertainly, assuming Ian's silence was somehow connected to his lover, Laura Craig. Laura was employed by the JU to organise union activities in the broadcasting sector. The government's recent ham-fisted efforts at censorship and control had given her several thorny problems to deal with. Lindsay had often heard Ian complain that he hardly saw her these days.

'I suppose it is,' he said coldly. A slight gap in the traffic opened up, and Ian accelerated jerkily to take advantage of it. As he drew close to the car in front, he braked sharply enough to throw them both against their seat-belts. 'Sorry,' he muttered, running a hand through his thick, straight salt-and-pepper hair.

'Problems?' Lindsay asked with sinking heart. She had enough on her own plate without having to bother with someone else's hard time, she thought bitterly. But Ian was a friend. She felt obliged to give him the opening.

'You could say that.' The news programme ended, and the jaunty signature tune of *The Archers* jangled in their ears. Ian's hand shot out and twisted the volume knob as far down as it would go. 'She's moved out,' he said softly in the sudden peace. His grey eyes stared straight ahead.

Lindsay tried out various responses in her head. 'When?' 'Why?' 'I never liked her anyway.' 'Is there . . . someone else?' She settled for, 'Oh, Ian. Poor you. What happened?' It seemed to combine solicitude with support. Please God, he wouldn't feel like telling her.

At first, it seemed as if Lindsay's prayer had been answered. Ian said nothing, simply concentrating on the road and the car in front. They started moving again, and, miraculously, whatever had been clogging the traffic vanished. Within minutes, the engine was in third gear, the tower was growing taller and Ian had become talkative. 'You know how you think you know someone? You feel comfortable with them? You could see yourself spending the rest of your life with them? Well, that's how it was with me and Laura,' he said.

And me and Frances, Lindsay echoed mentally. 'You seemed to get on so well together,' she said.

Ian gave a hollow laugh. 'Just shows how blind you can be, doesn't it? What a mug.' He took a deep breath, then broke into a fit of coughing. As he recovered, his hand went out automatically to the glove box. He opened it and took out a blue plastic tube with an angled end which he put in his mouth. Lindsay tried not to look as if she was paying attention as he used the inhaler and chucked it back in the glove box.

'Is my cigarette bothering you?' she asked.

Ian shook his head, holding his breath. He let the air out in a controlled gasp. 'Cigarette smoke doesn't set my asthma off. Now, if you were wearing Rive Gauche or you had a dog at home, I'd have to strap you to the roof-rack. Poor Laura could never treat herself to a new perfume without consulting me first. Oh well, that's one thing she won't have to worry about any more.'

The bitterness in his tone shocked Lindsay. It seemed so alien from Ian, that most gentle of men. It was hard to square with the devoted adoration he'd always displayed when he'd talked about Laura in the past. He was one of those men who carry photographs of their lovers and find the most tenuous excuses to pull them out of their wallets and display them. Long before she'd

15

ever met Laura in the flesh, Lindsay had seen Laura in Greece, Laura in Scotland, Laura on horseback, Laura in a sailing dinghy, Laura in evening dress and Laura asleep.

'When did all this happen? You haven't mentioned it at work,' Lindsay said.

'I could do without the snide jokes. Worse than that, the pity,' Ian said. He wasn't misjudging their colleagues, Lindsay thought sadly. 'I threw her out three weeks ago last Saturday,' he added.

He threw *her* out. It took a moment for Lindsay to grasp what Ian had said. Given his devotion, it could only mean Laura had been seeing someone else and Ian had found out. With her looks, and the force of her personality, she couldn't have been short of other offers. And although you'd go a long way before you found a kinder man than Ian, not even his own mother would have described his sharp features, beaky nose and long, skinny body as handsome. Lindsay had occasionally wondered what had attracted them to each other in the first place. Laura Craig was a woman who liked beautiful things, if her clothes and jewellery were anything to go by. But Ian wasn't given to superficial judgements so Lindsay had always thought that must mean that there was more to Laura than the stylish, hard-edged exterior she presented to the world. She flicked a sidelong glance at Ian. His mouth was clamped shut, his lips a thin line. Clearly, he didn't want to dissect what had happened. Lindsay breathed a silent sigh of relief. The sordid details of Laura's infidelity she could do without.

The car had slowed again as they reached the centre of the town. The pavements were thronged with day-trippers, enjoying the brief moments of sunshine that escaped from the drift of cloud. Like any British Bank Holiday crowd, people were dressed for extremes. It was either cap-sleeved T-shirts or macs as far as the eye could see.

'The street map's in the glove box,' Ian told her as they emerged on the Golden Mile in all its tacky glory. Ian turned north, the tram-lines and the sea wall to the left, the endless string of cheap hotels, amusement arcades, Gifte Shoppes, pubs and fast food outlets to their right.

Lindsay studied the photostat sheet that had been enclosed in their delegates' fact pack. Efficient as ever, Ian had marked the Princess Alice hotel with a red cross. Lindsay checked the name of the next side street they passed.

'About another mile to go, I'd say,' she estimated. The Golden Mile's attractions petered out, giving way to more hotels, boarding houses, and bed and breakfast establishments. 'There it is,' Lindsay said at last, pointing to a huge red brick edifice whose five storeys looked forbiddingly over the grey Irish Sea. 'It looks more like a Victorian asylum than a hotel.'

'Couldn't be more appropriate for a JU conference, as you'll discover soon enough,' Ian replied. 'And as you've probably noticed from the map, it's conveniently situated only two miles from the conference centre itself. Bloody hell,' he exclaimed as he pulled off the road on the forecourt. 'They weren't joking when they said there was limited car-parking, were they?' The whole area in front of the hotel was asphalted over to provide spaces for cars, but it had clearly never been a majestic sweep of lawn to start with. Ian inched forward, looking for a space.

'Over there. Right by the wall, look, someone's pulling out,' Lindsay said. Ian shot forward and squeezed his Ford Escort into the narrow gap.

'Well spotted,' he said, opening his door and getting out. He raised his arms in a long stretch and yawned. Then he opened his eyes and froze. 'Jesus Christ. What the hell is she playing at?' he whispered.

Lindsay turned to look at the woman who had caught his eye. Laura Craig strode up the short drive of the hotel, wavy brown hair lacquered solid against the whipping westerly wind. But Laura wasn't alone.

2

'Delegates are reminded that their duty is to follow debates and cast votes on behalf of their members. However appealing the bars, cafés, fringe meetings, gossip sessions and members of your gender of choice, the conference hall is where you should be. We know it can be boring; we even know of delegates who prefer hanging around at Standing Orders Sub-Committee rather than staying in the hall. In the interests of preserving your SOS members' sanity, please do not attend our sessions unless you are entitled to a voice [see SO5(b)(ii) and Footnote xiv]. Flattered though we are to be the centre of delegates' attention, this does not help the smooth flow of conference order papers!'

from 'Advice for New Delegates',
a Standing Orders Sub-Committee booklet.

Lindsay sighed. In spite of sitting up past midnight ploughing through the final conference agenda, with all its proposed amendments, she still hadn't a clue what this discussion was about. She was sitting on the margin of a group of a dozen delegates arguing with Brian Robinson, the Standing Orders Sub-Committee member responsible for preparing the industrial relations order-paper.

As Brian wiped his perspiring pink face with a flamboyant silk handkerchief, Ian leaned over and said quietly to Lindsay, 'With it so far?'

'Not really,' she admitted. 'What exactly are they arguing about?'

'Manchester Branch and Darlington Branch have both submitted motions on the same broad topic, and Brian wants to amalgamate them into one composite motion. Now they're each arguing about what they think their motion really said. Brian has to make sure they end up with something that includes all of the key points in the two original motions, without incorporating anything that wasn't there to start with.'

Lindsay shook her head. 'I can't believe grownups think this is a reasonable way to spend their time,' she muttered. 'It's like an Oxford tutorial without the relevance to real life.' She tried to concentrate on the obscure negotiation that continued like some quaint ritual dance whose meaning was lost in the sands of time. But it was no use. There wasn't enough meat in the argument to occupy her mind, and her grief kept butting in like an anarchist at the trooping of the colour. After another half hour, she leaned towards Ian and muttered, 'I'm going to get some air.'

She emerged into the foyer of the Winter Gardens with a sense of relief. The large committee room had begun to feel unreasonably oppressive. Oblivious to her surroundings, she wandered down towards the stands of the assorted pressure groups who had rented space for the conference. She didn't notice the chipped tiling on the walls, the scruffy paintwork or the garish posters for the forthcoming summer attractions. She paused long enough to buy an enamelled metal badge proclaiming 'Lesbians and Gay Men Support the Miners' before walking back into the stuffy hall to rejoin her colleagues.

No one glanced at her as she slipped into her seat. Only five others of the twelve-strong delegation from her branch were at the table. One of them was fast asleep, head pillowed on his arms. Another two were reading the morning papers. That left two who actually seemed to be following the debate. Lindsay shook her head. For weeks, every chapel meeting had been dominated by the impending annual conference. They had discussed their attitudes to motions, the importance of driving through certain policies, the crucial impact of decisions taken here in Blackpool. She'd spent the first morning taking notes on the debates and the results of the votes, until she had realised that she couldn't see another soul in the hall doing anything with a pen except the *Telegraph* crossword. She could only assume that the real politicking was going on elsewhere, perhaps in those tight huddles that seemed to spring up all over the place every quarter of an hour or so. As she looked around, Lindsay spotted one of her own delegation coming away from a group clustered around the platform.

Lindsay watched Siobhan Carter, a feature writer on the *Sunday Trumpet*, weave through the delegation tables and wondered how long it would be before she understood what the hell was going on around her. Siobhan seemed to fit in perfectly, yet it was only her second time at conference. She flopped into the seat next to Lindsay and fanned herself with an order-paper.

'Whew! It might only be the second day of conference, but there's already enough scandal going the rounds to keep a clutch of gossip columnists going for a month.'

'Is that what you've been doing? Gossiping?' Lindsay asked.

Ignoring the note of censure in her voice, Siobhan giggled. 'What else? You surely don't expect me to listen to this boring load of crap?'

'I thought that's what we were here for,' Lindsay said.

'What? To die of boredom listening to some obscure, incomprehensible motion that's only relevant to television journalists in the Republic of Ireland? No way! Listen, Linds, you stick with me. I'll keep you on track. I'll tell you when you need to be listening, okay? Trust me. I once screwed a doctor!'

Lindsay looked dubious. 'I don't know, I feel guilty if I don't get involved.'

'Fine. Get involved. But stick to the stuff that's got something to do with you. I mean, tell me the truth. Did you enjoy SOS?'

Lindsay pulled a face. 'Enjoy. Now, there's a word. You'd need to have a mind more twisted than a corkscrew to get off on Standing Orders. I had to get out before my brain blew a fuse.'

'Exactly. You're getting the idea. And you missed a wonderful bit of goss while you were gone,' Siobhan said eagerly, completely ignoring the passionate debate on the platform about whether the union's perennially troubled finances could stretch to a major publicity campaign in Eire. Siobhan wasn't the only one, Lindsay realised, glancing round the hall. She reckoned that less than ten per cent of the delegates even knew which motion was under discussion. Why should she join yet another minority group?

'Tell me,' she asked, putting Siobhan out of her obvious misery. 'What have I missed?'

'You know Jess, don't you? Jess Nimmo, from Magazine Branch?'

'How could I not?' Lindsay said with feeling, recalling the braying upper-class voice that had dominated every meeting of the JU Women's Caucus that she'd ever attended. 'She thinks consensus is a head count the government takes every ten years.'

'And you know Rory Finlayson, the Glasgow

Broadcasting Branch heart-throb?' Lindsay nodded. Everyone knew ITN's Scottish correspondent, who gazed lovingly out of their TV screens several times a week on *News At Ten*. It was obvious to anyone who had ever encountered Rory in the flesh that his biggest fan was himself.

'Well, Jess has been trying to get into Rory's knickers for a million years now, just like half the other women in the country. And in spite of throwing herself under his feet at every available opportunity, she'd never managed to get him to pay her the slightest bit of attention.'

'I suppose she's no competition if there's a mirror around.'

Siobhan giggled. 'Nice one. Anyway, last night, she finally cracked it. They left the bar together about one, and they were last seen canoodling in the lift. End of scene one. Scene two. About half an hour later, Paul wakes up to the sound of someone banging on his door.' Siobhan gestured with her head in the direction of their delegation leader, branch chairman Paul Horne, the thirty-something social policy editor of *The Watchman*, who was one of the handful absorbed in the debate.

'So he gets up and opens the door,' Siobhan paused for effect.

'Yeah?' Lindsay urged her.

'And there, wearing nothing but a parka, is Jess. 'I went for a pee and now I can't remember what room Rory's in,' she wails and marches past Paul into his room. He's completely bewildered by this apparition and by the time he gets his head together and follows her into the room, she's helped herself to his bed, the parka's on the floor and she's telling him he's got the choice of climbing in beside her or finding Rory.'

Lindsay's mouth fell open. 'You're kidding!'

'It gets better, believe me. It turns out she's not even had a legover with the man of her dreams so she's in an absolutely filthy mood. Poor Paul ends up getting dressed, going down to reception, finding out what room Rory's in, trekking back up there and knocking on Rory's door. Rory, of course, is spark out in a drunken stupor by this time, so he doesn't answer his door. And by the time Paul gets back to his room, Jess is comatose in his bed. He can't even go and take over Jess's room because, of course, her keys are in her handbag in Rory's room. So poor old Paul ends up spending the night in his armchair while Jess snores in his bed.'

'She doesn't snore, does she?' Lindsay asked, glancing over at the Magazine Branch table where Jess sat, immaculate in a sweater so baggy and shapeless it had to have a designer label, black leggings and ankle boots. 'I bet she's even more pissed off about people knowing that than she is about missing a legover with the fabulous Finlayson.'

Siobhan giggled again. Lindsay had a feeling

she was going to become very fed up of that giggle by the end of the week. 'You're not kidding. By the way, how's Ian? Has he recovered from discovering the new love of Laura's life?'

While she enjoyed the sharp savour of gossip about people she either disliked or knew only by reputation, Lindsay was less keen to dissect the private life of a friend as close as Ian. 'He seems fine,' she said stiffly.

Either Siobhan didn't notice, or else she was in investigative journalist mode. 'He must have been pretty demoralised to find he'd been replaced by a golden retriever. I thought at first it must be a guide dog. I mean, there must have been something wrong with her eyesight, fancying Ian enough to have lived with him all these years.'

'That's the trouble with you feature writers,' Lindsay said. 'You're all so superficial. Image, image, image, that's all that excites you. It takes a news reporter to penetrate below the surface and discover the truth.' It was an old argument, but none the less attractive. It had the advantage of shifting the conversation away from Ian, and it kept the two women occupied until the end of the order paper.

'Coming for a drink?' Siobhan asked as they shuffled their papers together.

'Tom Jack's speaking at a fringe meeting,' Lindsay replied, thinking that answered the question.

Siobhan looked horrified, then her face relaxed into a grin. 'I keep forgetting it's your first time,' she said patronisingly. 'I bet you still think fringe meetings are a vital part of conference business.'

'They aren't?'

'They're a distraction from the serious business of drinking and socialising,' Siobhan told her. 'Come on, let's go and have a hair of the dog. Whoops, remind me not to say that to Ian!' She giggled.

'Thanks, but no thanks. He's talking about how workforces cope when they get bought up by media buccaneers. Since we're still reeling from being taken over by Carnegie Wilson, I feel obliged to go and see what Union Jack's got to say for himself. God knows, he's said little enough at the meetings in the office.'

Siobhan winked. 'Say no more. I can read between the lines. You want to find out what he's not been telling you guys, then you can slip a banana skin under the sexist pig at your next meeting.'

Before Lindsay could deny it, Siobhan had slipped away. With a sigh, Lindsay headed for the committee room. She still felt she had a duty to the colleagues she was supposed to represent. Like the rest of them, Lindsay was worried about her future following their recent invasion by the New Zealand media tycoon. As well as being the senior JU official at Nation Newspapers, Union Jack headed the loose federation of the seven different unions represented there. If anyone could speak from experience about the implications of take-overs, it was him.

The meeting had attracted a large crowd, unlike the previous lunchtime's meeting where six women had gathered to hear a talk on 'Media Language and Gender Bias'. Not surprisingly, more journalists were concerned about potential damage to their pay packets than about the pursuit of equality. By the time Lindsay arrived, all the seats in the small committee room were taken. She slipped down the side of the room and leaned against the wall near the front. Union Jack leaned against the edge of a table facing the room. Shanti Gupta, one of the two candidates running for JU vice-president, was already intro-ducing the meeting, her strong voice rising above the desultory chatter of the audience.

'Brothers and sisters, I don't need to remind you of the dangers we face at the hands of asset strippers and fast-buck merchants who pin their dreams of profit to the rise of new technology at the expense of the health and welfare of their workers,' she said, scarcely pausing for breath.

'Tom Jack, the National Executive member for national newspapers, has recently had firsthand experience of negotiating with one of the new breed of newspaper proprietors, the profit pirates, the men who care more about the bottom line on their balance sheets than they do about their readers. We can all learn from the experiences of

Nation Newspapers, and there's no one better equipped to teach us than Tom.' Shanti stepped back and gestured towards Union Jack. 'Over to you, Tom,' she said, sitting down behind the table.

Tom Jack pushed himself upright and fixed the audience with his burning brown eyes. His thick brown hair was brushed back from his high fore-head, and his full beard almost obscured the collar of his Tattersall-check shirt and the knot of his tweed tie. He looked slowly round the room, as if committing every face to memory, slotting them into his mental filing cabinet till he was ready to take them out, scrutinise them, temper them in the fire and lead them to glory like some irre-sistible nineteenth-century zealot. He thrust one hand into the pocket of his moleskin trousers, and started to speak. His voice was deep, intense and unmistakably Yorkshire.

'Colleagues,' he intoned. 'We're facing the biggest threat to our journalistic livelihoods that I can remember. I know you've heard that before, and probably from me, but nevertheless, I'm not a man given to crying wolf. Shanti here has raised the spectre of new technology, and I'm here to tell you that the combination of Tory government policies, new technology and proprietors who understand nothing of the proud traditions of British newspapers could mean the end of our working world as we have known it. All the ben-efits we have struggled to bring our members could be lost like that' – he snapped his fingers like the crack of ice hitting gin – 'unless we pick our ground carefully and fight to win.'

The speech continued in predictable vein. The audience were exhorted to hold firm to their hard-won agreements on pay, conditions, and redundancy; to stand up to their new proprietors and show them who really ran the newspapers; and not to concede so much as a matchstick of dead wood to new technology. The rounds of spontaneous applause that greeted Union Jack's cries to arms astonished Lindsay. It was a long way away from the stony silence that he'd had to face when he returned to office meetings with news of yet more concessions that Carnegie Wilson's henchmen had wrung out of him. It was easy to see there weren't many *Daily Nation* staff members at the meeting.

With an unobtrusive glance at his watch, Tom Jack wound up. 'At the end of the day, we're the ones with the ink in our veins. We know how newspapers work. Carnegie Wilson made his millions out of butchering sheep, and he's found out the hard way that we're no lambs to the slaughter. Carnegie Wilson and his like have to bow the knee to us, because without us, newspapers can't exist. We have to remember, colleagues. They'll never invent a machine that can knock on doors or comfort a grieving widow. They'll never invent a machine that can persuade governments to change the law. Whatever the Carnegie Wilsons of this world would like to think their fancy computers can do, we have to remind them again and again, day in and day out, that without us, they have nothing to show for their millions of pounds of investments.'

It was a rousing finish, and some people even stood as they applauded Union Jack. Lindsay looked around and noticed with interest that Ian Ross and a handful of other *Daily Nation* journalists had not joined in the frenzy of applause. Tom held his hands up in the air, accepting the plaudits. As the applause continued, she remembered a rumour Ian had mentioned in the car. The JU's long-serving National Newspaper Officer had suffered his second major heart attack the day before conference began. The word was he would be offered early retirement and the obvious man to step into his shoes was Tom Jack. He'd filled every significant post open to part-time lay officials. There was nowhere left for his ambition to go unless he moved into a full-time paid official's job that could lead one day to the top job of them all – general secretary. Lindsay wondered if she'd just heard the first speech in an election campaign.

Tom sat down next to Shanti, who patted him on the shoulder as the applause finally died away. 'I know some of you may have questions for Tom,' she said. 'We have ten minutes left . . .'

A couple of the audience had clearly been primed with questions that managed to make Tom look even more statesmanlike than his speech already had. Disgruntled, Lindsay pushed herself away from the wall and stuck her hand up. Shanti nodded to her, after a quick glance at Tom, whose eyebrows lifted in acquiescence. Clearly he expected no trouble from one of his own flock.

'What advice can Tom offer to other chapel officials to help them avoid losing the ground we at Nation Newspapers have already lost? I refer specifically to the fifty per cent reduction in maternity leave, the cut in holidays from eight weeks to seven, the ending of time off in lieu for overnight stays away from base, and the freezing of expense allowances at 1982 levels.' She could see Tom's eyes narrow and his thick eyebrows descend, but she carried on. 'As far as I'm concerned, that is a lot more than the thin end of the wedge.'

Tom was on his feet, all traces of his momentary anger gone. His voice was conciliatory, aimed at the expressions of uncertainty that had appeared on the faces of some of his audience. 'Colleagues, Lindsay's making a point here that none of you can afford to ignore. And that point is that even with a strong chapel and experienced negotiators, you have to give a little ground. But against that, we have to weigh the fact that I personally sat across the table from Carnegie Wilson and persuaded him to drop his plans for ten per cent redundancies across the board at Nation Newspapers. We also now have a deal that no element of new technology will be introduced without a fully negotiated agreement between management and workforce.' He was blustering now, desperately trying to make it look as if he hadn't rolled over like the lap-dog Lindsay suspected he was. She could imagine only too well the 'good old boys' atmosphere of the negotiations, and the amount of alcohol that had flowed to ensure good working relationships.

As he carried on trying to win his audience back, Lindsay pushed herself away from the wall and walked out in disgust. Her departure made her point more forcefully than her words, but she was past caring about the effect. She wandered back towards the main concourse, desperately wishing Frances was only a phone call away.

She had reached the door of the conference hall when she was stopped by a member of the JU Women's Caucus, canvassing support for some motion or other. Absently, Lindsay listened to the familiar litany, nodding non-committally when some response seemed to be called for. She was shocked back to full attention by a heavy hand clamped on her shoulder and Tom Jack's voice in her ear. 'Just whose side are you on, Lindsay Gordon?' he asked menacingly.

Lindsay looked over her shoulder. Tom was flanked by a handful of his sidekicks. Ian was hovering on the edges of the bunch, trying to work his way round to her. She spoke softly, so her words wouldn't carry farther than their small group. 'Keeping the truth from people doesn't solve anything, Tom,' she said wearily. 'It tends to filter through in the end. Then what people will remember is that you bull-shitted them over your deal with Wilson.' She would have said more, but Ian put a warning hand on her arm.

'You're too bloody smart by half. You should remember whose side you're on. Leave playing devil's advocate to that fancy lawyer you're shacked up with. You've been spending too much time listening to Miss Frances Collier.'

Lindsay felt suddenly light-headed. Tom Jack's mouth carried on moving, but she could hear nothing. It was as if a glass bubble had enclosed her, cutting her off from the world around her. Without a word, she pulled away from his restraining grip and pushed through the group of men behind him.

As she began to run down the hall, the wall of silence shattered and she heard Ian Ross shout at Tom Jack, 'You stupid, insensitive bastard. You're about as out of touch as you're out of order. Don't you know anything about your chapel members? Frances Collier died six weeks ago. How could you not know that?'

3

'An inevitable consequence of the volume of work demanded of conference delegates is that they will suffer from a lack of sleep as conference week progresses. In order to avoid feeling like dead dogs, we recommend you bring a substantial supply of Vitamins C and B Complex as well as the painkiller of your choice.'

from *'Advice for New Delegates'*,
a Standing Orders Sub-Committee booklet.

The shingle crunched beneath Lindsay's feet as she charged headlong down the beach. At the water's edge she stopped, her chest heaving for breath, her eyes stinging with unshed tears. She stared out at the grey Irish Sea, glad of its bleakness. Recovering herself, she squatted down to make herself a smaller target for the sharp northerly wind. She pulled a crushed packet of cigarettes out of her pocket, straightened one out, cupped a hand round her lighter and inhaled deeply. In spite of the cancer that had taken three months from its diagnosis to kill Frances, Lindsay still couldn't bring herself to quit. Most days she felt only the nicotine and the caffeine were holding her together.

Three hellish months, trying to come to terms with the one adversary that wouldn't accept anything other than total surrender. Three months watching death inch closer and closer to the woman she loved. Three months trying to accept the unacceptable. Then that last week, when Frances was beyond words, beyond the defiance that had insisted on Lindsay's rights in the face of her intransigent family. They had done what neither life nor cancer could; they had separated Lindsay and Frances. When the news finally came, it had been from one of the workers at the hospice. At the funeral, Lindsay had stood apart, flanked by a couple of close friends, the ultimate spectre at the feast. That had been five weeks ago, and nothing was getting any easier.

She dragged the last lungful of smoke out of her cigarette and flicked the stub into the waves. Moments later, she jumped with shock as a warm wet tongue licked her ear. Lindsay straightened up, nearly toppling over in the process, and stared down at a golden retriever, tongue hanging out, shaggy coat dripping with salt water, tail wagging amiably.

A breathless voice behind her called, 'Becky! Come here.' Lindsay turned to see Laura bearing down on her. The dog didn't move. 'Oh, Lindsay, it's you. I'm sorry, she thinks everybody was put on the planet to play with her.'

'No problem. I was miles away, or I would have heard her.' Lindsay reached down and fondled the dog's damp, silky ears. 'She's a beauty,' she added rather stiffly.

'I couldn't resist her,' Laura admitted. 'She belonged to a friend of mine who was transferred to Brussels. Of course she couldn't take Becky with her. She was about to advertise for a good home for her when . . . well, when my circumstances changed and made it possible for me to have her. But then, I suppose you know all about that,' she said in tones of resignation.

'I just don't understand how you could do that to him,' Lindsay said in a much cooler tone than the dog had been granted. She studied Laura, speculating how much time it took in the morning to shape that flowing crest of chestnut hair, and how much of the problem with the ozone layer could be laid at the door of her hair spray. Even walking the dog on Blackpool beach, Laura had managed to achieve an air of elegance that Lindsay would have been hard pressed to match at a formal dinner.

Laura raised her perfectly shaped eyebrows. Beneath them, her eyes were wary. 'So he's been discussing our private business with all and sundry,' she said coldly.

Lindsay felt the colour rise in her cheeks. 'You

screw around with someone else behind his back and you expect him to keep his mouth shut for the sake of your reputation?'

Laura took a startled step back. 'He told you that?'

'He had to talk to someone, Laura. And in spite of what you think, I'm not all and sundry. Ian's my friend, and as far as I'm concerned, what you did to him is a shit's trick. And on top of it all, to turn up with Becky in tow, when you of all people know how allergic he is to dogs. What a slap in the face! You couldn't have made it clearer that you've no intention of trying to sort things out with him.'

Laura ground the heel of a brown boot into the shingle. When she spoke, her voice was harsh. Not for the first time, Lindsay wondered at the capacity betrayers have for anger against the betrayed. 'There wasn't any going back from the moment he threw me out. He left me in no doubt about that. He wasn't interested in my explanations, so why the hell should I kid myself?'

Lindsay looked up at the beautiful face, clenched tight in an expression of bitterness. Then, suddenly, it was gone, and the Laura Craig cool mask was back in place.

'Well, I hope he's worth it,' Lindsay said harshly.

She turned away, giving the dog a final pat and strode up the beach as fast as the shingle would allow. She didn't grant Laura a single backward glance.

By the time she returned to the Winter Gardens, Lindsay's run-in with Union Jack was already history. At least half a dozen things had happened which had grabbed the attention of delegates desperate to be riveted by anything other than conference business. But although the rest of the world seemed oblivious to Lindsay's highly charged encounter with the father of her chapel, it was still vivid in her mind. It didn't need Ian's solicitous enquiries as she sat down to remind her of the wound that Union Jack had so callously opened.

'Are you okay? Bloody Union Jack. I can't believe he could be so bloody insensitive,' he said, but not quietly enough to avoid arousing the interest of other members of the delegation. 'Even though he didn't know about Frances, he still had no right to drag her in like that.'

Lindsay rubbed a hand over her face. Any good the fresh air had done her vanished like mist in sunshine. 'He was just trying to discredit me, that's all. Making sure that anyone who didn't know I'm a dyke knows now. That and telling everyone that I'm somebody else's puppet. Why should I expect him to have known about Frances?'

By now, the entire table had given up any pretence of listening to the debate. Lindsay and

Ian were the centre of everyone's attention, even Paul leaning forward to hear better.

'Because he bloody should have. Because you're a member of his chapel, and for three months your partner was fighting a losing battle against cancer. He should have made it his business to see you had any support you needed.'

Lindsay sighed, and patted the fist Ian was banging on the table. 'I got the support I needed from you and the rest of my friends. You know I didn't want a big song and dance about it. Frankly, if Union Jack had been forced to swallow his prejudices and offer me sympathy, the sight of so much hypocrisy would have made me vomit.'

'Maybe so, but you shouldn't let it rest here. Union Jack treated you abominably, bringing up Frances like that, and I want to take it to the chapel committee. You deserve an apology,' Ian said defiantly. He had not noticed that Laura had come up behind him while he spoke.

'And that'll really make Lindsay feel better,' she said sarcastically. 'For Christ's sake, Ian, let the woman bury her dead in peace.'

Ian whirled round in his seat, the chair legs screeching on the floor. He faced Laura, his face flushed scarlet. By now, the surrounding delegation tables were agog. Lindsay felt a slow anger burn in her. How dare Laura use her pain as a stick to beat Ian with?

'What the hell has this got to do with you?' he demanded belligerently.

'Exactly as much as it has to do with you. Christ, Ian, you're just as bad as Union Jack. You're as willing to use Lindsay's grief for your own political ends as he is,' Laura snapped.

'Stay out of this, Laura,' Lindsay butted in. 'This is nothing to do with you.'

'You don't even know what we're talking about,' Ian said in exasperation, getting to his feet.

Laura made a deliberate point of stepping back and tilting her head upwards to look at his skinny frame towering above her. 'You think not? Let me tell you, Ian, if there's anyone in this hall who's caused a lot of heartache by jumping to conclusions, it sure as hell isn't me.' Her voice was low and dangerous.

The pair of them held each other's gaze. Ian's ears were scarlet, Laura's mouth set in a sneer. The stalemate might have continued indefinitely had it not been for the call for a vote. The muttering and rustling as delegates quickly checked which way they were voting and raised their hands shattered the moment. Ian turned away and picked up his voting card. Laura smiled ironically at the rest of their delegation and walked off towards the platform.

'What a prize bitch!' Siobhan muttered in Lindsay's ear. 'He's well shot of her.'

'Almost makes you feel sorry for the new man in her life.'

*   *   *

Lindsay didn't want to think about how much whisky she'd drunk. She knew she'd only had three and a half hours sleep after the Scots/Irish ceilidh, but lack of sleep was only a tiny component of the pounding, gut-churning hangover that had invaded her body. She felt like the ball in a rugby match somewhere towards the end of the first half: it was bad already, but she knew it was going to get worse. At least it was the final morning of the conference. She could probably lay her head on her arms and sneak a couple of hours' kip at the delegation table. Someone would happily hang on to her card and vote in her stead. The hangover would pass. Her guilt at not being in a fit state to carry out her duties as a delegate would probably hang around for longer.

As she slowly crossed the hotel dining-room, she managed to grasp that she was far from the only one who looked like they used to be members of the human race. As she passed the buffet table laden with fruit juices and cereals, she gave a shudder and slunk into her seat at the table she shared with Ian, Siobhan and a sub-editor from the *Evening Standard* who hadn't yet managed to make it to breakfast. 'Coffee?' she croaked. Siobhan passed her the pot. Lindsay's shaking hand knocked over the salt-cellar as she reached for the milk. Ian moved his pot of hot water out of Lindsay's line of fire.

'You're not fit to be let out,' he commented, looking up from his copy of *The Watchman*. 'And that poison won't help.' Self-righteously, he dunked his herbal teabag in his cup, then dropped it in the ashtray.

Ignoring him, Lindsay drained her first cup of coffee and shuddered as the shock hit her system. 'Come on then, Siobhan, don't keep me in suspense. Did you crack it?'

Siobhan giggled. 'Sure did. Four men in four nights.' She ticked them off on her fingers. 'Monday, Toby Tranter from Brighton; Tuesday, Peter Little, the Manchester branch chairman; Wednesday, Danny Stott, that radio reporter from Newcastle with the cutest bum at conference. And then last night. I'll be glad to get home. I need the rest.'

'So who was the lucky guy last night?' Lindsay asked.

'Search me. I went for a meal with the Racial Equality Caucus, and I got pissed as a newt. We ended up back in my room, and when I awoke, he'd gone,' she reported.

Ian tutted. 'I don't know, you spent the seventies slagging us men off for treating you like sex objects, and the minute you get liberated, all you do is do exactly what you gave us a bad time for,' he said in mock reproach.

'Shut up, Ian,' they choroused.

Lindsay added, 'You're failing to understand that by definition, the oppressed cannot themselves be oppressors. Go back and read your Germaine Greer again.'

Ian pulled a face. Then he said, 'You sure you did it? I mean, if you can't even remember the guy's name, I'm not sure we can award you the Legover of the Conference award.'

Siobhan giggled. The sound was like a hot wire splitting Lindsay's head in two. She'd been right about that giggle. 'Oh, we did it all right. Take my word for it, Ian, I know we did it. Let me tell you, it's only his name I can't remember. I can recall *everything* else about him.' She ticked items off on her fingers. 'He was Irish, he had freckles, he had brown hair and ginger pubes . . .'

'Enough, enough,' Lindsay groaned. 'I already feel nauseous.' She eyed a piece of toast, wondering if she could stand the noise crunching it would make inside her skull. Before she could decide, Ian helped himself to the last piece. Lindsay looked around for a waitress, and spotted Laura standing a couple of tables away, talking to one of the delegates.

Their conversation ended, and she walked towards the exit. As she approached their table, she turned back to call something to the man she'd been talking to. She carried on walking and cannoned into their table, sending Ian's plate of toast, his cup of rosehip tea and his pot of hot water flying.

The confused hubbub that followed made Lindsay feel like her ears were bleeding. Ian was on his feet, shouting more from shock than anger. 'You stupid, clumsy, bitch,' he yelled. 'You could have really hurt someone. Why don't you look where you're going, for Christ's sake?'

'Oh for God's sake,' Laura said in exasperated tones. 'It's only a bit of water. It hasn't even splashed your trousers. Do you have to make such a fuss?' She crouched down and picked up the empty pot. 'If it's such a big deal, I'll fetch you some more.' She marched past a waitress who had scurried up, and straight through the door into the kitchen.

The waitress brought Ian clean crockery, but before she could bring fresh supplies, Laura had returned with a rack of wholemeal toast and a fresh pot of hot water. She dumped them unceremoniously on the table, saying, 'I didn't do it deliberately, you know. There was absolutely no need to make such an exhibition of yourself. Why don't you grow up, Ian? Most women prefer men to small boys, you know.'

Laura marched off, head held high. Grimly, Ian stared at the table as he poured himself a cup of water and dropped his herbal teabag in.

'At least you know she didn't do it deliberately,' Siobhan said.

'How d'you figure that out?' Lindsay said, right on cue.

'If she'd done it on purpose, his balls would be in the burns unit by now!' Siobhan said raucously as Ian winced.

Lindsay cautiously worked her way through a slice of toast, discovering that if she sucked it

45

before chewing, the noise was just about bearable. Ian sipped his tea in silence, absorbed once more in his newspaper. Siobhan shovelled a cooked English breakfast down her neck, eyes swivelling constantly round the room in search of potential prey.

At five to nine, Ian glanced at his watch, folded his paper and got to his feet. 'I'll see you two at the Winter Gardens in a bit,' he said. 'I've got to pop to the shops. I promised my sister's kids I'd bring them back a present from the seaside. Somebody told me there's a really good toy shop up the back of the town, so I'm going to take a drive up there.'

'I wish he'd said a bit sooner,' Siobhan grumped as Ian strode off. 'I was relying on him to give us a lift. Now we're going to be late.'

Lindsay and Siobhan slipped into their chairs at twenty past nine. The hall was less than half-full, which was more than could be said for the platform. A man with a hoarse voice was proposing a motion which appeared to have something to do with child care. Lindsay shoved her voting card at Siobhan, made a pillow of her forearms on the table and carefully lowered her head. She was drifting in the comfortable half-world between sleep and wakefulness when Siobhan dug her in the ribs and announced in a voice loud enough to turn heads three tables away, 'That's him, Lindsay! That's the man I was with last night!'

Siobhan's urgent revelation caused enough stir to ripple forward to the platform. The young man at the podium was thrown off his stride mid-sentence as he struggled to see what was going on. He clearly couldn't believe it was the power of his oratory that had caused the commotion. It took only moments for him to realise who was at the centre of it. Even at that distance, Lindsay could see him flush. A slow ripple of mirth began in the corner of the hall.

Overcome with confusion, he gabbled, 'Support the amendment,' turned tail and fled. By then, the ripple had become a wave of laughter. The noise around their table was so loud that Lindsay could scarcely make out the words of Paul Horne, who arrived at the delegation table pale and sweating.

'Say again?' she said.

Paul's lips trembled as he struggled for his rapidly disintegrating self-control. 'It's Ian. He's dead.'

4

'In view of the increasing tendency of delegates to sneak off before conference ends at Friday lunchtime, SOS is considering methods of enforcing delegates' attendance. We await with eagerness reports of experiments in the probation service with electronic tagging; not that we imagine for one minute that we would want to know exactly where people are at crucial moments. Meanwhile, as a trial deterrent, this year delegates will not be paid their conference lunch expense allowance until noon on Friday. So be there or be poor.'

from *'Advice for New Delegates'*,
a *Standing Orders Sub-Committee booklet.*

It was hard to imagine the crumpled concertina of red metal had ever been a Ford Escort. It didn't look as if it could ever have been longer than a Mini. The signpost it had hit first had sliced the car almost in two, before the brick wall of the

48

shopping centre had compressed it to half its length. As she watched a salvage crew struggle to get the wreckage away from the shattered wall, the churning in Lindsay's stomach had nothing to do with the amount of alcohol she'd consumed. She turned away and threw up unceremoniously in the gutter.

When she recovered herself, she saw Paul had turned away and was staring unseeingly at the traffic.

'I was passing when it happened,' he said emptily. 'I'd popped out for five minutes to buy some rock for the kids. He came round the corner at the end of the street there like a bat out of hell. The car was fishtailing all over the road. I didn't even realise it was Ian. If I thought anything at all, I thought it was some teenage joyrider.'

Lindsay tentatively put out a hand and touched Paul's arm. He gripped her fingers tightly.

'He just kept going faster and faster. Then he tried to take the bend, but he must have been doing seventy, and it's a really tight turn. He was completely out of control. He just kept going faster and faster.' Paul shook his head. 'Then I saw his face, in a kind of blur, and I realised it was Ian. I knew he didn't have a chance.'

'Let's go somewhere and have a cup of tea,' Lindsay suggested gently, steering Paul towards a nearby café. Luckily, it was the lull between morning coffees and lunches, and they had no trouble finding a quiet table. Because Paul's dramatic announcement hadn't penetrated the general laughter, Lindsay had been able to get the shocked branch chairman out of the hall before he could cause general consternation. Outside the conference, he had simply said, 'Come and see,' and led her in silence to the scene of the accident.

As they waited for the waitress to bring them a pot of tea, Paul started to shiver, like a dog in a thunderstorm. 'He looked . . . he looked really weird,' he said in a puzzled voice. 'His eyes were really staring, and it was like he was pushing himself up on the steering-wheel. And he'd gone a funny colour. Sort of purply.'

'He had bad asthma,' Lindsay said. It didn't seem very helpful, but she couldn't think of anything else to say.

'I know,' Paul said. 'Ian's been my friend for years. But I've never seen him in a real state with it. Not like that.' The waitress deposited a tray on the table. Lindsay poured the tea and Paul instantly clutched a cup, warming his hands like a man dying of cold. 'He looked completely out of control, and I've never seen him like that. He always had his drugs with him, always.'

Lindsay sighed and lit up a cigarette. 'Maybe he didn't take them soon enough. I don't know. I don't know anything about asthma.'

Paul shook his head. 'I do. My eldest son is mildly asthmatic. But I've never seen him like that either, not even when he was a baby and he couldn't use inhalers. But Ian was always really careful, really methodical. Well, he would be, wouldn't he? Look what an organised branch secretary he was.' Paul gave a hysterical laugh. 'Listen to me. The poor bastard's in the past tense already.'

'You're sure he was dead?' Lindsay asked, clutching at straws.

Paul gulped his tea. 'I'm sure. No one could get the door open. We tried. The fire brigade had to cut it open. When they finally got him out, they . . .' His voice cracked. He cleared his throat noisily and said, 'He didn't come out in one piece, Lindsay. His face was covered when they took him away. They didn't have their siren going or their light flashing.' He stared into his cup.

Lindsay felt numb. It was too much, after Frances. Her grief had overloaded in an emotional short circuit that left her incapable of feeling anything more. In self-preservation, her mind was moving only in practical channels. 'I think you should go to the hospital, Paul. You're in shock.'

Paul gave a short sharp bark that was a long way from laughter. 'I can't go to hospital. You think I'm in a state? You just wait. Who's going to tell Laura? I should do that, I saw him die, I was their friend.' The shivering started again.

Lindsay gently took the cup from him and placed it on its saucer. She took his hands in hers. 'You're not the person to tell her, Paul. Not right now.'

She saw a sudden flash of relief as his eyes met hers. It disappeared as suddenly as it had come. 'But I should,' he said guiltily.

Lindsay shook her head. She took a deep breath and let it out slowly. 'I'll tell her,' she said softly. She released Paul's hands and lit another cigarette. 'I know what it feels like,' she added distantly.

Though she'd never have admitted it to Paul, it was a secret relief to Lindsay when they returned to the Winter Gardens and discovered that the bad news had travelled with its usual swiftness. The hall was virtually empty. Standing Orders Sub-Committee were in a huddle by the door, discussing whether to move suspension of standing orders; to bring conference to an end; or simply to make a brief announcement from the stage, followed by a minute's silence.

The delegates stood around in subdued groups, talking softly about what they'd heard had happened. Lindsay couldn't help noticing that there wasn't a national newspaper reporter in sight. She knew exactly what most of her delegation would be doing now – they'd either be at the hospital or the police station. And she knew that any minute now, her newsdesk would start looking for her to write the definitive piece on the life and death of Ian Ross. Part of her wanted to go on the missing list, but the other, professional part of her wanted to be the one who would give shape to the way Ian would be remembered.

Leaving Paul in the capable hands of the JU's assistant general secretary, a former colleague from *The Watchman*, Lindsay systematically worked the fragmented groups to discover where Laura was. It soon became apparent that the police had been led to the conference as a result of the organ donor card Ian carried. The card still gave Laura as his next of kin. Since her business card and a selection of photographs were also in his wallet, it hadn't taken them long to work out she was likely to be at the JU conference. Once they'd got that far, it had been straightforward. Instead of the tragic news being broken by someone she knew, Laura had heard about Ian's death from a strange police officer. Lindsay could only imagine what that had felt like. Even in imagination, it made her shudder.

There was no reason to hang about at the Winter Gardens, so Lindsay slowly walked back to the Princess Alice to collect her bag. She wandered through to the bar and checked out their selection of whiskies. She ordered a large Glenfiddich, the only malt on offer, added a dribble of water to the pale liquid and took a small sip. As she took a cigarette from her packet, a hand snapped a flame into life in front of her. She looked up into the dark blue eyes of Shaz Morton, who was noted for managing the seemingly impossible, blending her job as a high profile television company press officer with her role as a campaigning lesbian. Wherever Shaz went, controversy followed. So, usually, did her girlfriend, a polytechnic lecturer in women's studies. But this week in Blackpool, Shaz was unaccompanied. Probably, Lindsay had decided, because her girlfriend knew how few opportunities Shaz would have to stray at a JU conference.

'I heard about Ian,' Shaz said, lighting Lindsay's cigarette. 'Not what you needed just now, right?'

'Right,' Lindsay agreed.

'Especially not after Frances.' Shaz took a deep drag of her own cigarette and ordered a large gin and tonic, and another malt for Lindsay.

'No thanks,' Lindsay started to say.

'You need it. I meant to speak to you earlier before about Frances, but you know how it is. I was really upset to hear about her death. She was very special,' Shaz said.

Lindsay looked surprised. 'I didn't know you knew her.'

Shaz smiled and topped her gin up with tonic. 'We did some work together on a briefing pack for lesbian mothers involved in custody fights. It was a few years ago, long before she met you. We bumped into each other now and again, at meetings. I don't know if anybody's thought to mention this to you, but she was really happy with you.'

Lindsay's throat closed in the familiar emotional uprising. One step away from tears, she forced a mouthful of whisky down, then sucked in the comfort of nicotine. 'Thanks,' she finally managed to say. 'I was really happy with her.'

Shaz nodded towards Lindsay's bag. 'What train are you catching? Fancy some company?'

'I'd like that. I don't have a reservation, though. I expected to be going back in the car with Ian.' An involuntary shudder set her whisky swirling in her glass. She put the glass down with a bang. 'I keep thinking how bloody awful it must be for Laura. I know they'd split up, and she treated him like shit, but they were together for years. You don't just switch off your feelings for someone after all that time. No matter what's happened between you.'

Shaz nodded. 'She'd have to have a heart of stone not to be upset. She'll feel guilty too, probably. You know, all that, "if we hadn't split up, it would never have happened", business.'

'Yeah.' Lindsay sighed. 'She's not one of my favourite people, but if she's feeling a fraction of what I felt about Frances, then my heart goes out to her.'

Before they could say more, there was a disturbance behind them. A familiar voice floated through the door, focusing every drinker's attention on the speaker. 'Will you for God's sake leave me alone, Tom? I'm not a piece of bloody china,' Laura Craig was shaking off Tom Jack's protective arm and stalking into the bar.

'But Laura, you shouldn't be left alone, you're

in shock.' For once, thought Lindsay, he actually sounded sincerely concerned.

'Tom, piss off,' Laura said slowly and clearly. 'Watch my lips. I want to be alone.' She sounded more like Margaret Thatcher than Greta Garbo.

Tom Jack stepped back. There was no mistaking the determination and anger in Laura's voice. He put his hands up at chest level, palms towards Laura. 'Okay. Okay. I'll be through in the lounge if you want me.'

She watched him leave before turning back towards the bar, face set in a hard, expressionless mask. Shaz leaned forward to say softly, 'Sounds like your sympathy might be a bit misplaced.'

Lindsay shook her head. 'She's in shock, like Tom said. Grief does funny things to you.'

When she realised who her companions at the bar were, Laura sighed in exasperation. 'Oh God,' she said. 'Is there no peace in this bloody town?' Lindsay opened her mouth to speak, but before she could say anything, Laura said sharply, 'Don't say it. Don't for God's sake say you're sorry. Is anyone serving here?' she demanded, turning to the barman. 'Good. Give me a very large vodka and ginger beer. When I say very large, I mean four.' The barman took one look at her face, decided not to comment and scuttled off towards his optics.

Lindsay moved towards Laura and said, 'Laura, I know what it's like. After Frances died, I sometimes felt it was only the anger holding me together.'

Laura shook her head, as if to clear the vision. 'That's what comes next, is it? People giving me permission for my emotions?' Lindsay felt as if she'd been smacked in the face, but tried to subdue her reaction. When Laura's drink came, she swallowed half of it in one. As the alcohol hit, her shoulders straightened.

A BBC radio producer chose that moment to come over and put his arm round her. 'Laura, love, we're all so very, very sorry,' he said.

Laura pulled herself clear. 'You're dripping beer on my suit. I doubt you earn enough to have it cleaned, never mind replaced. Now piss off,' she hissed.

The man dropped his arm as if he'd been stung. He backed away, his face a mask of shock.

Laura finished her drink slammed the glass down on the bar. 'What a waste,' she said bitterly. 'What a bloody, bloody waste.'

'I know,' Lindsay persisted. 'I can't believe it either. I can only imagine how much worse it is for you.'

'Can you?' Laura asked dangerously. 'Can you? Sure you're not just fishing for an angle for your story, Lindsay?'

Lindsay clocked the look of shock on Shaz's face, and suspected it was mirrored on her own. 'For Christ's sake, Laura,' she protested.

'How come you didn't make it to the hospital like the rest of the pack, Lindsay? Oh, of course! You came in *Ian*'s car, didn't you? You didn't have

57

any wheels to get there. Well, you missed a great show. Your cronies were in fine form. "How do you feel, Laura? What was the last thing he said to you, Laura? What was he really like, Laura?"' she mimicked. 'My God, to think my job puts me on the same side as you vultures!' Laura turned away and signalled to the barman. 'Just a double this time, please.'

Lindsay moved forward, shaking off Shaz's restraining arm. 'Whatever you might think, Laura, I'm not interested in sneaking a couple of juicy quotes out of you. Ian was my friend, and in case you hadn't noticed, you don't have a monopoly on grief.' She spoke softly, but there was no mistaking her sincerity.

Laura turned to face Lindsay and looked her up and down. 'My god,' she said, her drawling voice heavy with contempt. 'I thought you were as bad as the rest of the vultures. I was wrong. You're a hundred times worse. You stand there, trading on the fact that Ian was too soft-hearted to treat you with the contempt you deserved. Have you any idea how much it pissed him off to have you hanging round, always badgering him with questions, thrusting your bloody grief down his throat? And now you stand there with your crocodile tears like he was something to you. Christ! You should get a T-shirt printed. Lindsay Gordon, queen of the jackal pack. Just for the record, Gordon, let me tell you that your pathetic posturings of grief made Ian sick. And not just

Ian. Let's face it, no normal person's going to shed a tear because there's one less dyke on the planet.'

Lindsay could feel the scarlet tide of anger and embarrassment that swept through her body. She was dimly aware of Shaz's hand on her arm again. This time she let herself be drawn away from the bitter, bereaved woman at the bar. 'Come on,' Shaz said. 'She doesn't deserve your support.'

At the door, Lindsay looked back, Laura was still leaning against the bar, the centre of all the other drinkers' wary attention.

'I'll never forgive her that,' Lindsay said, her voice cold, her face set. 'I don't care how shocked she is, she's gone too far. One day she's going to regret this.'

PART TWO

Sheffield, April 1993

1

'Tempting though it is for fringe groups to regard conference as a captive audience, only authorised conference material may be distributed inside the hall itself. Any other leaflets, flyers, etc. will be removed and shredded, thus resulting in needless death to trees. Non-authorised material may be distributed outside the hall, though those distributing it should be warned that hung-over delegates who have unwanted bumf thrust upon them can often react violently. SOS and the Amalgamated Media Workers' Union can accept no responsibility for any injuries thus caused.'

from *'Advice for New Delegates'*,
a *Standing Orders Sub-Committee booklet.*

The custody sergeant picked up his pen and gave Lindsay a shrewd look of appraisal. 'Been drinking?' he asked. It was the first indication he'd given that she wasn't invisible. The two

63

detectives who had brought her into the police station also turned towards her. She'd listened patiently while they'd informed the sergeant she was required for questioning relating to a suspicious death. The stocky detective sergeant had grumbled at her refusal to say anything, either at the scene of the death or in the car on the way to the station.

In answer to the custody sergeant, Lindsay nodded. 'I had a few whiskies earlier.'

The custody sergeant nodded grimly. 'Okay lads, no questions for a couple of hours. Give the lady time to sober up.'

'No problem. We've got plenty to keep us busy back at the scene of the crime,' the detective constable said.

'Alleged crime,' the custody sergeant corrected him absently.

The two detectives shouldered their way past Lindsay. She heard the DS mutter, 'Bollocks to that,' as he opened the door.

'A few details, if you please, miss,' the custody sergeant said.

'I'd like a lawyer,' Lindsay said.

'Do you know one locally? Or would you prefer me to call the duty solicitor?'

'The duty solicitor will do fine,' Lindsay sighed. 'Thanks.'

The custody sergeant picked up the phone on his desk and dialled a number. Almost immediately, he spoke. 'Pager number 659511. Please call

Sergeant Meadows, Central Police Station. End message.' He paused. 'That's right. Thanks.' He put the phone down and smiled at Lindsay. 'Now, while we're waiting, a few details.'

'Name, rank and serial number, that sort of thing?'

'Name, address and fingerprints, more like. And you don't get Red Cross parcels here, neither.'

The cell they took her to was cold and smelled stale. The solicitor had agreed to come soon, so she could interview Lindsay before the police decided she was sober enough for interrogation. She sat down on the edge of the narrow bed and stretched in a huge yawn. Then, elbows on her knees, she rubbed the sleep out of her eyes with her knuckles. She had sobered up the moment she had realised what the jagged hole in her window meant. But that couldn't stop the drink taking its physiological toll. Besides, it was nearly six in the morning. She was entitled to feel tired. She should be tucked up in bed, fast asleep, not locked up in some scruffy, dismal cell.

Lindsay began to wonder if leaving her to kick her heels was a deliberate ploy; perhaps they intended her to become more nervous and panicky the longer they left her. Then the voice of realism shouted down the paranoia. She knew how chronically understaffed the police always claimed to be. These guys were investigating what was either a highly dramatic suicide, a mystifying accident or a horrific murder. Maybe they simply had more pressing things to do before they were overtaken by events. After all, they knew she wasn't going anywhere now.

A dull ache had started behind her eyes. The classic whisky hangover was starting to bite. Lindsay had learned at an early age the technique of drinking large quantities of whisky without becoming either aggressively drunk, maudlin or catatonic. She'd also learned that there was only one way of dealing with the after-effects. Two pints of cold tap-water. Then ten hours sleep followed by a substantial meal – preferably the traditional Scottish New Year's Day dinner of steak pie, mashed potatoes and peas, followed by sherry trifle.

They did things very differently in California. Now, on the rare occasions when Lindsay had more than a couple of drinks, it was more likely to be white wine spritzers. And the morning after cure consisted of a handful of vitamins washed down with a litre of fizzy mineral water. Lindsay shuddered. She should be kicking down the door of this cell, demanding a lawyer right this minute. Somehow, she just couldn't summon up the energy. Instead, she swung her feet up on to the bed and lay back. She closed her eyes, placed her hands palm down on the rough blanket and breathed deeply. Area by area, she deliberately relaxed her muscles, mentally repeating, 'I love and approve of myself, right where I am.' Within five minutes, the pain had eased.

Cautiously, she opened her eyes. The light in its mesh cage seemed painfully bright, so she closed them again. One of the reasons she'd left Britain was because she'd had one too many close encounters with police interviewing techniques. Because her investigative journalism had once poked the authorities in the eye with a sharp stick, it had become clear to her that she was always going to be top of the list when the command came to 'round up the usual suspects'. It wasn't a role she relished. Moving to California might have been a leap into the dark, but at least the cops wouldn't be breathing down her neck every time something criminal happened within a mile of her.

Their relationship had only just begun to find its rhythm and shape when Sophie had been offered the sort of opportunity that comes along only a couple of times in a consultant gynae-cologist's career. A leading hospital in San Francisco was head-hunting an experienced team to staff a new unit, and Sophie's work in Glasgow with HIV positive mothers-to-be made her the ideal choice. She had leaped at the chance and Lindsay, only too glad to escape the bitter memories Glasgow now held for her, had chosen to trust enough to go too.

They'd moved into a wood-framed house above the beach, an hour's drive from the city, with a view of the Pacific that made Lindsay feel instantly at home. The best times in her life had been lived by the sea. First, growing up in a small Scottish village on the Atlantic coast. Later, learning to be a journalist in the cosy picture-postcard world of Cornwall. And later still, escaping from the security services' awkward questions and restoring herself to sanity in a humble and repetitive daily routine on the Adriatic coast. For the first few weeks in America, she'd been happy to put her mind on hold again while she sanded and sealed floors, stripped and painted woodwork and walls, and learned the basics of surfing. She'd hardly even begun to get to know San Francisco in all its glorious charm. Then suddenly, she'd woken one morning, alert and restless, needing to find something that would give her the same fulfilment that Sophie found in her harrowing role at the hospital.

Strangely, she found it in passing on the very skills she'd declared redundant in herself. Although she knew she could never again be a working journalist, Lindsay had never doubted her abilities. Her background in mainstream newspaper journalism coupled with her single foray into enemy territory, treading on the toes of the security services, made her the ideal choice for the job she landed as a university lecturer in journalism and media studies. Although she'd been apprehensive about moving into the world of higher education, it had been less of a shock to the system than she had anticipated. University life in California couldn't have been more different from the memories of her own student days at Oxford. Somehow, Lindsay couldn't imagine her former tutors in Bermuda shorts, playing volleyball at a Sunday afternoon beach barbecue.

The one fly in the ointment was the pressure to pile up qualifications and publications. Publish or be damned was an expression that could have been coined for her new world instead of her old one, Lindsay often thought. But when she'd chosen to write a doctoral thesis researching women's roles in the trade union movement, she hadn't expected it to be a straight road back to a police interrogation.

Her thoughts were interrupted by the sound of the door opening. Lindsay's eyes snapped open and focused on the woman who had just walked in. She was tall to start with, but the three-inch stilettos she had chosen put her near six feet. Her hair was short and neat, emphasising the kind of bone structure that has generated the fashion industry's demand for striking black models. Her skin was the colour of copper beech leaves in summer. Lindsay took in a pair of sharply tailored trousers in hounds-tooth check, a black matador jacket and a spotless white blouse open at the neck. Lindsay jumped to her feet. 'You must be my solicitor,' she said as the woman moved towards her.

The solicitor shook her hand and perched on the edge of the bed. 'Right. I'm Jennifer Okido,' she said.

Lindsay shuddered at the thought of how she must appear to this woman who couldn't have looked less like she'd been dragged out of bed in the middle of the night. 'Lindsay Gordon,' she said. 'Sorry you had to be called out so early.'

'It's no problem, Ms Gordon. I'm used to it. There aren't many firms in the city who do criminal work any longer, thanks to the Legal Aid changes. We're the largest, and I'm the senior criminal partner. By the way, I'm sorry about this, but we'll have to talk in here. Since the Strangeways riots, our police stations are so overcrowded with remand prisoners that there are no more secure interview rooms. They've all become holding cells. Now, if I can just sort out some details?' She took a pad from her briefcase and moved swiftly through the formalities. 'So what brings you back to Britain?' the solicitor asked.

Lindsay ran a hand through her hair and pulled a wry face. 'I'm beginning to wonder myself,' she said. 'My doctoral thesis is a study of how women have worked within the trade union movement to achieve changes in media attitudes towards them. That's why I came back for the Amalgamated Media Workers' Union's first annual conference. Years ago I used to be active in the Journalists' Union, which has been swallowed up by the new union, and I needed to talk to people who were involved in the equality struggles of the seventies and eighties. I thought that coming to the conference would be a good way of catching several of them in the same place.'

Jennifer nodded as she jotted notes with a shiny silver fountain pen. 'And you arrived here when?'

Lindsay closed her eyes and rubbed the bridge of her nose. 'Monday afternoon,' she said.

The foyer of Wilberforce Hall was buzzing. But the focus of attention wasn't the long trestle table where arriving delegates were registered and supplied with their conference packs. It was the photocopied A4 sheets that the earlier arrivals were waving under the noses of their friends and acquaintances as soon as they put their noses across the threshold. As Lindsay joined the queue, the pony-tailed young man behind her was accosted by a woman in her mid-forties.

'Have you seen this, Liam?' the woman demanded in a harsh Ulster accent. 'It's outrageous! Look what they're saying about Fearghal O'Donovan!'

Lindsay sneaked a look over the young man's shoulder as he took the brandished sheet of paper. She read:

When Irish Ayes Are Lying?

Some of us were more than slightly gobsmacked at the turn-out in the election for an assistant general secretary (Ireland) last month. For those of us more familiar with the depressingly low numbers of members who normally vote in elections for fulltime officials, seeing returns of sixty-two per cent was pretty astonishing. And a staggering eighty-nine per cent of them voted for former despatch worker Fearghal O'Donovan.

The reason for O'Donovan's phenomenal success, however, has more to do with chicanery than popularity. O'Donovan has always performed better in secret ballots than in workplace shows of hands.

The reason for this is that in Irish secret ballots, the ballot papers never actually reach the voters, particularly in the offices of more remote local papers where there is traditionally a low or non-existent turn-out in union elections.

And in the major newspaper offices where the forms are actually handed out, Fearghal's cohorts simply make sure they collect up any unused forms, then put the crosses in Fearghal's box.

What's in it for them? Well, guess who controls all the highly-paid casual Saturday night-shifts at the Sunday Sentinel? *None other than Dermot O'Donovan, brother of the more famous Fearghal.*

Of course, Fearghal will deny **Conference Chronicle**'s *claim. Maybe it's time someone went through the ballot papers and compared how many were filled in with the identical pen and the identical cross.*

Lindsay reached the end of the piece ahead of the young man. She couldn't keep a smile from her lips. There were a lot of journalists who'd be walking round with sanctimonious smirks on their faces when they saw that. All their wild claims about the corruption and nepotism of the traditional print unions would be vindicated by that one anonymous article. The air would be thick with the sound of 'I told you so'.

'Sure, they can't prove a thing, so,' the young man protested in the softer Dublin accent. 'They shouldn't be let away with the likes of this, though. Fearghal'll be biting the carpet. Where did you get it?'

The woman, red-faced in her anger, said, 'It was shoved under my bedroom door. Everybody's got one. It's a scandal, so it is.'

'Who's behind it?' the young man asked, handing the sheet back as the queue moved forward.

'It'll be them bloody journalists, trying to run everything their way. As if it's not enough that their man got the general secretary job, they have to stoop to telling lies about a decent man who'll stand up to them.' She was building up a fine head of steam. Lindsay hoped the woman wouldn't round on her and demand to know which sector of the union she belonged to.

'What's Fearghal saying to it?' the young man asked.

The woman snorted. 'Let me tell you, that man's a saint. He's gone to see Standing Orders Sub-Committee about an emergency motion to clear his name. And in the face of this,' she added, waving the offending article, 'I don't doubt they'll see things his way. I've never seen the like, not in all my years as a union official. What we've got to do is, we've got to organise a proper investigation into who's doing this.'

The young man shrugged. 'It'd be a waste of time, Brid. Anybody could have done it.'

'Only someone with access to a photocopier,' she said triumphantly.

'Brid, think about it. There must be half a hundred places in a city the size of Sheffield where you can get photocopying done. If it is a journalist, they could have pals on the local paper who are only too happy to run them off copies in the office. Plus, don't forget, you can get these wee portable ones now, just the size of a briefcase. I bet half the journalists here, if they haven't got one, they'd know where to hire one from. It'd be like looking for a needle in a haystack.'

'I don't know what this union's coming to,' the woman said. She continued grumbling, but Lindsay tuned her out, scanning the room for anyone she knew. She was dying to find someone who could fill her in on all the latest gossip. She had enough experience of the internecine warfare of union politics to know that **Conference Chronicle** would be the one topic of conversation in the bars that night. There would be plenty of candidates for the position of scapegoat, she felt sure.

It was a long time since Lindsay had watched a witch-hunt. This time, she wanted a front row seat.

2

*'Remember conference lasts for a week. Pace your-
selves. And remember that fights you pick on
Monday night will surely return to haunt you by
Friday morning.'*

from *'Advice for New Delegates'*,
a Standing Orders Sub-Committee booklet.

Jennifer crossed her legs and propped her notepad
on her thigh. Lindsay had fallen silent. 'It would
be helpful if you could run through what's
happened since you got here,' she said, gently.

Lindsay rubbed a hand over her face and
muttered, 'Sorry. I'm shattered. Monday. Well,
I hadn't even signed in before I saw the first
issue of 𝕮𝖔𝖓𝖋𝖊𝖗𝖊𝖓𝖈𝖊 𝕮𝖍𝖗𝖔𝖓𝖎𝖈𝖑𝖊. The place was
jumping. I kept having conversations with
people I hadn't seen for five years that all began,
'Lindsay! It's been ages. Have you *seen* 𝕮𝖔𝖓𝖋𝖊𝖗𝖊𝖓𝖈𝖊
𝕮𝖍𝖗𝖔𝖓𝖎𝖈𝖑𝖊?'

*   *   *

She'd been deep in thought when a loud shriek closely followed by a bear-hug brought her sharply back to the here and now. Kathy Dean, a civil service press officer was bouncing up and down in front of her. 'Lindsay!' she yelped. 'Lindsay Gordon! Is it really you? Hey, no one said you were coming! Are you back for good?'

Lindsay shook her head. 'Just for conference. I'm only here as an observer.'

'It's great to see you,' Kathy said with a wide smile. 'It's been . . . what? Three years since you were last at conference. And judging by this,' she continued, waving a copy of **Conference Chronicle** 'it's not going to be short of controversy.'

'I've seen it,' Lindsay admitted. 'I don't remember anything this wild in my days as a young radical.'

'I tell you, when they find out who's responsible, I'm going to hire them to come and work in my department and produce scurrilous gossip sheets about my bosses,' Kathy said with a chuckle. 'Look, I've got to run now, Lindsay, but it's great to see you. The bar tonight?'

Lindsay nodded as Kathy hurried off. 'The bar tonight.'

'Typical,' a loud voice boomed in her ear. 'Not back five minutes and you can't wait to get wide-eyed and legless.'

Lindsay whirled around to face another old friend. Stan Merton was an East Ender who'd worked his way up the journalistic tree the old-fashioned way, starting as a tea boy and reaching his present position as city editor of a national daily. When Lindsay had been a junior reporter on the *Daily Nation*, she'd worked on the city desk for a few weeks, and she'd realised very quickly that under Stan's loud-mouthed and heavy-handed humour there was a shrewd mind that could teach her a lot. She'd been a quick learner, and the mutual respect the pair had for each other had been more than enough to counterbalance their political incompatibility.

'Stan!' Lindsay exclaimed. 'What a lovely surprise.'

'Sight for sore eyes, you are, girl,' Stan said. 'You seen the error of your ways, then? You come back to grace our shores? Or did you come back to get your own back?' He waved 𝕮𝖔𝖓𝖋𝖊𝖗𝖊𝖓𝖈𝖊 𝕮𝖍𝖗𝖔𝖓𝖎𝖈𝖑𝖊.

'Only wish I'd thought of it years ago,' she said. 'Buy you a drink later?'

'What about tomorrow morning? The second order-paper looks like the kind of bleeding-heart liberal crap that builds up no end of a thirst. I don't know why I come to these conferences. I really don't.'

'You've said that at every one of the half dozen I've been to. You're only here for the beer, Stan.'

'Tomorrow then? Half past eleven? In the bar?'

Lindsay shuddered inwardly but managed a smile. 'Great. See you then, Stan,' she said, as Stan moved off, giving her a smacking kiss on the cheek as he passed.

By the time she reached the registration table, Lindsay had chatted to half a dozen old acquaintances who were, in a triumph of hope over experience, still union activists. She'd also studiously pretended not to have seen a couple of others she'd hoped never to encounter again. As the queue snaked forward, she spotted one or two familiar faces among the union clerical staff who were dishing out the delegate packs. Even though the full Afro had been replaced by a sharp Grace Jones flattop, Lindsay instantly recognised Pauline Hardy. The black woman looked astonished. 'Lindsay Gordon!' she exclaimed. 'I thought you'd abandoned us for good. Hey, it's good to see you!' The warmth in her voice was genuine, there was no mistaking that.

'You really thought I could stay away? And never feast my eyes on you again?' Lindsay replied, falling straight back into the old teasing habit of years ago. She and Pauline had always flirted, each knowing that it was nothing more than a game. Pauline's devotion to her husband and son was legendary, but that didn't stop her enjoying a joke that had shocked dozens of prejudiced union hacks over the years.

'I didn't think my humble attractions could drag you back from California,' Pauline replied archly.

'Wild horses couldn't keep me away,' Lindsay said, taking the bulky plastic wallet of information that Pauline handed her. 'Not from you, or from the delights of conference. I tell you, though, it's depressing how many of the old familiar faces are kicking around. Hasn't *anyone* moved forward?'

'Oh, there are always plenty of old stagers around. They can't stay away, just like you,' Pauline teased.

'Are you two going to stand there blathering all afternoon, or what?' the Irishman behind Lindsay interrupted. 'Some of us have got delegation meetings to go to, you know, so. Women,' he added under his breath.

'Sorry, pal,' Lindsay said. She turned back to Pauline. 'We'll have to have a drink later, catch up on all the gossip.'

Pauline smiled. 'Have a read of **Conference Chronicle**' she said with a throaty laugh. 'That should bring you bang up to date. I'll be in the main bar about eight, provided we've finished tomorrow's order-papers.'

'See you then.' Lindsay picked up her holdall and studied the plan of the 1960s campus that occupied one wall of the foyer. The map was laid out as a Romanesque mosaic, with the borders of the buildings picked out in different colours and identified in a key alongside. She worked out how to get to her room, and headed out into the spring afternoon. Immediately, she had to lean into the wind that was flattening the clumps of daffodils dotting the grass. The buildings seemed to have been cunningly laid out to maximise their aerodynamic effect. It was like walking through a wind-tunnel the wrong way. She thought with longing of her own campus, where a fresh breeze from the bay was often a welcome relief, where the buildings looked as if they'd actually been designed rather than thrown together by a bad-tempered child with a box of Lego.

Lindsay eventually reached the lee of a tower block and looked up at its name plaque. Maclintock Tower. 'Not so much a redbrick as a breeze-block,' she muttered and pushed the door open. She joined a bunch of strangers by the lifts which ran through the centre of the modern tower block. As she waited, she pulled out the '*Advice for New Delegates*' booklet from her folder. It looked suspiciously similar to the old JU one. She couldn't imagine how something so heavily laced with irony could have been positively vetted by the po-faced men in suits who had been print union officials when she'd been a JU activist. Maybe they'd taken it seriously. She boarded the lift, stuffing the booklet back into the folder. By the tenth and final floor, she was alone in the lift, and she emerged into a corridor that seemed about as lively as the deck of the Marie Celeste. She walked slowly along it, checking the door numbers against her key, trying to ignore the slight squeal that her trainers made on the shiny vinyl flooring.

Maclintock Tower, one of five students' resi-dences at the newly upgraded Pennine University, was constructed as a series of concentric squares. In the centre were the lifts, the toilets, showers and bathrooms and a small kitchenette. Lindsay stuck her head round the door and saw a tall fridge, two gas rings and a kettle. By the kettle were a catering tin of cheap instant coffee, a box of sugar cubes and a jar of coffee whitener. Above them a sheet of A4 paper was taped to the wall. It read, 'Sheffield welcomes the Amalgamated Media Workers' Union'. But not very heartily, Lindsay thought. She almost caught herself longing for a cup of wild strawberry tea.

The corridor surrounded this central block, and the rooms were on the outside. Lindsay found hers as she rounded the third corner. She unlocked the door and stepped into the small room, skidding on a sheet of paper that had been slipped under the door. Picking it up, she immediately recognised the **Conference Chronicle** she'd already seen downstairs. With a wicked smile, she picked it up and placed it on the desk. There were quite a few activists from the former Journalists' Union who deserved to get their come-uppance. It looked like **Conference Chronicle** might just provide that as the week went on. Now that was something to look forward to!

The room seemed even more basic than the ones she'd inhabited as a student. The chair by the desk was plain wood, with no padded seat to ease the long hours that went into the produc- tion of an essay. Maybe the former polytechnic actively discouraged its students from writing lengthy analyses, she thought. The theory gained more weight as she noticed the room contained only one bookshelf. A wobbly armchair had a rip in its cracked plastic, revealing a lump of yellowish wadding. Lindsay slid open the wooden door of a built-in unit, to reveal a small hanging space, a few drawers and a tiny wash-basin with a tarnished mirror above it. The off-white walls were pockmarked with grey hollows where the adhesive pads that held up student posters had been removed. Considering how modern the block appeared from the outside, everything inside was astonishingly tatty. At least the room was light. A tall window stretched the width of the room, high as the ceiling, ending about two and a half feet above floor level.

Lindsay swiftly unpacked her bag. Two pairs of leggings, a pair of jeans, a pair of black needlecord trousers. Two sweatshirts, three polo shirts, two oversize washable silk shirts (one cream, one russet). A handful of underwear, another of socks. Sponge bag, towel, black leather cowboy boots, a swimsuit and a dressing-gown. Two paperback novels, a box of microcassettes for the tape recorder in her handbag, a couple of spare note-books and three litre bottles of Badoit. Lindsay pulled a face as she stowed the last of her things. Why was it that you needed as much for a week away as you did for six months?

Then she'd headed back to the lifts, pricked by

her Calvinist conscience to seek out someone who could give her impending thesis the blast from the past it so desperately needed. There would be plenty of opportunity for play; all she had to do was justify it with a little work.

'I take it the deceased was one of those faces from the past you were looking for?' Jennifer asked, underlining something in her notes.

'Not exactly,' Lindsay said. 'I mean, I knew him from way back, but he wasn't high on the list of people I was eager to see again. This thesis is about how the cause of women has been furthered, not hindered,' she added, acid in her voice.

'So when did you meet up with him again?'

'It was in the bar that evening. I'd noticed him earlier, when I was going into dinner. He was in a huddle in a corner with Laura Craig and Andy Spence. Andy used to be the deputy general secretary of the National Union of Printworkers. When the NUP amalgamated with the JU and the other print unions, their general secretary retired and Andy stood against Tom Jack for the AMWU top job. He lost that election, but he was definitely the people's choice for the number two job.'

'You seem very well informed, considering you live in San Francisco,' Jennifer observed.

'I'm still a member of the union, so I get my monthly copy of *Media Worker News*. It's usually only a couple of months out of date. That keeps me in touch with the factual stuff. As far as gossip's concerned, I rely on global village syndrome,' Lindsay said. 'San Francisco's one of those cities where people are always happy to scrounge a bed for a couple of nights.'

'I see. So, you saw Tom Jack with Spence and . . . now, who exactly is Laura Craig?'

Lindsay rubbed her eyes hard with her knuckles. Anything to put off thinking about Laura. There were silver threads in that flowing crest of wavy brown hair now, and the laughter lines round the blue eyes were fast approaching crows' feet. But the rest of the picture stayed the same. That mouth that could smile or sneer, but not much in between. Good figure, convention-ally elegant clothes. It was hard to imagine Laura Craig in a pair of jeans and a T-shirt up a ladder painting the ceiling.

'I don't suppose you smoke, do you?' Lindsay asked.

Jennifer shook her head. 'I carry them for clients, though,' she said, taking a packet of Benson & Hedges out of her briefcase. She tossed them to Lindsay with a brushed chrome Zippo. Lindsay noticed a chased silver ring on the third finger of her left hand.

She opened the packet and slowly drew out a cigarette. 'I haven't smoked for over two years,' she said. 'Funny, I couldn't have imagined anything making me start again. Sophie'll kill me.' Jennifer raised an eyebrow plucked to a smooth arc without a stray hair in sight. 'Sophie is the woman I live with. She's a doctor.' Lindsay lit the cigarette and cautiously inhaled. Her head seemed to float away like a helium balloon on a piece of string, but the smoke was less irritating than she'd feared. She knew then that, like an alcoholic, she'd never be able to have the odd one. She was an addict. Only the nightmare thought of having to rerun the battle to give up made her crush out the cigarette on the floor after the third drag.

Jennifer recrossed her legs and said, 'Laura Craig?'

'She's been a full-time official in the JU since the late seventies, responsible for about half the journos in broadcasting. The rest of them were in a different union, and when the JU merged with them, Laura decided she was going to be the one in sole charge. So she made sure that everybody who mattered was convinced that the other official was an idle sod who didn't have the confidence of his members. He took voluntary redundancy with record speed.

'I take it she's not one of your favourite people,' Jennifer said mildly, making another note on her pad.

'I've never been crazy about empire builders. Besides, we've got history,' Lindsay said abruptly.

'Relevant history?'

'I can't imagine how it could be,' Lindsay said. 'Call it a clash of personalities.'

'So, you didn't interrupt them to say hello?'

86

'No. I went on into dinner with a few cronies from the old days that I'd run into in the bar. It wasn't till a lot later that I actually managed to have a chat with Tom.' Oh boy, the euphemisms were piling up. Lindsay thought. 'Having a chat' was one description of what she and Tom had been doing. She'd put money on that not being the words the witnesses would come up with.

The bar was a seething mass of thirsty activists. Lindsay pushed her way through the crowd, making slow progress. If she'd had a drink for every person who'd hugged her, shaken her hand or clapped her on the back and asked how San Francisco was, she'd have been drunk before she was half-way across the room. Suddenly, it began to feel uncomfortably like she'd never been away.

She spotted the gap at the bar between the two men, each waving money at the harassed bar staff and shouting orders incomprehensible in the general hubbub. Lindsay ducked under their arms, brandished a tenner and made eye contact with one of the barmaids. After the woman had finished pouring the three pints of bitter in her current order, she glanced across at Lindsay, who mouthed 'Budweiser', held up two fingers and pointed to the familiar red, white and blue can. She smiled sweetly at the scowling men flanking her, paid for her beers and resumed her search for Pauline.

She found her in a distant corner with half a

dozen other women, all of whom Lindsay recognised from her JU days. Three of them were clerical and administrative workers like Pauline, and the others were lay officials from the book and magazine sectors of her old union. Even from a distance, Lindsay could see this wasn't a cheerful girls' night out. In a serious huddle, heads close together, the women were speaking forcefully to each other, fingers jabbing at the table top, cigarettes, dragged on furiously. They were so engrossed that no one even noticed Lindsay till she said, 'Is this a private council of war, or can anyone join in?'

Sally, a book editor who had represented the staff of a major publishing conglomerate for as long as Lindsay had known her, growled, 'Anyone who isn't one of the bosses.'

Pauline squeezed up to make room for Lindsay, who said, 'Surely you're not expecting the bosses here?' She waved at the room in a gesture that would have been expansive if she hadn't clobbered a lager-drinking woman with a Sinead O'Connor haircut, black leggings and a short black skirt. She looked like a punk Tinkerbelle in mourning. 'Sorry!' Lindsay exclaimed.

'S'all right,' the woman said. 'She means that lot,' she added, gesturing over her shoulder with her thumb across the room at a group of National Executive Council members who surrounded Tom Jack and Andy Spence.

'The management,' Sally said, her voice even

more hostile than the poisonous look she cast at Union Jack as he threw his head back and guffawed. 'Call themselves trades unionists? If Margaret Thatcher stood as this union's equality organiser, they'd vote her in.'

'I guess I'm a bit out of touch,' Lindsay said. 'What's been going down?'

'It's the same old story,' one of the other clerical workers piped up. 'If you're looking for a lousy boss, pick a trade union baron.'

'After the merger, there was a surplus in the new joint staff pension fund,' Pauline explained. 'We're talking millions, not thousands. We wanted to use the money to improve benefits, but Union Jack and his buddies on the NEC decided instead that in their role as our employers, they'd take a pensions holiday.'

Lindsay shook her head. 'You've lost me,' she said. 'I need the idiots' guide.'

Pauline grinned. 'Sally's the expert on that.'

Sally leaned back, closed her eyes and recited. 'A company pension fund is financed by contributions from employers and employees. The money is invested to provide pensions. If a fund accumulates more money than it needs to fulfil its existing obligations, there are various options. One, improve benefits and entitlements. Two, the employer takes a pensions holiday and suspends his contributions till the surplus is eaten up. Three, the employer gives the employees a pension holiday, which is, in effect, a pay rise funded out of the pension fund, a useful option in times of recession when business is bad and a rise can't be paid for out of current profits.'

'Alternatively, the boss-man takes the whole kitty, blows it on new toys, then jumps off the back of his yacht. This is known as "doing a Maxwell", and is, unfortunately, slightly less than legal,' the young woman in black chipped in.

Pauline took up the tale again. 'So we suggested they give us a pension holiday too, since that was the only way we were going to get a rise, given the state of the union finances. They said no. But now they've actually done their sums, they've decided to shed a lot more jobs than they'd originally planned. And surprise surprise. Every single one of us who'd kicked off about the pension situation is on their hit list. Me included.'

Lindsay drained her first can and crushed it in her fist. 'Wild,' she said. 'Surely the redundancies are voluntary?'

Sally snorted. 'You were one of the ones that got the golden handshake from the *Daily Nation* in their new technology purge in '86, weren't you?'

'More gilt than golden,' Lindsay said. 'Yes, I was one of the lucky ones, though it didn't feel like it at the time.'

'And wasn't that supposed to be a voluntary deal?' Sally demanded.

Lindsay popped the top of her second Bud and took a long swig. 'I take your point,' she said finally. 'Voluntary as in press gang.'

'Exactly. And Tom Jack managed to make that shitty *Daily Nation* stitch-up look like the best possible deal for the majority. Now he's using what he learned back then to shaft the union's own staff. Anyone who looks like they might be a trouble-maker is going out the door,' Sally said.

'So I'm supposed to accept the tin handshake gracefully, as of the end of next month,' Pauline said.

'They won't get away with it,' the woman in black said defiantly. The others looked at her as if she'd dropped in from the planet Out To Lunch. 'Well, they won't,' she added, uncertainly.

'I take it there's action planned?' Lindsay said.

Sally smiled grimly. 'Oh, there's action planned all right. Union Jack and his buddy boys won't know what's hit them before this week's out.'

3

'It was strange, you know,' Lindsay said, gazing
into the middle distance somewhere beyond
Jennifer. 'Sometimes it was like we'd all been
frozen in aspic some time in 1984. The rhetoric
was the same, the attitudes, even the faces. As if
the last nine years just hadn't happened. And
then I'd look around, and suddenly it was all
different. There we were, sitting in a conference
hall with the very same people who'd supposedly
been our enemies and our rivals. Talking about

streamlining our administration, improving our public profile, developing new services to meet changing needs, like some post-Thatcherite corporation. And Union Jack still at the heart of it, cutting his coat according to what would keep him in power.'

'When did you actually first speak to him?' Jennifer glanced at her watch as she asked the question.

'I'm sorry, I keep getting side-tracked. It's probably the drink. I've had more than I should have tonight. On Monday evening, after the women told me about the redundancies, I went over to the bar to get a round of drinks in. On the way, I had to pass Tom and his NEC cronies. Being Tom, he couldn't let me pass without getting into my ribs.'

'Ey-up lads, lock up your daughters. The Gay Gordons are back in town,' Tom roared as Lindsay tried to slip unnoticed past the bunch of fixers gathered round the general secretary. 'What happened? The Yanks realise they'd been sold a pup?'

'Nice to see you too, Tom.' Lindsay tried to carry on towards the bar, but he moved to block her way. He was trying to push her into behaving like some butch blundering dyke, trying to make her shove him out of the way. As if she'd make any impact on that stocky, bullish figure in her path. Lindsay smiled sweetly, shaking her head. 'Still the same old charmer, eh?'

'Well, Lindsay, it's a dirty job, but somebody's got to do it, haven't they? Otherwise, we'd fall into the hands of some of them dangerous radicals. You know the ones – they're out there, ready and waiting to turn us into a matriarchy, leaving us lads to be nothing but the playthings of you lasses,' Tom said, leaning so close she could smell the beer on his breath and see the individual hairs in his thick, curly beard. He hadn't changed much, she thought, either superficially or more deeply. These days, there were grey hairs among the brown in his hair and beard, but his warm brown eyes were still the same, holding the eyes of his audience, whether it was one person or a thousand, forcing them to be the ones to look away first.

'You should be so lucky, Tom,' she said.

He smiled the familiar smile, his full sensual lips barely parting. His crooked teeth were the only chink in his armour that Lindsay had ever noticed. But even that he turned to an advantage. She had heard him once in full flood, explaining how he would never have his teeth fixed because every time he looked in the mirror they reminded him of the importance of a free National Health Service, and of how his working-class roots had prevented him from having the gleaming white smile of the bosses. It was a performance that had to be seen to be believed. He winked confidentially and said, 'Oh, but I am lucky, Lindsay, I'm a very lucky man.'

'I wonder if you'll still be saying that at the end of the week,' Lindsay mused softly.

Jack's brows dropped in a frown that seemed to promise the wrath of God. 'I hope you're not threatening me already, Lindsay. Bloody hell, woman, you've only been back in the country five minutes.'

'You sound very paranoid, Tom. Fancy you feeling threatened by a little woman like me! As it happens, it's not me you've got to worry about. Maybe you should have taken more time to consider the consequences when you decided to behave like management.' Lindsay moved to one side, hoping to get away.

Jack's scowl deepened and his nostrils flared. 'You always were full of piss and wind,' he said. All the fun had gone out of it now. The rest of the group had fallen silent, shifting uneasily, almost imperceptibly moving back from the two antagonists.

'It used to take more than that to rattle you, Tom,' Lindsay said matter-of-factly. 'I didn't realise that dumping union staff on the dole queue was such a sore point with you.'

'Just what gives you the right to come back here and monopolise the high moral ground? You've got no right, no right at all to treat me like a piece of shit. If you were a bloody delegate at this conference, I might just listen to what you have to say. But you're a nobody now. Do you hear? A nobody!' Jack shouted at the top of his powerful bass voice.

Taken aback by the force of his onslaught, Lindsay held her hands up, palms facing him. 'Hey, Tom, cool it. I was just putting a point of view.'

'You've got no right to a point of view in this union any more. You don't even live in this bloody country. Listen to me, Lindsay Gordon, and listen good. You've done your share of trouble-making in this union. You and your cronies wasted enough of the JU's time and money with your daft feminist schemes and gay rights propaganda. Well, you're not going to hijack the AMWU. So you can stop right there.'

Lindsay tried the deep-breathing techniques she'd learned at a seminar in Sausalito. They failed. She flushed a deep scarlet and took a step towards him. 'Don't you dare talk to me like that, you conniving turncoat bully,' she said in a low voice that attracted more attention in that crowded bar than shouting would have done. 'And don't try blowing smoke in everybody's eyes. What you and that National Executive you've got tucked in your back pocket are doing to the head office staff is nothing to do with feminism, and you know it. It's to do with good old-fashioned bad management and the broken promises between employer and employee. The only reason most of the people you're getting rid of are women is the age-old reason. They're cheap to pay off. How did you put it to me back in '86, when the *Daily Nation* were making me redundant? Let me get it right . . .' Lindsay closed her eyes momentarily, as if deep in thought. 'Oh yes, now I remember. Quote: "The reason why women get paid less than men is that they will keep taking these low-paid jobs." End quote.'

For a brief, terrifying moment, she thought Tom Jack was going to hit her. His eyes widened and his hands bunched into fists at his side. He staggered slightly, then, with perceptible effort, he regained control of himself. 'If you've got the sense you were born with, you'll stay out of my road,' he said quietly, his voice tight with suppressed anger. 'There's plenty of rules in the rulebook for getting rid of the likes of you.'

Lindsay shook her head theatrically, playing up her air of astonishment as she moved past Jack and made for the bar. '"A working-class hero is something to be", right enough,' she said to no one in particular.

'Not what you'd call a private confrontation, then,' Jennifer said wryly. 'Have another,' she said, pushing the cigarette packet towards Lindsay.

'I'll pass, thanks all the same. Not only was it not private, it hit the headlines. By breakfast next morning, everyone in the place knew we'd had a run-in.' Lindsay summarised the couple of paragraphs that had appeared about their fight in **Conference Chronicle**'s 'Gossip and Innuendo' section.

Jennifer looked alert, like a cat hearing the tinopener at the opposite end of the house. 'Who produces this **Conference Chronicle**, then?' she asked.

Lindsay shrugged. 'I wish I knew. And so does everyone else. Half of the delegates and officials want to lynch whoever it is, and the rest want to buy them a large drink. I've never known any fringe publication generate this kind of interest. You always get the odd scurrilous flyer round conference, but nothing this organised. It's incredibly well-informed. It takes on the left as well as the right, it has a go at full-time officials, lay activists, the lunatic fringe, the boringly predictable establishment. I know it's a dreadful old cliché, but truly, nothing seems to be sacred to **Conference Chronicle**. It's reasonably witty, it's competently put together, and it's delivered as if by a band of paper-boy fairies that no one's seen or heard. Certainly, the distribution's a hell of a lot more efficient than the members of the old distribution union ever managed!'

'But no one knows who's behind it?' Jennifer persisted.

'Nope. It could be anyone. Photocopiers are ten a penny these days, and you wouldn't need a great deal of skill to produce the master copy. All you'd need is a couple of hours with a lap-top and a decent DTP package. Fingers have been pointing all over the place, and there are obviously one or two complete loops who'd like us all to think it's them, but nobody's got any serious idea who's behind it. I'll tell you one thing, though. It's the only topic of conversation in the bars and the smoke-filled rooms.'

'You're telling me that this . . . newsletter is the issue that everyone at conference is getting worked up about?' Jennifer asked. There was a note of incredulity in her voice that Lindsay found reassuring. It meant she wasn't the only one who was aware that in the big bad world out there, whatever appeared in **Conference Chronicle** was even less interesting or significant than the marital relations of the royal family.

'That's right. There are three million unemployed, the government's threatening legislation that will be the effective end of trade unionism in this country, and my union's got its knickers in a twist because someone is getting their kicks from taking the mickey. It makes little sense to me these days either, Ms Okido, but that's what's been going on. But I don't think it's got anything to do with Tom Jack's death, except that the article in **Conference Chronicle** makes it sound like I had a better motive than most for wanting rid of him.'

'You think that's why the killer chose your room?'

Lindsay sighed, perplexed. 'It's the only thing I can think of. God knows, it's little enough reason. There must be a lot of people in the motive queue ahead of me. Union Jack's machinations were ruffling a lot of feathers among the rank and file. I was one of the lucky ones – I didn't have to work with him on a regular basis any more. But a lot of the ones who did were getting pretty wound up. Let me tell you, Ms Okido, I'm not the only person who would have been happy to see the back of Union Jack as AMWU's general secretary.'

'And if our general secretary wasn't so concerned with furthering the sectional interests of our so-called brothers and sisters from the former Journalists' Union – an organisation that was more like a gentlemen's club than a union, by all accounts – those of us who are facing redundancy on a massive scale in the print would not be in the mess we're in. They were happy enough to grab our historic traditions and a bank balance that was in the black, unlike their own, and now they want to grab our very jobs. Colleagues, it's time the National Executive and the general secretary adopted the policy of the greatest good of the greatest number and started remembering who's been paying their wages.' The red-faced man pounded the lectern, causing a shriek of feedback that cut through a couple of hundred hangovers like broken chalk screeching on a blackboard. 'Colleagues, vote for the London Central Print Division's amendment to motion thirty-two. Thank you.'

Lindsay pressed 'play' on her Walkman. Anything had to be better than this debate. She shifted in her seat again, trying to find a comfortable position on the hard chair. As an observer, she was seated apart from the main body of delegates, on a small raised dais at the back of the octagonal conference hall. The observers didn't rate tables, unlike the delegates, so they were condemned to shuffling constantly through their agendas, order-papers and copies of **Conference Chronicle**. The latest edition had been the sole topic of conversation over breakfast for the members of the paranoid tendency, with its 'revelation' that Laura Craig was a Special Branch plant. As the voices droned on around her, Lindsay amused herself by flicking through the dozen paragraphs again.

We can exclusively reveal today that full-time official Laura Craig gets more than one pay packet. The tough-talking broadcasting journalists' organiser has another full-time job – stool pigeon for the Special Branch.

For the last fifteen years, her role has been to undermine the whole trade union movement by working to ensure that the former Journalists' Union was such a laughing-stock that its own members could only hold it in contempt. That in turn meant that influential media figures judged the rest of the TU movement by the pathetic and politically naïve behaviour of their own union.

So those journalists in turn helped create the climate of opinion which allowed the Thatcher

government to systematically strip working people
of their rights and demolish their confidence in
the whole TU movement.

Craig orchestrated the damaging strikes at BBC
TV in 1984, ITN in 1986, IRN in 1988 and BBC
Radio in 1990 and '91. All of these actions
damaged the union both financially and politi-
cally. She has also been a vociferous supporter of
strikers in other sectors of the JU, an invariable
face on every picket line. One opponent of her
hard-line approach, general secretary 'Union'
Jack, once said, 'You'll never see a bandwagon
rolling past without Laura clinging to it by her
beautifully painted fingernails.'

Craig, 40, was recruited to secret government
service when she was a student at the LSE. She
was planted on the BBC graduate training scheme,
and quickly became actively involved in the JU.
In spite of that, she also achieved rapid promotion
in the radio news field, something so unusual for
a union official at Broadcasting House that BBC
bosses are still citing her as an example that being
an activist doesn't stop you being a success.

When she applied for the job as full-time
organiser for the broadcasting sector, she seemed
the obvious choice. And so another union was
infiltrated by those who have a vested interest in
the status quo.

Lindsay couldn't help smiling. Pure garbage, but
it was good to see Laura get a good slagging off

in print. At the very least, it must have sent her blood pressure up a few notches when she'd seen it that morning. Lindsay only hoped that **Conference Chronicle** could maintain credibility after a crazy leap in the dark like this. Fringe scandal sheets always got carried away by the need to be more and more shocking. But if it managed to stay more in touch with reality, the flyer had the potential to be the shit-stirrer conference needed. Lindsay was wondering idly what Laura had done to upset the writer of **Conference Chronicle** when a familiar voice interrupted her thoughts.

'Better than the bear baiting?'

Lindsay looked up in surprise. 'Dick? What are you doing here? You used to think the union was one of Britain's last bastions of conservatism!' She switched off the Walkman.

'Aye, along with the Reform Club and the House of Commons. What's so fascinating?' he asked, pointing to her headphones.

Lindsay pulled a wry face and shrugged. There was no way she was going to admit to Dick McAndrew that she'd been relaxing to the sound of whale music. 'Anything's better than the massed drones of trade unionists. But you didn't answer the question. What are you doing here?'

'I'm here to see Tom Jack get his come-uppance,' Dick said bitterly, his Glasgow accent lending a threatening edge to the words. 'Him and his cronies have done for me and my team, so I came along to try to do the same for him. And how's California?' Dick eased his large frame on to the chair next to Lindsay. He looked absurd, like a Hereford bull on a bicycle.

'I'm thinking of having a flyer printed. "California's wonderful, I love the job, we've got a terrific house on the beach where the fog rolls in just like Argyllshire, no, I don't miss running with the pack, no, I don't miss British sausages, beer or sitcoms." How about you?' Lindsay gave him an affectionate hug. She and Dick had met years before in the Glasgow Labour Party, and had stayed friends ever since. And she owed him. A few years before, when she'd been eagerly pursuing the spy scandal that had sent her into her first overseas exile, Dick had stuck his neck out for her. She'd never had the chance to repay him. 'Is *Socialism Today* still keeping the kids in shoes?'

'You're well out of touch, Gordon,' Dick replied, a scowl changing his amiable face into the grimace of a Sumo wrestler. 'There is no *Socialism Today*. Just like Kinnock purged socialism from the Labour Party, Union Jack and his cronies purged *Socialism Today* from the newsagents. So I am no longer the news editor of a radical monthly magazine. I'm just another freelance desperately scratching a living off a shrinking market.' Dick stared at the floor, hands involuntarily bunching into fists.

'What's that got to do with Union Jack? Did

the union refuse to bail you out of trouble?'
Lindsay asked. For as long as she could remember,
Socialism Today's finances had been less stable than
Mexico's. The difference was that banks didn't fall
over themselves to lend billions to struggling left-
wing publishing houses.

Dick snorted. 'What are you on? One of they
weird American pills that warp your sense of
reality? Tom Jack didnae wash his hands of us
when we were in trouble. That I could have
understood, though forgiving would've been
something else again. Naw, it was Union Jack
himself that put the shaft in.'

'Going to stop talking in riddles and tell me the
story?' Lindsay asked, the brisk words softened
by her tone.

'Nothing much to tell. We ran a story about
eighteen months ago alleging that Tom Jack was
going behind the backs of the union executive
and dealing directly with the firm of accountants
who were putting together the statements of
accounts prior to the merger with the other
unions. Nothing wrong with that in itself, except
that the piece went on to reveal that Union Jack
was suggesting all sorts of creative accounting
tricks to make our finances look a lot healthier
than they really were. Some of the wee tricks
he'd thought of were borderline illegal.'

Lindsay sucked her breath in sharply. 'Pick the
bones out of that, eh?'

Dick nodded grimly. 'We thought we had it

copper-bottomed, but Union Jack insisted it was a set-up. He announced he was going to sue, and our source inside the accountants got cold feet and bottled out of going in to bat for us. So Union Jack took us to the cleaners. We couldn't even pay the lawyer's bills, never mind the damages. The four of us that owned the magazine on paper all had to dive headlong into bankruptcy.'

Dick's blue eyes had a new bleakness Lindsay had never seen there before. It wasn't surprising. He wasn't some reckless kid with no one to worry about but himself. He was an experienced professional, a man who knew the risks, but had always managed to avoid exposing his wife and children to them.

'Helen and the kids?' she asked.

'We're okay. We managed to keep the house. When I joined the *Socialism Today* management collective, the office lawyers recommended that we put it in her name, that and the car. So it could have been worse, I suppose.'

Lindsay felt anger rising, a taste as distinctive as bile. 'And the union just stood by and let this happen?'

'Lindsay, the executive committee were in Tom Jack's pocket. He said crawl, they said, how low. Sure, there were plenty of people in the union jumping up and down about it, but nobody walking the corridors of power gave a shift about a wee magazine with a dozen journalists and a nasty habit of bursting balloons. The trouble is,

Lindsay, this union isnae for the rank and file any more. And until we get rid of Tom Jack once and for all, nothing's going to get any better. He's got to go.'

Lindsay stood up and stretched. 'I don't think I can take any more of this debate. Are they open?'

Dick glanced at his watch. 'Ten minutes ago. What are we doing, wasting good drinking time?'

In spite of the earliness of the hour, the student union bar was doing a brisk trade. Dick ordered a pint of bitter and turned to Lindsay. 'What're you for?'

'D'you know, I don't think I can face drink,' she said in a tone of incredulity. 'You'd better make it a mineral water.'

Dick shook his head in sorrow, but ordered it nevertheless. 'You've been away too long.'

Before Lindsay could leap to her own defence, the double doors of the bar swung open and Laura Craig strolled in. Her tailored trousers and long sweater were as close as Lindsay had ever seen her to casual clothes. 'Hey, Laura,' one of the delegates at the bar called. 'Shouldn't you be buying the drinks? We've all read **Conference Chronicle** – you're the only one here that's on expenses!'

Laura smiled. 'I wish,' she said. 'Mine's a vodka and ginger beer. Make it a large one, or else I'll set Miss Moneypenny on you!' She moved across to the group of men, succumbing willingly to their raucous teasing.

'Played the room like a fiddle,' Lindsay said.

'You've always had the knife into the Vogue Vamp. You're not seriously telling me you believe that guff?' Dick asked.

Lindsay sighed. 'Of course I don't. Even her worst enemy couldn't have come up with something that ludicrous.'

Dick emptied his glass and dumped it on the bar. 'I'd better be on my way. I've got to go down to Standing Orders Sub-Committee. I've got an emergency motion to propose for the membership and organisation order paper.'

'Oh? What about?'

'As well as having branches organised locally and according to sector, we should set up unemployed branches, since that's what this union seems to be best at presiding over.' Dick pulled a lopsided smile.

'I'm sorry about *Socialism Today*,' Lindsay said.

'So'm I. And about the philosophy, not just the magazine. See you around.'

Dick lumbered off. As he reached the door, he came face to face with Tom Jack. Lindsay saw their mouths move, but they were too distant for her to hear what they said. Not for the first time, she wished she could lip-read. Suddenly, Dick's right arm shot out, and he pushed Tom hard in the chest, so the union leader stumbled and fell back against the wall. It wasn't the first bit of rough stuff she'd seen so far at the conference. There had been a few punches flung in the bar in the early hours between warring factions. But this was the first time she'd seen anyone lay a hand on the man who seemed to be at the centre of every divisive and damaging row she'd witnessed. Lindsay couldn't help feeling worried that it had been Dick who'd thrown the first blow.

4

Lindsay tried unsuccessfully to stifle the yawn that gripped her suddenly. 'Aagh,' she groaned. 'I'm really sorry, the night's beginning to catch up with me.'

'It's okay. I'm in no hurry,' Jennifer reassured her. 'What's most important is that we get as many of the facts clear at this stage so we can convince the police there's no point in holding you here.'

'Okay. I can't think of anything else that happened during Tuesday that has any bearing on anything. I spent most of the day doing interviews for my thesis with the women who were around during the big equality issue rows of the eighties, getting them to dredge their memories for the human stories behind the dry recorded facts of motions passed and leaflets issued. All very boring stuff to someone who wasn't involved at the time, I suspect.' Lindsay avoided the revelation that she too had found much of it excruciatingly tedious, and was beginning to wonder how she was going to give her supposedly groundbreaking thesis the bite she wanted it to have. 'Anyway, while I was interviewing, one of the guys I used to work with in Glasgow when I was a reporter on the *Scottish Daily Clarion* came over and invited me to the Scots-Irish Ceilidh Night.

'The JU always held one. You could only go if you were Scots or Irish, regardless of where you worked. A handful of outsiders always used to get invited if they were prominent in the union and had the right political credentials – and I mean right. In spite of which, I'm ashamed to say I've always enjoyed it. The music was always terrific – we've got some really talented singers and musicians in the union, and it always felt to me like the music and the dancing was at least as important to the people there as the rest of the Celtic male-bonding stuff. So when I was invited, I handed over my tenner like a shot. We each chip in a tenner for the drink.'

Jennifer couldn't hide the look of surprise. 'That's a lot of drink,' she commented.

'The Celts are a thirsty people. Historically, we've got a lot of sorrows to drown. Anyway, it always used to be one of the few events at conference where political differences were forgotten as we forged our sentimental bonds of spurious camaraderie. Unfortunately, like so many other things in the trade union movement, it's changed beyond recognition.'

The joyous energy of the jigs and reels that filled the room did nothing to dissipate the atmosphere of simmering rancour that filled the post-graduate common room of Wilberforce Hall. For once, the old Celtic alliances were failing to diminish the strains of AMWU's newly discovered tensions. The brains who had dreamed up the terms and conditions of the most complex merger in the history of the British trade union movement had somehow failed to consider the volatile effect of lumping printers, clerical workers, broadcasters, researchers, journalists, camera crew and distribution workers together to find common cause, something they'd signally failed to achieve in the 500-year history of the mechanical mass media.

As the drink flowed, so too did the old resentments. At first, Lindsay had managed to steer clear of disputes by grabbing a bottle of White Horse and squeezing into the corner behind the fiddler, two guitarists, concertina player and tin whistle blower who were currently providing the music. But her hiding place was exposed soon after mid-night when the impromptu band took a break and gave way to a Newcastle printer who played the Northumbrian pipes. Their mournful notes always made her feel melancholy. Or maybe it was just the whisky. Either way, she wished Sophie was with her, instead of at a conference a hundred miles away. If Sophie was here, the atmosphere would be irrelevant, Lindsay told herself.

Her maudlin thoughts were interrupted by a familiar face, bleary with drink. Stewart Grant had been one of her fellow reporters on the *Daily Nation* in London years before. A diehard misogynist, Grant had been one of those who had exploited her grief at Frances' death in a series of supposedly innocent remarks whose barbs twisted like fish hooks in her stomach. Even before then, she'd never liked him. But his behaviour when she'd been at her most vulnerable had turned dislike to contempt in a handful of sentences.

'Hey, if it's not Lindsay Gordon, come back to lord it over us. You've got some nerve, lady,' he slurred.

'As usual, Stewart, you make as much sense as a square toilet-seat. Go away and bother somebody else, eh?'

He giggled, a high, edgy sound. 'Cannae face the truth, eh?' He turned back to face the room. 'Hey, guys, come and see this. It's no' often you get a chance to see one of the rats that deserted the sinking ship. They're usually running too

113

damn fast. Get a load of this.' He turned back to Lindsay and leered. 'You always did wish they all could be California girls, didn't you? Mind you, I cannae imagine them going for the likes of Flash Gordon. A wee bit more taste they've got over there, I'd say.'

'Do us all a favour, Stewart. Go and find a tall building and jump off.' She got to her feet and tried to push past him, but she was too late. A handful of his cronies had moved forward to form a tight ring around her.

'D'you know the boys, Flash?' Stewart demanded. 'All *real* journalists. None of your equality reps here, eh, boys?' There was a chorus of 'no way's. 'Naw, we get out there at the rock face and do the business. Out there, stitching up the punters, shafting the oppos, getting stuck into the real job. But you couldnae hack it, could you, Flash? Naw, it all got too much for you. You had to go running off with your tail between your legs to the soft life in the States.'

'Not that we've got anything against America,' one of the other drunken Scots piped up. Lindsay vaguely remembered the face. He'd been a reporter with the *Glasgow Tribune* when she'd worked for the *Scottish Daily Clarion*.

'Of course not,' another added. Lindsay recognised Chic McBain, a down-table sub-editor on the *Clarion*. 'Some of my best pals work in America now. You know why that is, don't you Flash? It's because there's no jobs here for them. And do you know why that is, Flash Gordon?'

'I'm sure you're going to give me the version according to macho man,' Lindsay said wearily, 'so why don't I just shut up and save time?'

'It's because when people like you were our union reps back in the eighties you were too busy playing politics and screaming about AIDS and sexism instead of fighting for jobs. Youse all just stood back and let Thatcher and Tebbit kick the union movement to death. Youse said yessir, no sir, to the Maxwells and Murdochs and Carnegie Wilsons while they decimated our jobs and wrecked our industry. And then you buggered off to a cushy number in the sun while we run about the country like headless chickens, desperate for casual shifts anywhere that'll pay our bus fare.' Chic stopped suddenly, his flow of invective in need of fuel.

He stumbled away, in search of more whisky, while Stewart, refreshed by support, returned to the attack. 'Squandered our birthright, you and your pals did,' he shouted, his bloodshot eyes blinking wildly as he thrust his purple face close to hers. For the first time since the harangue had started, she felt slightly nervous, not convinced that she could get out of this unscathed. 'Did you come back to laugh at us? Is that what you're doing here, drinking our whisky?' Stewart yelled. 'It's not on, you bitch, it's not on!'

Lindsay's heart sank even further as she saw

Tom Jack shoulder his way through the men who surrounded her. All she needed right now was for the general secretary to add his weight to the bully boys.

'You're damn right it's not on,' Union Jack roared loud enough to stop the Northumbrian piper in mid-phrase. His pipes died with a wheezing groan.

Lindsay steeled herself for his onslaught. But to her astonishment, he moved to her side and grabbed Stewart Grant by the shirt-front.

'This is supposed to be a ceilidh,' Union Jack growled. 'Who the hell do you think you are, turning it into a war? Bloody hell, it's come to a pretty pass when a Yorkshireman's got to tell a bunch of drunken Jocks how to behave at a ceilidh.'

Stewart's mouth kept opening and closing without a sound.

'This isnae anything to do with you, Tom,' Chic said, his voice placatory. 'We were just having a wee word with Lindsay here.'

'Anything you've got to say to Lindsay, there's a time and a place for, and it's not here. And as long as I'm general secretary of this union, anything that happens at conference is to do with me. You'd all do well to remember that. Now, Lindsay, I want a word with you.' Abruptly, Tom pushed Stewart away from him and steered Lindsay across the room to a quiet corner.

'I'll not forget this, Tom Jack,' Stewart spluttered vainly at their retreating backs.

'Neither will I,' Lindsay said. 'Thanks. I appreciate it.'

'Oh, I'll want paying back,' Tom said with a broad wink. 'I've not got where I am by giving owt for nowt. There's something I want to discuss with you. What you might call a proposition. Something you can help me with.' He looked around and realised there were eager ears all round. He drew Lindsay close and said softly in her ear, 'I've had a few drinks, so this isn't the time. Tomorrow, during the first order-paper. There's a coffee shop about half a mile down the hill from the conference centre. Polly's it's called. I'll see you there.' He stepped back. 'I'll see you later, Lindsay. I know we can do business together.'

Jennifer leaned forward with the look of a prospector who's just spotted the glister of gold. 'Did anyone hear him make this arrangement?'

Lindsay shrugged her shoulders. 'I suppose someone could have. There were plenty of people around.'

'Can you think of anyone who was particularly close to the pair of you at that time?'

Lindsay closed her eyes and tried to visualise the scene. She could almost smell the smoke and the alcohol, she could picture Union Jack's unflinching eyes, but the other figures were unidentifiable blurs. Reluctantly, she shook her head again. 'I'm sorry. The room wasn't well lit, and I'd had a few drinks. It was all I could do to concentrate on what Tom was saying.'

Jennifer tapped her pad with her pen. 'What I'm far from clear about is why Tom Jack was in your room later that same night when he'd made an arrangement to meet you the following day.'

'You and me both,' Lindsay said. 'I haven't a clue. Maybe he decided that what he had to say to me wouldn't wait. Or maybe he was on that floor for reasons that were nothing to do with me. After all, there are another dozen or so delegates with rooms there. He might have had an assignation with any one of them.'

'But wasn't your door locked?' Jennifer asked, with that tone of despairing incredulity that lawyers reserve for clients who appear to be clinically brain dead.

Lindsay shrugged. 'Probably not. The lock was really fiddly, so half the time I didn't bother. I wasn't the only one who'd been having a problem. It was the main topic of conversation at breakfast on Tuesday once we'd all exhausted **Conference Chronicle**. I just took to carrying my passport and traveller's cheques around in my bag.'

Jennifer began to look as if she wished she'd stayed in bed and let someone else have the joy of handling Lindsay Gordon's little problem. She massaged the back of her neck with one hand. 'Okay, let's go back to this ceilidh. What happened after you and Jack had arranged to meet?'

'The music started up again, and Tom went off to talk to some of his cronies from the print sector. I was collared by some Irish guy who's been short-listed for a job in Minnesota teaching journalism. He wanted to pick my brains about doing the business in the States. Anyway, we couldn't hear ourselves talk, so after about ten minutes, we went outside. We walked across to the fountain in that sort of plaza in the middle of the campus. I don't know if you noticed, but it was a really mild night. Either that, or we'd both had enough drink not to notice the cold. Anyway, even the breeze felt warm, and my new friend had a quarter bottle of Irish, and so I just sat there and had the odd swallow and told it like it is in the US of A.'

'Okay. Two things. Did you leave before Tom Jack? And how long did you sit talking to this Irishman?' Jennifer asked, flipping back a couple of pages in her notebook and checking her notes of what Lindsay had already said.

'Tom was still in a huddle when we went out. As for how long, I can't be sure. What I can tell you is that I parted company with the Irishman just after three o'clock. And before you ask, the reason I can be so precise about it is that I'd run out of things I felt I could usefully tell him, but he seemed happy to rabbit on all night. So I asked him what time it was and he looked at his watch and said it was ten past three. So I did the "Good God, is it really that time? I have to be up in the morning" routine and got to my feet. His room wasn't in Maclintock Tower, so we said our good-byes and went our separate ways.'

'His name?' Jennifer asked, pen poised like a stake over a vampire's heart.

Lindsay pulled a wry face. 'Good question. I wish I knew the answer. He's the nearest thing I've got to an alibi, since there can only have been a few minutes between me leaving him and screaming my head off to raise the alarm.'

Jennifer looked close to exasperation. 'You mean, your alibi witness is a man you've never met before, whose name you don't know, and who was quite probably drunk?'

'That's about the size of it.'

5

'The rooms we offer delegates typically don't offer a high degree of security. We therefore urge you not to bring your diamonds along on the off chance of being invited to the Broadcasting Branch dinner. By Friday morning, chances are even your paracetamol won't be safe.'

from *'Advice for New Delegates'*,
a *Standing Orders Sub-Committee* booklet.

Jennifer breathed deeply through her nose. Lindsay felt six years old, as uncomfortable and inadequate as her primary schoolteacher had always made her feel.

'Okay,' Jennifer said, the strain starting to edge into her voice. 'What happened next?'

'I walked to Maclintock, pressed the button for the lift, waited for the lift and ascended to the tenth floor. And no, I didn't see anyone close enough to identify them, so I doubt they could do that much for me. When I got out of the lift, I

121

was aware of somebody disappearing round the corner of the corridor to my left, but I couldn't really see who it was, since the main lights had gone off and it was just those dim blue emergency night-lights that were on. I've got this feeling at the back of my mind that there was something else I noticed, but the more I try to pin it down, the more elusive it gets. I'm sorry, Ms Okido, I'm not giving you much to go on, am I?'

From somewhere, Jennifer pulled a smile that demonstrated a lot more conviction than she felt. 'Don't worry,' she said automatically. 'I've heard worse. Carry on, Ms Gordon. I know this is the hard bit, but once we get to the end, we'll be a long way towards getting you out of here.'

Lindsay nodded. 'Maybe I will have that other cigarette,' she said, half to herself as she reached for the packet. 'As I got closer, I could see my door wasn't quite closed. The tongue of the catch was sitting on the edge of the hole, if you see what I mean. I pushed it open, half-expecting to find I'd been burgled. The first thing I noticed was that the breeze was blowing in my face. I felt a bit muddled, because I was sure I hadn't left the window open when I went out. I switched the light on and realised that there was a bloody great jagged hole where the window should have been. It took me a moment to register that there was no glass on the inside of the room, so whatever had broken the window had gone from the inside out.'

She inhaled deeply on the cigarette and closed her eyes, determined to be as accurate as she could be about her thoughts and actions. 'I looked round the room, trying to work out what was missing, but everything seemed to be where it should be, except that the chair was lying on its side and the clothes that I'd dumped on it were all over the floor. I walked across to the window and . . .' She paused and inhaled more smoke. 'I didn't want to look down, but I made myself. It was a long way down, and I could see the car roofs glinting in the glow from the lights that line the paths. Only, one car wasn't shining. There was something light coloured on it, like . . . like a shirt when you've thrown it on the floor. That's when I started screaming.' Lindsay leaned back and rested her head against the cold cell wall, staring up at the ceiling bulb in its wire cage.

'It felt like I was standing there for ages, but it can't have been long before other people arrived. I didn't take much notice, to be honest. There was a lot of shouting about calling the police, which someone must have done. The rest you know,' Lindsay nodded.

Jennifer Okido nodded approvingly. 'Good. Okay, Lindsay, what's going to happen now is that the police are going to interview you. I strongly urge you at this stage to assert your right to silence. What that means is that, whatever they ask you, you must say, "No reply". Now, are you familiar with the TV show *Take Your Pick*?'

Lindsay looked at her as if she'd gone mad. 'Yes,' she said dubiously.

'You know the section at the beginning where contestants are asked questions in an attempt to get them to say "yes" or "no"? Well, this interview will be rather like that. They'll try to trick you into giving an answer other than "no reply", and as soon as you do that, in law you are deemed to have given up your right to silence. They'll say things like, "Has your solicitor instructed you to say no reply", and "Is it the case that whatever I ask you, you're just going to say, no reply". You mustn't fall into the trap. I can protect you to some extent, because they're not allowed to put you under undue pressure, but I'm afraid most of the burden rests on your shoulders. Are you clear about what you have to do?' Jennifer asked.

Lindsay nodded. 'I'll do my best.'

'I know you're tired, but the sooner we get this over with, the sooner I can set about tracking down your alibi witness. I'm afraid they're not going to release you till we can establish that. Hopefully, though, they're not going to charge you either just yet. If you're ready, I'll go and tell them, and we can maybe get started soon.'

Jennifer got up and knocked on the cell door. After a few moments, feet tapped up the corridor, and the Judas window slid open. Satisfied that the right person was about to leave the cell, the officer opened the door. The solicitor turned back and gave Lindsay a smile before the door banging shut cut her off from sight.

Left to herself, Lindsay curled into a ball on the hard bunk and closed her eyes. When the custody officer came to get her fifteen minutes later, he had to shake her awake.

Conference Chronicle
The Paper Off The Record
Did He Fall or Was He Pushed?

They scraped him off the tarmac like a lump of strawberry jam, just like the song says. It may not have been 20,000 feet without a parachute, but it was far enough to spell 'Good night, Vienna' for General Secretary Tom 'Union' Jack. Our late unlamented leader always thought he could walk on water. But in the early hours of this morning, he proved he couldn't fly without one of those planes he was so fond of spending your union dues on. Now everyone will remember the inaugural Annual Delegate Conference of the Amalgamated Media Worker's Union as the one that gave a whole new meaning to plummeting membership figures.

Union Jack was discovered spread over a sizeable acreage of the car-park behind Maclintock Tower about twenty past three this morning when former journalist and conference observer Lindsay Gordon raised the alarm, claiming she'd returned to her room in the student's residence to discover a man-sized hole in the tenth floor window.

This unlikely tale follows the stand-up fight between Gordon and Union Jack on Monday evening (reported in yesterday's **Conference Chronicle**). *According to our sources, the pair have a history of falling out over a wide variety of issues over the years, ranging from feminism to feminism.*

Gordon, who can resemble a one-woman monstrous regiment, had spent the evening at the notorious Scots-Irish Night, a tradition of the former Journalists' Union that has been claimed eagerly by enthusiastic haggis-bashers and bog-trotters in AMWU. There, Gordon and her compatriots did their level best to drink Sheffield dry. This monument to sexism (the women get groped) and racism (non-Celts are barred) was held in the post-graduate common room in Wilberforce Hall.

Union Jack had been invited to the bash in spite of a lifetime of playing the professional Yorkshireman born, bred and buttered up by everyone after a political favour. Some say he got the invitation out of respect for his exalted office as elected General Secretary of our recently amalgamated dog's dinner of a union; others, because his attitude to women and ethnic minorities made him a natural candidate for adoption to the Celtic fringe. While there, he demonstrated a third qualification for membership by drinking the lion's share of a bottle of Black Bush.

Gordon, meanwhile was conducting a scientific comparison of as wide a range of Scotch and Irish whiskeys as she could get her hands on. Eye witnesses say she was more than holding her own under attack from several Fleet Street hacks who berated her for abandoning Her Majesty's Gutter Press just so she could sit in the sun in California teaching journalism to Yanks. (New readers unfamiliar with Gordon's background should ask any newspaper journalist with more than five years' Fleet Street experience for the 'cashed in, sold out' version and any former member of the Equality Committee of the dearly departed Journalists' Union for the 'paid her dues, deserved the break' version.)

Strangely, given their past history, informed opinion (i.e. one step up from gossip, two up from rumour, three up from innuendo) reveals that Union Jack and Gay Gordon had a reconciliation at the Celtic thrash. **Conference Chronicle** *spies tell me that the pair were seen in a huddle after Union Jack sprang unexpectedly to Gay Gordon's defence when one of her ex-colleagues began to question her nerve.*

'She might have less judgement than a Lancashire batsman, but tha' cannot call her for lack of bottle,' he reputedly said angrily. 'Any lass that'll stand up to me's got more nerve than you bunch of jessies.' Union Jack then launched into one of his familiar rants against the self-seeking fat cats of Fleet Street and their craven capitulation over free collective bargaining. When the revellers awoke from the coma this induced, Union

127

Jack and Gay Gordon were heard arranging to meet to discuss unknown matters.

Two hours later, Union Jack lay dead. As we go to press, Gordon is 'helping police with their inquiries'. A fiver says she's being about as helpful as a Trappist monk.

Legovers – Latest!

Liverpool Branch and London Graphical might have been at daggers drawn over the industrial councils proposals, but a certain branch chair and branch secretary are definitely working on building bridges of the hump-backed variety . . . What was a BBC researcher doing taking such an interest in the affairs of the horny-handed sons of toil in the print? . . . No prizes for guessing which Central Lancashire branch delegate is going for the record of most notches on the bed-head at conference. So far, I'm told she's had a floor manager from Carlisle, a sub-editor from Nottingham and a researcher from Aberdeen. And it's only Wednesday! . . . In an attempt to get in on the act, there's to be a meeting of the newly formed Gay And Lesbian Action group tomorrow at six. Just a warning in case you come upon them unawares – they'll be in the lounge bar of the Flying Parrot pub down the hill from the conference centre.

Gossip and Innuendo

If we ever get back to conference business, look out for an unholy alliance between the former

Stalinist Petra O'Dwyer and the careerist Larry Knox that's set to sabotage the fragile truce in Central Magazine branch . . . I'd watch my back if I were one of those who have ever fiddled a union expense docket . . . Coming soon – more exclusive revelations about secret service plants in your very own union . . . I hear that a certain clerical section are planning some serious horse-trading to win support for Motion 48C, so if there's something you badly want from your local friendly office support staff, now's the time to stake your claim . . . Union Jack's death will almost certainly scupper moves by AMWU staff to disrupt conference by staging a lightning strike protesting at the union's redundancy plans. Word is the action will be postponed, not cancelled, so deputy general secretary Andy Spence better not breathe too many sighs of relief . . .

The hand pulled the A4 sheet that contained the Wednesday morning edition of the anonymous **Conference Chronicle** out of the satchel and slipped it under the next door on the eleventh floor of the student residence. A quick glance at the watch. Time was running short. Soon, the early birds who took the po-faced view that conference was for conference business only would be up and about. Still, this door was the last in the block. Only one more building to go, and that was only five storeys high. The author of the scurrilous daily commentary on events political, social and sexual at the first ever Annual Delegate Conference of the Amalgamated Media Workers' Union looked cautiously around then walked briskly towards the lifts.

'No reply,' she said for the twenty-second time. Concentrating on counting her replies made it easier to ignore the questions. She just kept saying the two words whenever there was a pause in the drone of the coppers' voices. In between the gaps, she simply kept reciting the numbers in her head.

The rhythm changed only when Jennifer Okido interrupted occasionally to protest that they were badgering her client, who was exercising her right to keep her own counsel.

It took an hour for the police officers to give up in frustration. The stocky detective sergeant pushed his chair back with a jerk that made its legs squeal on the vinyl floor tiles. He leaned over the tape recorder and said 'Interview terminated at 8.10 a.m.'

'Can I go now?' Lindsay asked, her voice shaky with exhaustion.

'No,' the detective sergeant said.

'You'll have to stay here till we can establish your alibi,' Jennifer said, leaning close. Lindsay smelled a light, citrus perfume and almost giggled at the incongruity.

Back in the cell, Lindsay stretched out on the

hard bunk, pulling the blanket over her. There was nothing that wouldn't look better after a good sleep.

It took Jennifer Okido less than ten minutes at the AMWU conference centre to realise Lindsay hadn't been exaggerating about the impact of **Conference Chronicle** on the hundreds of delegates. In the foyer of the hall itself, it seemed there were copies at the heart of every babbling huddle as the union representatives discussed the death of their general secretary and the implication that Lindsay had had more than a hand in it.

As she pushed her way through the throng, Jennifer heard snatches of conversation.

'. . . dark secrets. The way things are being revealed in **Conference Chronicle**, he could have jumped rather than face the music . . .'

'Maybe he made a pass at her and she decked him, only the deck was further away than she thought . . .'

'Come on, even Tom Jack wouldn't top himself just to drop Lindsay Gordon in the shit . . .'

'It's going to be another mystery like Maxwell and the yacht . . .'

'He'll have been pissed out of his head. He could easily have fallen . . .'

Everyone had their own theory, and the volume increased by the second as everyone tried to make theirs the one that was heard above the

others. Jennifer made it to the door of the conference hall, where the clerical staff were under siege
as they tried to hand out order-papers for the
morning's business.

'For the last time, we don't know what's
happening,' one said sharply to a bunch of determined journalists who had abandoned their role
of delegates for the far more exciting one of on-
the-spot news reporters. As their baying rose to
a crescendo, she shouted, 'I don't give a damn
what your news-desks want to hear, we haven't
got anything to tell you. All we know is what you
know. If you want to hassle someone who might
have some answers, why don't you go and find
the Standing Orders Sub-Committee? They're
meeting right now to decide what's going to
happen to conference.'

The pack were gone faster than Jennifer would
have believed possible.

'Excuse me,' she said in a low voice to the
harassed woman. 'I'm Lindsay Gordon's solicitor.
I rather think I need to speak to your Standing
Orders Sub-Committee. They may be able to help
me. Can you give me directions?'

The woman gave a wicked grin. 'Well, you
won't find them in their committee room. All
you'll find there is a shower of frustrated journos.
They needed to meet in peace, so they went off
somewhere else. But I don't think they'll object
if I tell you.'

*   *   *

Ten minutes later, Jennifer stood in the doorway of Burger King. A quick glance was all she needed to spot the seven members of the committee that was responsible for the smooth running of the first annual conference of the AMWU. The four women and three men had taken over two tables and each had a bundle of papers in front of them. Although, like all Standing Orders committees, they were generally credited with possessing the sharpest brains in their union, right then they all looked like bankers with indigestion.

Jennifer walked confidently up to the table and gave them her best professional smile. 'I'm sorry to intrude,' she said, 'but I think I need your help.'

They gazed at her with expressions that ranged from bewilderment to relief. Jennifer sat down on the vacant chair and introduced herself. 'What I need desperately is to find the Irishman that Lindsay was talking to between leaving the ceilidh and entering her room. I know it's rather like asking you to produce a needle from a haystack, but I hoped you'd be able to indicate the best way of achieving this.'

A middle-aged man with a crew-cut and a flamboyant silk waistcoat snorted. 'Dear lady,' he drawled in the cultivated tones of a Radio Three announcer, 'we find ourselves desperately searching the rule book for something that might conceivably cover the eventuality of the suspicious death of a general secretary in the midst of conference. We'd got as far as a two-minute silence. You have no idea how welcome it is to be asked to do something so simple and straight-forward as to find one Irish drunk among so many!'

Jennifer smiled with relief. For the first time, she was beginning to think she'd be able to get her client out of her cell without being charged.

6

'While SOS will do everything in their power to ensure the smooth running of conference, we cannot control Acts of God. In the event of an earthquake, a nuclear attack or an American decision to bomb some God-forsaken part of the globe, we ask delegates to observe the conventions of conference, to be patient and not to shower us with pointless emergency motions.'

from *'Advice for New Delegates'*,
a Standing Orders Sub-Committee booklet.

Jennifer had never heard a silence more eloquent than the two-minute tribute to the memory of Union Jack. It felt like a balloon whose surface had been so stretched that a whisper of air would explode it into shreds of twisted rubber. The delegates stood, heads bowed, the bright colours of their clothes lending the scene the air of a Billy Graham crusade at prayer.

The platform party were uncomfortably at

135

attention, a few of them failing to avoid the temptation to glance at their wrists. The union president stared down at the table where he'd had the foresight to place his own watch. As the hand crawled round the dial and reached twelve for the second time, his shoulders straightened and he lifted his head. He leaned forward over his microphone and said, 'Thank you, brothers and sisters. I'll hand you over now to Brian Robinson from Standing Orders Sub-Committee.'

The man who had first spoken to Jennifer in the Burger King got to his feet and composed his face into a mask of solemnity as the delegates subsided noisily into their seats. She noted that multi-coloured silk had given way to a more sombre black leather waistcoat.

'I realise that many of you will feel uncomfortable about continuing with conference under the circumstances,' he began. Judging by the faces Jennifer could see, he was well wide of the mark. 'But those of you who had known Tom Jack for as long as I have will realise he was a man who always demanded most forcefully that the show must go on; except, of course, when it was a matter of getting a paper out during an industrial dispute,' he continued, raising a murmur of appreciation from his audience.

'My colleagues on SOS and I are attempting to ensure that conference will therefore continue. But before we proceed with this morning's first order paper, I have an appeal to make to you all.

Police inquiries into Tom's death are proceeding, and one of our number is, as they say, helping with their inquiries. Many of you will know Lindsay Gordon of old, and I for one am convinced that she had nothing whatsoever to do with an event that I feel certain will finally be seen as a tragic accident rather than something more sinister. Those of you who don't know Lindsay may have noticed her sitting among the observers at the back of the hall yesterday. She's the one with the rather noticeable Californian suntan; medium height and build, short brown hair, blue eyes, Scottish accent. There is a point to this,' he added peevishly, frowning down into the floor of conference, where delegates had begun to move around and chat excitedly to each other.

The mutter subsided and Brian resumed. Jennifer couldn't help being impressed by his stage presence, since delegates deprived of conversation appeared to be like plants deprived of light and water.

'Lindsay was at the Scots-Irish Ceilidh last night, and in the early hours of the morning, she was introduced to a delegate who has been offered a job in America. They left the ceilidh together so she could offer him some tips about working among the barbarians, and they chatted for some time. Unfortunately, it's been so long since Lindsay was a working journalist that she's forgotten some of the cardinal rules. She failed to ascertain the name of the person she was talking to, and it is imperative that her solicitor talks to the gentleman in question. Ms Okido, if you could just step forward . . .?'

Feeling more self-conscious than she ever had in court, Jennifer stepped away from the group of people round the door at the rear of the hall. Hundreds of heads swivelled round to look at her. She smiled bleakly.

'Ms Okido up at the back there is the person in question. So if you were at the Ceilidh last night, and you know the identity of the Irishman Lindsay was talking to, or if indeed you are that soldier, please let her know. I can't stress how important this is, and I know you'll all be as eager as I am to ensure that Lindsay isn't in custody for a moment longer than necessary.'

'Don't be too sure of that,' Jennifer heard in a rumbling baritone by her side. She turned in surprise to see a tall, burly man who resembled a battered teddy bear. 'I'm a friend of your client,' he said as Brian moved on to run through the order-paper.

'What exactly did you mean, Mr . . .?' Jennifer asked.

'McAndrew. Dick McAndrew. Well, somebody killed Union Jack,' he said. 'And whoever it was, the cops are leaving them well alone while they give Lindsay the heavy-duty hassle. Besides, if what I hear about the hooly last night is anything like the truth, there were plenty of people at that ceilidh who wouldn't piss on Lindsay if she was

138

on fire. Which it sounds like she might be. How bad is it looking?'

Jennifer shrugged. 'I've seen worse, Mr McAndrew.'

'The word on the street is that the police have a witness from the ninth floor who says she was woken up by the sound of breaking glass. According to her clock, it was five to three. I take it you're looking for an alibi witness who was with Linds then?'

Jennifer smiled. 'Whether you're asking as a friend or as a journalist, you must be well aware I can't answer that.'

As she spoke, a man shuffled up to them. He looked like he'd just crawled out of bed, his shirt rumpled and his eyes red-rimmed. 'Excuse me,' he said in tones so soft he was barely audible. 'I think you want to talk to me.'

Jennifer said, 'Are you the man Lindsay Gordon was talking to?'

He nodded, then immediately looked as if he regretted a motion so violent. He closed his eyes momentarily then said. 'I am.'

'You two need to get away from this mob,' Dick said, his reporter's eye noticing the attention they were attracting. Almost imperceptibly, people were shifting closer to the three of them, desperate for any gobbet of gossip that would put them in pole position among their peers.

'I couldn't agree more,' Jennifer said. 'Where can we . . .?'

'You can use my room,' Dick fished a key out of the pocket of his jeans. 'It's in Wilberforce Hall, second floor. If I'm not here when you've finished, just leave it with one of the head office staff in the conference office.'

'Thanks,' said Jennifer, unable to keep the surprise out of her voice. Looking at the state of her potential witness, she could only imagine what his room looked and smelled like.

'No bother,' said Dick. 'Just get my buddy out of jail. That'll do me fine.'

Dick's room managed to look as if he'd been at home there for months. There were a dozen books on the shelf, a Tandy computer and printer on the desk beside a pile of typing paper. On the window-sill, a queue of used mugs displaying a bewildering range of political slogans sat beside a framed photograph of a woman and two children. The Irishman made straight for the armchair and collapsed into it.

'I'm sorry,' he mumbled. 'After Lindsay went off, I went back to the ceilidh. My head feels like it's got an army of elephants doing the rumba in there.'

Jennifer couldn't have cared less. She perched on the edge of the neatly made bed and pulled out her note-pad. 'First, let's get your name.'

'Desmond Joyce,' he said. 'I'm a freelance in Birmingham. I work two days a week at the university in the media studies department.'

'Tell me about last night.'

Hands shaking, Desmond fumbled a cigarette into his mouth and lit it. When he stopped coughing, he said, 'I was at the ceilidh, and a woman I used to work with in Dublin introduced me to Lindsay. I've been offered a teaching job in Minnesota, you see, and Rose thought Lindsay might be able to give me a wee bit of a notion what it would be like working in America.' He rubbed a hand over the bright ginger stubble on his chin that looked the more disreputable because of the contrast with his chestnut hair.

'We couldn't talk properly, what with all the music, and Lindsay had just had a bit of a head-to-head with some of the jackals from the Street of Shame, so we went outside.'

Desmond continued with the story that Jennifer had already heard from Lindsay. She registered gratefully that there seemed to be no significant discrepancy.

'She asked me what time it was. My watch said ten past three. She said she had to be going because she had things to do in the morning. So I said cheerio and went back to the ceilidh. That was my big mistake,' he groaned. 'I never could tell when to call it a night. Half past five I got to my bed.'

'And you're quite sure about the time?'

'Half past five? That's right, a bunch of us left the ceilidh together not long after I went back. We all went to Rose's room because she had a

141

couple of duty-free bottles of Black Bush there. That's how come I didn't hear about this business till I got up this morning and read the **Conference Chronicle**.'

'Not half past five. The time when you left Ms Gordon,' Jennifer said, unable to hide the note of exasperation in her voice.

'Oh. Sorry. Yes, sure I'm sure. I remember because I thought to myself that it was a bit early to be heading for bed when there was a good time going on. I was thinking that if that was what living in America does to a person then maybe it wasn't for me after all.' He gave a feeble smile.

'Right. Well, Mr Joyce, what I need is for you to have a shower, a shave, a clean shirt and two asprin.' She glanced at her watch. 'How long will that take you?'

'About half an hour, I suppose,' he stuttered.

'Fine. Well, when you've done all you can to make yourself look like a respectable citizen whose word could be accepted by a police officer, we will go to the police station where you will tell them exactly what you have told me,' Jennifer said briskly.

She got to her feet. 'I have some calls to make, since I'm clearly not going to be at the magistrates' court this morning. I will see you outside the conference hall in thirty minutes.' As Desmond hauled himself out of the chair and moved towards the door with all the care of a man balancing a tray of eggs, she said, 'And Mr Joyce? Thank you for coming forward. I appreciate that, and so will my client.'

'What do you mean, she isn't there?' Sophie demanded of the telephone. 'You took her into custody, didn't you? Well, what have you done with her?'

Whatever the beleaguered police officer on the other end of the phone was saying, it was clearly what Sophie wanted to hear. Her shoulders dropped back from their stiff, hunched position and her breathing became more calm. 'I see. And when exactly was this?' As she asked the question, the sixth sense that informs lovers of each other's presence checked in. She swung round to see Lindsay walk into the conference office. Sophie's face broken into a huge grin of welcome and relief. 'It's okay,' she gabbled into the phone. 'She's just walked in. Thanks.' She dropped the phone back into its cradle. For a moment, the two women simply stared at each other. Then Lindsay opened her arms and they fell into a hug.

The atmosphere their reunion created was so tangible that a handful of the clerical workers in the room broke into spontaneous applause. 'Thank God you arrived when you did, Lindsay,' Pauline Hardy called across the room. 'I thought she was going to throw that phone through the wall.'

Sophie laughed. 'Sorry. But you must know

what Lindsay's like. I had visions of her starting to tunnel out of her cell. Either that or doing the usual Scottish trick of remonstrating with the arresting officer with a chair leg.'

Pauline winked as she headed for the door. 'Didn't they tell you that's why they released her? The council tax payers of Sheffield couldn't afford to pay for any more damage to their cop shop. I'm off to the station to pick up some parcels of stationery,' she added, 'otherwise I'd offer to buy you a celebration drink. So have one for me!'

'It wasn't a drink I had in mind,' Lindsay murmured in Sophie's ear.

'I had a feeling it might not be,' Sophie replied. 'That's why I took the precaution of booking into a hotel.'

Sophie, had barely closed the door behind them before Lindsay was pulling her clothes off.

'Hang on,' Sophie protested mildly. 'At least give me a chance to phone room service for a bottle of bubbly.'

'Feel free,' Lindsay said, dragging her shirt over her head. 'But I've got to get out of these clothes. They stink of sweat and smoke and drink and police cells.'

Sophie giggled. 'And there was me thinking you were desperate for my body.'

'Oh, I am, I am. So get the fizz on ice while I wash away the night.'

'Yes boss,' Sophie said, snapping to mock

attention and waving a vague salute at her partner.

As Lindsay towelled her hair dry, she heard the blissful sound of the champagne cork easing out of the bottle with a soft pop. 'Have I told you lately that I love you?' she inquired as she emerged into the bedroom.

Sophie, by now naked too, handed her a glass and said, 'Actions speak louder . . .' She held out her arms and Lindsay stepped into her embrace.

After the love came the tears. Lindsay sobbed and rocked in the safe circle of Sophie's arms.

'I don't know, I let you out of my sight for two days, and you end up embroiled in another murder,' Sophie said gently, trying to lighten the atmosphere. 'I'm beginning to wonder if I need danger money to live with you.'

Even Sophie's embrace and the surge of desire that accompanied it couldn't stop the shadow that passed through Lindsay's mind. 'Tell me about it,' she murmured. 'Sometimes I feel like the bloody angel of death.' She sighed, and stroked the smooth, cool skin in the small of Sophie's back. 'I was so bloody scared,' she gulped. 'And I couldn't show anyone how scared I was in case they thought I'd done it. Oh, Sophie, you'll never know how pleased I was to see you when I walked through that office door. It was like the light coming on.'

Gradually, Lindsay grew calm, and they lay

quietly together sipping champagne. 'How did you find out about it?' she asked.

'You know Helen,' Sophie said. 'The world would end if she didn't wake up to Radio 4. I was spark out in the spare room, sleeping like the dead after a night on the jungle juice with her and Ros when the whirling dervish bounced in.'

'Oh God,' Lindsay groaned. 'What a start to the day! You know, I sometimes wonder how you managed to live with her for so long without caving her head in one morning.'

'You're not the only one,' Sophie said with a grin. 'Anyway, she announced that the general secretary of AMWU had perished in suspicious circumstances during the night. Before my eyes were even open, she was informing me that I'd better get down here, given your track record of sticking your nose in wherever it's none of your business. We both agreed there was no way you'd be able to stay out of this one.

'Of course, neither of us had any idea exactly how far your nose was already in. So I borrowed Helen's car and agreed to keep her posted. You can imagine how I felt when I walked into the conference office and they told me you'd already managed to get yourself arrested! I thought you'd given up cosy chats with policemen.'

'Be fair, Sophie, you know I never wanted to hear about another murder after Alison Maxwell. And I swear that if Tom Jack's killer had chosen any other window to throw him out, I'd have given the whole thing a body swerve.'

'But . . .?' Sophie said, her heart sinking. 'I hear a but in there, Lindsay.'

'Well, I feel like I'm involved whether I want to be or not. Let's face it, my love. Unless the police actually find out what went on in my room last night, there are going to be a lot of people wandering around convinced that Lindsay Gordon really had a lot more to do with it than she's letting on. Besides, I've got my own suspicions.'

Sophie moaned. 'Oh, Lindsay. Can't we just get in the car and go back to Glasgow? I mean, does it matter if the entire AMWU membership thinks you pushed Tom Jack out of the window? You don't work in this country any more, you'll never have to see any of them again. Who cares what they think?'

'I do,' said Lindsay stubbornly. 'I care. I'm sorry, Sophie, but I want to stick around long enough to see which way the wind is blowing at least. Besides, I'm on police bail. I'm not supposed to leave town without their say-so.'

Sophie smiled and cuddled into her. 'I had this feeling you were going to say something like that,' she said ruefully. 'Oh, well, why worry? You've only got about 400 potential suspects to offend.'

'Should be a piece of piss, then, shouldn't it,' Lindsay said sweetly.

Sophie gave a sigh of resignation. 'In that case,

I'd better ring Helen and check it's okay to leave her without wheels for a few days longer.'

'Just a minute,' Lindsay said, pulling Sophie back as she moved towards the bedside phone. 'Helen can wait.'

'Shouldn't that be, heaven can wait?'

'You want heaven? Then come back here.'

7

> *'Your Standing Orders Sub-Committee must advise
> you that we are extremely reluctant to accept emer-
> gency motions, which disrupt the smooth running
> of conference. Emergency motions will only be
> accepted if they relate to a genuine emergency. The
> definition of a genuine emergency is laid out in
> SO9(a)(ii), but in practice, it is "a set of circum-
> stances about which the chair of SOS could not
> conceivably have had prior knowledge". Delegates
> should bear in mind that the chair of SOS is not
> a registered psychic.'*
>
> from *'Advice for New Delegates'*,
> a Standing Orders Sub-Committee booklet.

'Emergency Motion 17. This conference deplores
the death of ANWU's General Secretary and
instructs the National Executive Council to
express the union's condolences to Tom Jack's
widow and family. It further instructs all delegates
and officials of the union to extend their full and

free cooperation to the South Yorkshire Police in respect of their inquiry into Tom Jack's untimely death. It further calls upon any person involved to come forward immediately.' Lindsay read the words with a sense of unreality. Only a trade union could believe an emergency conference motion was the way to handle something like this, she thought, looking around to check there wasn't a white rabbit or a hookah-smoking caterpillar around.

She was standing in the shadows at the side of the stage with Sophie, reluctant to return to her exposed position among the other observers on their dais. She was going to have to face the questions of the mob sooner or later, but the longer she could postpone it, the happier she'd be. Silently, she handed the copy of the motion, currently being proposed by Central London Print Branch, to Sophie, who couldn't keep a bemused grin from lips that felt bruised from their recent close encounter. Suddenly, a man Lindsay vaguely remembered having seen waiting for the lift on her floor of Maclintock Tower ran up the steps of the opposing podium and seized the microphone.

'Jed Thomas, London Broadcast Journalists Branch, proposing an amendment to the motion.' In spite of the cries of 'Out of order' from the handful of procedural bureaucrats on the floor, he persisted. For some reason, no one on the platform cut off his mike. Scarlet, he said. 'This Annual Delegate Conference offers its

150

congratulations to anyone who was involved in ridding this union of a man who was largely responsible for the dissent, disorganisation, dishonesty and dissatisfaction he presided over. While we regret the undemocratic methods chosen for his removal, we applaud the result and the benefits that will accrue to the union as a result.'

Jed Thomas stood defiantly at the podium, through a stunned silence that lasted longer than anyone who hadn't experienced the earlier two-minute version would have believed possible. Then, as the room erupted into shouting, booing and even a few calls of 'Hear, hear!' he turned and bolted, not down the stairs and into the body of the hall, but down the side of the platform, towards the doors at the rear.

'What the hell was that all about?' Sophie asked. 'I've never heard anything like it in my life.'

'I've no idea,' said Lindsay. 'But I'm going to have a bloody good go at finding out.'

Lindsay and Sophie's attempts to catch up with Jed Thomas were thwarted as soon as they emerged from the side exit into the corridor. One of the delegates who had missed the outburst was hurrying back towards the hall clutching a handful of the now familiar flyer sheets of **Conference Chronicle**. When he saw Lindsay, he stopped short and said, 'Lindsay Gordon, isn't it? Charlie Dominic, *Sunday Trumpet*. I'm really glad they saw sense and released you. Have you got a minute?'

'No comment,' Lindsay said. Turning to Sophie, she added, 'You can have no idea how much I've longed to say that to a journo.'

'Aw, Lindsay, just a word,' Charlie pleaded, eager beaver from head to foot. 'Unless I get something to myself, I'm going to look a real dickhead to my newsdesk. I mean, here I am, right on top of the best trade union story of the decade, and the daily boys will have left me not a sausage.'

Against her better judgement, Lindsay relented. She could still remember the pressures inside the hothouse of national newspaper journalism. Besides, Charlie was one of the few Fleet Street hacks at the conference who hadn't tried to give her a bad time; and it was already too late to catch Jed Thomas.

'Just a word it is, then. And if it makes you any happier, I won't talk to the rest of the pack. All I ask is that you keep quiet about me saying a dicky-bird to you until I've left Sheffield. Deal?'

'Deal!' he agreed fervently. She wondered how long it would take the hammer of newsdesk attrition to beat him into the cynical mould of his colleagues.

'Five minutes, then,' she said. Sophie stifled a sigh and leaned against the wall. Lindsay threw her an apologetic look.

'Who do you think killed Tom Jack?' he began, inevitably.

'I don't know that anyone did. I only know for sure that I didn't. I arrived back in my room to find the window broken and Tom's body lying in the car park below. It was one of the worst moments of my life,' she said, unconsciously slipping back into the tabloid prose that had earned her living for years.

'But there was no love lost between you, was there?' Charlie asked.

'No, but that didn't mean I was glad to see him dead. Sure, we'd had our disagreements in the past, but not the sort you'd even swing a punch about, never mind push someone out of a tenth-floor window. If I went around killing everyone I thought was sexist or racist, that hall in there would be littered with corpses.'

Charlie scribbled furiously on the back of one of the **Conference Chronicle**s he was carrying. With a shock, Lindsay realised it was a different edition from the morning one she'd seen in the conference office earlier.

'By the way,' he said, 'rumour has it that the forensic lads have found traces of blood in one of the shower cubicles on the tenth floor.'

'Really? Do we know whose blood?' Lindsay asked eagerly.

'No idea. But it sounds serious. The *Daily Mail* guy was saying that they'd found a couple of splashes on the shower curtains, traces between the tiles on the wall and some in the drains. So maybe they'll have to get into DNA testing and take blood samples from all of us.' Charlie sounded like he couldn't wait to get in the queue for the needle.

'What do you think, Sophie?' Lindsay asked, adding, for Charlie's benefit, 'she's a medic.'

Sophie shrugged. 'Depends how much blood they found. I suppose if Jack cut himself on a major artery as he went through the window it might have sprayed his killer with blood. More likely, though, whoever pushed him cut himself or herself on a shard of glass. Frankly, I can't see them running DNA tests on anyone other than a prime suspect, though. The test costs far too much to run a screen through the whole conference. Besides,' she continued, 'it could have nothing to do with the killing. Maybe someone who was having a heavy period had just used the shower.'

Both women tried not to grin at Charlie's look of shocked squeamishness.

'Yeah, well, thanks,' he said unenthusiastically. 'I don't suppose you saw any blood-stained killers heading for the showers?'

'No, I didn't. Besides, everyone was either asleep or so pissed that a naked murderer covered in blood could probably have run from one end of the campus to the other without anyone noticing,' Lindsay said.

'And you didn't see anyone else who might have had anything to do with it?'

Again, that niggling feeling of having noticed something she couldn't quite get hold of came back to Lindsay. Not for the first time, she wished she'd stuck to her new habits of sobriety. 'No,' she said hesitantly. 'At least . . . as I came out of the lift, I had the impression of someone turning the corner, but nothing I could positively identify.'

Charlie looked like a dog with two bones. 'That's tremendous,' he enthused. 'That gives me a great line for Sunday – "Prime Suspect Spots Mystery Figure".'

'Gee, thanks, Charlie. Couldn't you really stitch me up instead?' Lindsay asked ironically.

He had the grace to look sheepish. 'Sorry. Just got a bit carried away. I'll tone it down a bit, promise. Now, was it a man or a woman you saw? Think,' he urged.

'No idea, really. It was something I caught out of the corner of my eye, that's all. Is that a new **Chronicle**, by the way?'

'Yup,' he confirmed. 'A bundle of them just appeared in the bar. I grabbed a handful for my delegation, since they'll vanish like snowflakes in a sauna soon as the word gets round. D'you want one?' He thrust a copy at her. 'Wild, isn't it? I wish I could get to whoever was doing it.'

Lindsay ignored him, absorbed in the front page of the **Conference Chronicle Evening Supplement**.

Now that Lindsay Gordon's been alibied by her mysterious stranger, who turns out to be yet

155

another of the USA Meeja Studies Mafia, police will have to make at least a pretence of looking elsewhere for their killer. Unless of course Desmond Joyce changes his mind about the accuracy of his fake Rolex.

𝕮𝖔𝖓𝖋𝖊𝖗𝖊𝖓𝖈𝖊 𝕮𝖍𝖗𝖔𝖓𝖎𝖈𝖑𝖊*'s spies report a signal lack of regret about the departure of Union Jack, a man whose recent popularity had plunged so low he made Arthur Scargill look like the Queen Mum. Street talk says Union Jack has left AMWU in administrative chaos. But the word is that deputy general secretary Handy Andy Spence is more than fit for the big man's shoes, and now that Union Jack is out of the way and can't throw any more spanners in the works or wobblers in the office, there is sure to be a complete and inescapable investigation of the Union's troubled finances.*

So if you were one of the ones who felt safe from scrutiny while Union Jack was still holding the reins, better start sweating. 𝕮𝖔𝖓𝖋𝖊𝖗𝖊𝖓𝖈𝖊 𝕮𝖍𝖗𝖔𝖓𝖎𝖈𝖑𝖊 *knows who the guilty are. But since the guilty don't know who* 𝕮𝖔𝖓𝖋𝖊𝖗𝖊𝖓𝖈𝖊 𝕮𝖍𝖗𝖔𝖓𝖎𝖈𝖑𝖊 *is, there's nowhere to post the used fivers, is there?*

Before she could finish reading, Sophie's voice insinuated itself into her consciousness with its best bedside manner.

'Lindsay, the man's asking you a question. You're wasting his five minutes.'

'Sorry. What was that, Charlie?'

'Will you be going to his funeral?'

Lindsay mentally shook her head in disbelief. Now she was out of it, it was hard to fathom how she'd done a job like Charlie's for so many years.

'I shouldn't imagine so for one minute,' she said. 'I never chose his company when he was alive, so I don't see any point in hypocrisy now he's dead. Now, Charlie. Time for me to ask a question.'

'Fire away.'

'Who's the clever money on now? I mean, leaving me out of the equation, of course.'

He ran a hand through brown hair that was already beginning to thin, though his unlined face looked no more than early twenties. 'You've got me there, Lindsay. I mean, there's a million crazy rumours in the naked city tonight, but nobody *seriously* thinks he was bumped off because someone wasn't happy with the merger, or because Andy Spence wants the job, or because Dick McAndrew wanted to get even for Union Jack closing down *Socialism Today*, or because he hadn't delivered one of his thousands of broken pre-election promises,' Charlie rattled off, enumerating the suggestions on his fingers. 'I don't know, maybe he had a mistress he'd given the elbow to. You know his reputation with women.'

Lindsay nodded. 'If it moves, it's there to be screwed. Unless it's a member of the Equality Committee, in which case, it's there to be put down.'

157

'Charming,' Sophie muttered. 'I know hospitals where he'd have walked into a consultant's job.'

'Word is,' Charlie added confidentially, 'it might be *cherchez la femme*. Only nobody knows who the *femme* in question might be. Before the merger, the clever money said he was conducting very close negotiations with Maureen Sloane, the former deputy general secretary of the broadcasting union, but that was over months ago. And she moved in with one of the floor managers from *Newsnight* just after Christmas, so she can't have been carrying that much of a torch. And there's been no recent goss about Tom. So your guess is as good as mine.'

'Oh well, thanks anyway, Charlie. And hey – don't make me look a complete bitch, there's a pal,' Lindsay said.

He grinned and waved his copies of **Conference Chronicle**. 'No way. Compared to this, I'm an amateur! See you.' He grinned and shot off back down the corridor to distribute the latest scandal among the other members of his delegation.

'Nice to know I'm not the only victim of the bad-mouth brigade, isn't it?' Lindsay said.

'Don't get too sanctimonious, Ms Gordon,' Sophie responded. 'Let's not forget how many years you spent earning a living doing exactly what young Charlie and his fellow vultures do.'

'Okay, okay. I'll leave the moral high ground to you people who've never lived in glasshouses.'

'What next?' Sophie asked. 'Do you still want to get hold of that guy who set the place by the ears just now?'

'Of course I do. He's got to have a hidden agenda behind that outburst. Even I wouldn't have had the bottle to stand up on that platform and say out loud what so many of us are thinking.'

'Bottle or stupidity,' Sophie observed. 'By the way, what was all that about shadowy figures disappearing round corners? You never said anything to me about that.'

Lindsay shrugged. 'It was the vaguest of impressions. Just a flicker in the peripheral vision. But there's something niggling at the back of my mind about it. I just can't get a hold of it.'

'Do you really want to get a hold of it?'

'Of course I do. That's a daft question,' Lindsay complained. 'If I could get a handle on something definite, something factual, I'd be as happy as a pig.'

'It's not a daft question, smartarse. The point I'd like to make is, if you suddenly remember something you saw or heard that you didn't tell the police earlier, they're going to be deeply suspicious on two counts. One, are you deliberately trying to draw suspicion away from yourself and towards someone else? And two, did you deliberately suppress the information earlier for some twisted reason of your own?'

'You mean, blackmail?'

'Or just to pass it on to one of your old journo cronies. For a fee, of course.'

'That's evil,' Lindsay said. 'I've lived with you for three years, and I never suspected you of possessing such a devious mind. Mind you,' she added, 'I never was much good at spotting devious women.'

'Water under the bridge, babe,' Sophie said, giving her a quick hug. 'There's nothing wrong with your judgement. So, are you sure you really want to dig up whatever it is you think you might have buried away in your few remaining brain cells?'

'Yes, I'm sure. After all, I don't have to tell the police right away, do I? I could just poke around till I found some more convincing evidence, couldn't I?'

Sophie groaned. 'That wasn't quite what I had in mind. God, Lindsay, you're incorrigible.'

'I know. Good, innit?' Lindsay said with a wink. 'So what did you have in mind?'

'Well, hypno, of course!'

'Oh *no*, you must be out of your California-crazed *mind*,' Lindsay groaned.

Sophie pressed on regardless. 'I use hypno all the time! I can get women to deliver their babies without drugs by using hypnosis, so I'm sure I can help you retrieve data that's only filed away in the drawer marked "alcoholic oblivion". What do you think?'

Lindsay closed her eyes. 'My eyelids are growing heavy,' she intoned, then slumped backwards against the wall.

'Quit clowning,' Sophie said. 'You know it works.'

Lindsay straightened up and pulled a face. 'I know. I just don't like that whole thing of handing over control. You could tell me to do anything you wanted.'

'I've told you a thousand times, you *don't* lose control. Your subconscious is in charge, not me. I can't get you to do anything that goes against your basic personality or principles. If you'd let me practise on you when I was training, it would be second nature by now.'

'Oh, all right,' Lindsay said grudgingly. 'Only don't blame me if it doesn't work.'

Sophie smiled. 'I won't.'

'And don't *tell* anyone, okay?' Lindsay scowled.

Sophie struggled to straighten her face. 'Your reputation is safe with me. You won't regret it, I promise you.'

Lindsay looked doubtful. 'Huh,' she said. 'But if I catch myself doing your ironing, there'll be trouble, I'm warning you.'

8

*'Head Office staff are present to ensure that SOS
has the clerical and administrative back-up it
needs to keep the wheels of conference turning.
The staff are not there to meet your every need
and solve your problems. This is* not *the time to
ask for one of those yellow forms to apply for a
Press card – if the staff don't cave your head in,
rest assured that the nearest member of SOS will.'*
from *'Advice for New Delegates',*
a Standing Orders Sub-Committee booklet.

As they walked towards the conference office,
Lindsay finished reading the 𝕮𝖍𝖗𝖔𝖓𝖎𝖈𝖑𝖊's latest
contribution to the troubles of the amalgamated
Union of Media Workers. She let out a soft whistle
and said, 'Hey, Sophie. Listen to this.

*Handy Andy's commitment to change in the union
is pointed up by the close eye he was keeping on
Union Jack and his yes-men cronies throughout*

the conference. As well as being overheard taking Union Jack to task about the amount of AMWU's limited cash flow the big man was putting across the bar in the course of his 'legitimate' conference expenses (in other words, buying drinks for everyone he could hope for support or favours from), the deputy GS somehow managed to be one of the first on the scene after Lindsay Gordon discovered her late general secretary had bequeathed her Yorkshire's answer to air conditioning – 'Open t' bloody window'.

One imagines the police are inquiring just what Handy Andy was doing at three in the morning on the tenth floor of a building that's a good 200 yards away from the bedroom where he should have been catching up on his beauty sleep. Perhaps they should remember that sometimes the alibi looks like provoking more trouble than the offence, especially now they don't string 'em up any more.

'Bloody hell! Someone's really got their knife into Andy.'

'No more than they did into you in this morning's edition. Now you seem to be in the clear, I suppose they've got to find someone else to sling their mud at. And who better than the one man who stands to gain most,' Sophie said.

'Well, he does and he doesn't,' Lindsay said. 'He'll only take over the top job on a temporary basis, till they can organise an election for a new general secretary. And there's no guarantee he'll win. Union Jack beat him last time, but even if he does do a good job as caretaker, there will be a lot of people who see him as being tarred with the brush of Tom Jack's appalling administration. I'll obviously need to talk to him, though. Maybe I can collar him this evening in the bar.'

They turned into the office. Most of the harried staff didn't even look up as they entered. Eyes were focused on word processors, duplicating machines and photocopiers as AMWU's administrative staff struggled to generate the mountains of paperwork that had to be reprinted because of the disruption Tom Jack's death had brought to the agenda. Brian Robinson from the Standing Orders Sub-Committee stood by one of the word processors, dictating an order paper to a clerk who looked as if he would have sold his soul to the Employment Minister in exchange for half a dozen hours of sleep. Brian sketched a cheery half-wave in the direction of the two women, before returning to his dictation. He'd already abandoned his black leather waistcoat for a more flamboyant paisley-patterned one.

Lindsay spotted Pauline threading a stencil on to the drum of a duplicating machine and crossed the room to her. Sophie dawdled behind, as always fascinated by other people's worlds, glancing idly at the computer screens as she passed.

Pauline snapped the metal strip over the

bottom of the stencil and turned away to start the machine running. She jumped at the touch of Lindsay's hand on her arm.

'God, Lindsay,' she gasped. 'You trying to give me a heart attack?'

'Sign of a guilty conscience,' Lindsay teased.

'You're not wrong,' Pauline replied, managing a tired smile. 'This stuff should have been ready half an hour ago. I completely forgot about it with all the aggro that's been going on. I thought you were the long arm of the SOS come to give me a bollocking for taking so long. What're you after this time? It can't be my body, now Sophie's here,' she added in a half-hearted attempt at their usual banter.

'Sorry to disappoint you,' Lindsay said. 'I just need a bit of information. Can you tell me what Jed Thomas's room number is? He's with London Broadcasting Journalists Branch, if that helps.'

Pauline pulled a face. 'What kept you, Lindsay? We've already had half a dozen hacks in here chasing him. I told them it was confidential information. A guy who manages to say up front what so many people are thinking deserves a bit of protection, don't you think?'

Lindsay shrugged. 'You know I'm not after the same thing as them.'

Pauline cocked one eyebrow. 'Do I?'

'It's been a very long time since I stopped being a card-carrying bloodsucker,' Lindsay was reproachful. 'As you well know.'

Pauline checked the copies rolling off the machine. 'Wait there,' she said, walking away and opening a cardboard filing box. She fished out a dog-eared bundle of paper stapled together and quickly flicked through it. She shoved the list back in the box and came back to the duplicator. 'Maclintock Tower. 1005. Just round the corner from you. Satisfied?'

'Fascinated. I owe you one,' Lindsay said. As she walked back across the office, she heard Brian say, 'Thank you, George. You've coped magnificently, as usual. Four hundred and fifty copies, please, by four o'clock. Thanks again, team.'

Sophie followed Lindsay out into the corridor. 'Got what you need?' she asked.

'More than I expected, actually. Our man also has a room on the tenth floor.' Before she could say more, Brian Robinson emerged behind them.

He touched Lindsay lightly on the shoulder. 'Word to the wise, my dear.'

'I believe I owe you a vote of thanks, Brian. My brief says you did me sterling service this morning,' Lindsay said.

'The least I could do, my dear. Let me tell you, you deserve some decent service from this God-forsaken union after all the work you and your colleagues did in the eighties.' He turned to Sophie. 'Your lady and her cohorts deserve the undying gratitude of all the old queens like me for the work they did in forcing some of those dreadful tabloid hacks to acknowledge the existence of our Ethics Code. Not to mention that marvellous pamphlet you produced on reporting AIDS. My dear, young Lindsay here got up at conference and positively lambasted them for their narrow-minded anti-gay hysteria. And of course, when AIDS turned out not to be the gay plague visited by God on the sons of Sodom, they all had to eat their words and go right back to the guidelines that Lindsay and her intrepid team on the Equality Committee had drawn up in the first place.'

'Yet another thing you never told me,' Sophie said drily.

'One has to keep the mystery alive, dear lady,' Brain said. 'But enough of that. I couldn't help overhearing what you were asking Pauline. I take it you wanted to talk to Jed about his little tantrum in the hall?' Lindsay nodded. 'I thought so. Might one ask why?'

'Because I don't think the police are going to make fast progress unless they have someone on their murder squad who's experienced in the internecine warfare of trade unions. Not only do I want to clear my name, I also want to be on a plane back to San Francisco next Tuesday.'

'So you've taken your investigative skills out of mothballs? Well, I wish you every success, my dear. Just don't tread on so many toes that you have to leave the country in rather more of a hurry than you'd anticipated! As for young Jed, you won't find him in his room. I collared him as he came out of the hall and told him to lie low for a few hours. He should be in my room, which is in Pankhurst Tower, room 403. Tell him I sent you. He's worked himself up into a real old tizzy, so be gentle with the boy.'

'I wouldn't dream of being otherwise, Brian,' Lindsay said, with rather less than complete honesty. 'I don't suppose you'd like to make things any easier for me by suggesting a line of questioning I might benefit from pursuing?'

Brian's mouth twitched as he looked consideringly at her. Then he cocked his head to one side and scratched his stubbled head, rather like a de-crested parakeet. 'I don't honestly know whether I should tell you this,' he said wistfully.

But you're going to, you old gossip, Lindsay thought affectionately. 'If you can't trust me, Brian . . .' She added a conspiratorial smile.

'Well, my dear, one certainly can't trust the police, can one? Not in a city where they arrested thirteen men in a raid on public toilets only last week. Ask him about Handy Andy.'

'Andy Spence?' Lindsay demanded incredulously.

'You absolutely didn't hear it from me. Nice to see you again, Lindsay,' he added over his shoulder as he walked away.

Lindsay stood staring after him, open-mouthed. Sophie jogged her arm gently. 'One of life's little surprises?'

Lindsay shook her head, still with the kind of

look she'd have had if someone had offered her documentary evidence that the Archbishop of Canterbury was a cocaine baron.

'One of life's complete gobsmackers,' she said. 'Well, I definitely think we need to talk to Jed Thomas. And right now. Desperately sorry, darling, but the hypno will just have to wait.'

Pankhurst Tower was a mirror image of Maclintock, right down to the scuffed paintwork and the slow lifts. In the middle of the afternoon session of conference, it was deserted. Room 403 seemed no different, for Lindsay's knock met with silence. She looked a question at Sophie, who shrugged eloquently, and tried the handle. The door was, unsurprisingly, locked. Lindsay cast her eyes upwards and hammered loudly on the door. Still there was no response. Exasperated, she took a quick look around to check they were still alone, then bellowed, 'Jed! I know you're in there.'

Her voice echoed in the corridor, but the door remained obstinately shut.

'Jed, open up!' Lindsay yelled through the keyhole. 'Brian sent me. I'm on your side, for God's sake! Come on, Jed.'

'Dear God, you sound like the Sweeney. Let me try,' Sophie said. She stooped and called softly, 'Jed, please open up and listen to what we've got to say. We're not going away until we've spoken to you, so why don't you just open up and we can have a quiet chat face to face rather than screaming through the door so the whole world can hear.'

She stepped back. For a moment, nothing happened. Lindsay had got as far as. 'So much for softly, softly . . .' when they heard the key turning in the lock.

'You were saying?' Sophie murmured as the door opened a couple of inches.

Jed couldn't keep his eyes still. They flicked between the two women nervously. 'Who are you? What do you want? I've got nothing to say,' he gabbled.

'I'm Lindsay Gordon. And this is my girlfriend, Sophie Hartley,' she said. 'It was my window that Union Jack was pushed out of this morning. I need to talk to you, Jed.'

'I've already told the police all I know. I was asleep. I'd gone to bed drunk and I didn't hear a thing.'

'Can we come in for a minute, Jed?' Sophie asked gently. 'I really don't think it's in anyone's best interests to have this conversation in the corridor. Anybody could step out of the lift, and we genuinely don't want to cause you any more awkwardness.'

Lindsay couldn't help admiring Sophie's style. Considering she was the one who'd made her living out of persuading the reluctant to talk, it was remarkable how much she still had to learn from her lover. Slowly, Jed opened the door and stepped back. Before he could have second thoughts, Lindsay was past him and sitting in the armchair.

Jed perched on the edge of the bed, his left leg twitching like a daddy-long-legs round a lamp-shade. His right hand fiddled with the dark blond curls on the back of his head. He had the kind of Greek god looks that become gaunt and raddled in the middle thirties. He looked as if he had maybe seven or eight years to go. His brown eyes still moved restlessly around the room.

'I don't understand why Brian told you I was here. I don't know what you want with me,' he said. Without the amplification of the conference hall, his voice sounded reedy, the traces of a West Country accent still audible in his vowels.

'I heard you propose your amendment. I need to know what made you do it,' Lindsay said.

'I don't see what it's got to do with you,' he said, his lower jaw jutting obstinately.

'Union Jack was murdered this morning. Whoever did it chose my bedroom window to throw him out of. From what I've seen of the police so far, and believe me, I've seen more than enough, they don't understand the situation anything like well enough to get the right person in the frame. And until they do, I'm one of the people the fingers are pointing at. That's not a situation I'm comfortable with,' Lindsay explained forcefully.

'So you think you can come along and play at being V I Warshawski,' he sneered. 'Well, excuse me if I don't fall at your feet and confess.'

171

'Jed, if I was in your shoes, I'd think twice about alienating me with your smart mouth,' Lindsay said. She tossed the afternoon edition of **Conference Chronicle** across to him. She waited for the words to sink in, then added, 'I could go to the cops right now and tell them exactly how Andy Spence came to be on the scene so quickly. Okay, I'd also be telling them that you and Andy had given false statements and wasted police time during a murder investigation, but if that's the way you want it, that's how I'll play it. I foolishly thought that talking to you first was a way of showing a bit of solidarity. Clearly I was wrong. Come on, Sophie, we're wasting our time here.' She got to her feet.

Jed looked up and caught her eye for the first time. 'You're a hard bitch,' he said. 'Wait.' He sighed. 'I'll talk to you.'

'No bullshit?' Lindsay asked.

'No bullshit,' he agreed.

Lindsay lowered herself into the uncomfortable chair again. 'Andy was with you in your room last night, wasn't he?'

Jed nodded. 'I'd been waiting for him since eleven o'clock. It was nearly two when he managed to get away. But I didn't mind, I was just pleased to see him.'

'How long have you two been lovers?' Lindsay asked.

'Just under three months. I work for the BBC, and I was researching a *Panorama* feature about

172

the use of illegal immigrants in printing sweat-shops, and I interviewed Andy. Like everybody else, I thought he was the archetypal macho man of the print unions. He suggested going for a drink afterwards, and I thought he'd made a mistake when we ended up in this little back bar in Islington that was wall-to-wall denim and leather.'

Oh God, thought Lindsay. It's always the same. First they won't talk, then they want to tell you their life story. At least it had stopped him twitching.

'Anyway,' Jed continued, 'he started asking how I'd come to be involved in setting up AMWU's Gay And Lesbian Action group. I didn't know he'd even heard of GALA, but he seemed really inter-ested, you know, not taking the piss, or being embarrassed. Then a couple of days later he rang me at the BBC and asked if we could have dinner to carry on what we'd been discussing. Over dinner, he told me he was gay, that he'd been in the closet for twenty years because of his career in the union, and he asked if I was involved with anyone. Well, I wasn't and that night, he came back to my flat, and we've been seeing each other ever since. It's been really difficult sometimes, because he's so paranoid, and that's hard for me to reconcile with my politics, but it's been worth all the hassle,' he ended defiantly.

'Wasn't it a bit of a risk for him, sleeping with you at conference?' Sophie asked.

'Not really. I mean, if you're not in your room, people assume you're having a legover with someone. And in Andy's case, they'd always assume it was a woman. He's very attractive to women, you know.'

Lindsay found it hard to imagine the beefy Scottish deputy general secretary fighting off women. His thick pepper-and-salt hair was cut in the straight lines favoured by Japanese tourists, his skin was scarred with the remains of teenage acne, his smile had always reminded her of the grin of a barracuda. Then she remembered those china blue eyes with their deep laughter lines. Maybe Jed wasn't so far off the mark after all.

'So what exactly happened this morning?' she asked.

'Like I said, he arrived about two. We had sex, then we fell asleep. I woke up when you started screaming. Andy leapt out of bed and started scrambling into his clothes. His first thought was to get out of there fast before anyone found him with me. He usually got me to check the corridor before he left, but this time he just shot off. Then the police hammered on my door, and I pretended they'd just woken me up.'

'And you're sure Andy hadn't already left and come back before I started screaming? I'm sorry, but I have to ask.'

'I'm sure. He was sleeping next to the wall. It's only a single bed, don't forget. He'd have had to climb over me to get out, and I would have

174

woken up,' Jed said. There was no hesitation in his voice.

'And you didn't see or hear anything else that might indicate what happened? You didn't hear any voices in the corridor outside or anything?' Lindsay asked.

Jed shook his head. 'We'd had some music on. Not very loud, but just loud enough to drown out any noise we were making. And then we went to sleep.'

'How are you going to explain your outburst this afternoon?' Lindsay asked.

He shrugged. 'I'll just say that I'd had a few drinks at lunchtime, and I was furious because I'd just discovered that Jack had vetoed our submission for funding for GALA. You know us media types. There'll be a new scandal by dinner time.'

Sophie picked up the **Conference Chronicle**. 'Unfortunately, it looks like the new scandal they've got is going to give you even more headaches. You and Andy are going to have to talk to the police again.'

His jaw set obstinately once more. 'I'm saying nothing until Andy asks me to. They don't seem very interested in him so far, so I reckon we can just keep our heads down and it'll blow over. They're bound to come up with the killer eventually. If there really is a killer.'

'Oh, I think there's a killer all right. Just pray that after they've seen **Conference Chronicle**, the cops don't decide it's Andy. Because if you wait till they've got their claws into him, it's going to be a lot harder to convince them that your alibi's for real and not just something you've cooked up to get him off the hook.'

9

'As this is the first conference following the forma-
tion of AMWU, there are bound to be procedural
confusions. We recommend that all delegates study
the new conference standing orders carefully. Then
restrain all urges to raise points of order, sit back
and let it all sink in at a subliminal level. If doubts
remain, SOS members will be happy to answer
any queries in exchange for a bottle of Appellation
Contrôlée.'

from *'Advice for New Delegates'*,
a Standing Orders Sub-Committee booklet.

As they stood waiting for the lift to grind its way
back up to the fourth floor, Sophie said, 'It's funny
how hanging out with journalists kills the myths
stone-dead.'

'What do you mean?' Lindsay asked defen-
sively, convinced she was about to be impaled on
the rapier of Sophie's wit.

'Well, I always had this romantic notion that

the BBC hired only the brightest and the best of our young British journalists. But frankly, if Jed Thomas is a typical example of the breed, I'm beginning to see why the Tory party feels it's time the BBC started operating in the real world of market forces,' Sophie replied, stepping into the lift.

Lindsay grinned as she pressed the button. 'I see what you mean. He isn't going to do too well on *Mastermind*, is he?'

'It's his lack of self-control I found so worrying. I suppose we can reluctantly assume he won't persuade Andy to trot along to the police with him and tell them the truth?'

'No chance. Did you see the look on his face when I suggested it? He looked like I'd just asked him to jump out a tenth-floor window without a parachute. No, if anyone's going to persuade Andy Spence that his only chance of avoiding being banged up in a police cell is to come clean, it ain't going to be Jed.'

Sophie sighed. 'Let me guess. We're going off to talk to Andy?'

'Well, you don't have to come along,' Lindsay said reasonably as she strode out of Pankhurst Tower and headed back towards the conference hall.

'Wild horses,' Sophie muttered as she followed.

Andy Spence was sitting on the platform next to AMWU's president. He was leaning back in his chair, giving every appearance of listening to the delegate who was standing at the podium proposing a stultifyingly boring motion urging the union to protest strongly about the lack of human rights in Burma. Lindsay could just imagine the military junta quaking in their boots at the prospect of being condemned by the AMWU. Lindsay ripped a page out of her notebook and scribbled, 'I have just come from Jed. I need five minutes of your time. I'll be waiting in the corridor behind the stage. Lindsay Gordon.' She handed the note to Sophie and said, 'Can you take that up to Andy? It'll be a bit obvious if I do it.'

'Whereas most people here don't know me from a hole in the ground,' Sophie finished. Lindsay waited till she saw Sophie slip up the stairs at the rear of the stage, then she went through to the corridor.

Sophie had only just found her when Andy appeared. He was wearing the scowl that had made dozens of newspaper managers wish they'd taken up a quiet, uncontroversial career in nuclear waste. His blue eyes looked as cold as an Arctic sky. 'What's the game?' he grated in a Glaswegian accent that fifteen years in England had done nothing to temper.

'Nice to meet you, too, Andy,' Lindsay said.

'Don't give me that. There's no way you and me are gonnae be pals, so gonnae no' play at it, eh? Now, what's the meaning of this?' He waved the note in Lindsay's face, so close she had to lean back to avoid it hitting her eyes.

'I would have thought it was obvious,' Lindsay said. 'Even to a printer,' she added, deciding that in his state of agitation it was easier to wind him up further rather than try to calm him down.

'I've had you smartarse hacks up to here,' he growled. 'Oh, youse were all our best pals when you were trying to get my union into bed with yours. Turns out all you wanted was the dowry. Union Jack and his pals thought they could muscle in on AMWU and run everything their way.'

'It seems to have been what the rank and file wanted. After all, they voted Union Jack in.'

'What the rank and file seemed to forget was that it was their way that had landed the JU in the cart in the first place,' Andy said. 'And it had to be stopped before AMWU ended up as bankrupt as those clowns made the JU.'

'I wouldn't go around shouting my mouth off like that if I was in your shoes, Andy,' Lindsay said. 'There's some who would think that would do as a murder motive for a man like you, a man married to the union in the absence of a wife.'

Andy looked disgusted. 'You make me sick, so you do. I've got nothing to say to you.' He turned on his heel and started to walk away.

'Jed's scared,' Lindsay called after him. 'Scared people do very stupid things, Andy.'

He turned back to look her in the eye. 'Any more out of you, lady, and you'll be finding that out from bitter personal experience.'

In that brief moment, transfixed by his cold gaze like a butterfly on a pin, Lindsay understood why the print union had won so many seemingly impossible victories over their years of confrontation.

Sophie stepped forward from the shadows and touched Andy's arm. 'It might not look like it, Andy, but she is trying to help.'

He looked searchingly at Sophie, as if trying to find the weakest point at which to target his next attack. 'And who the hell might you be?' he challenged.

'My name is Sophie Hartley. I'm an obstetrician and gynaecologist. And before you ask, it's got fuck all to do with me, except that I'm with her and when you kick her, we both limp. Which rather seems to be the case with you and Jed.'

'What's with this Jed stuff? You talking about that heid-the-ba' that got up to bury Tom Jack? What's that got to do with me?'

'Enough to make you come out of the hall to talk to me, evidently,' Lindsay said. 'Look, Andy. Jed's told me the whole story. How you met, what happened last night, and the bits in between. **Conference Chronicle**'s chosen you as suspect of the day. I don't know what if anything you've told the police, but sooner or later, they're going to be kicking your door in and shining the spotlight in your bonny blue eyes.'

'You're fu' o' shite,' Andy said disgustedly. But his eyes had grown wary, and his body had unconsciously shifted into 'fight or flight' mode, balanced on the balls of his feet, hands bunched loosely at his sides, shoulders slightly hunched forward.

'Am I? Please yourself, then. But Jed's too scared to do the sensible thing, which is to persuade you to go to the cops with him, now, before they come to you. You need to get in first, and tell them what you were really up to when somebody shoved Union Jack through my window. Face it, Andy, chances are they might just believe you, and the pair of you can walk away and nobody else will have to know the truth. Whereas, if they do take you in and you try to pull your nuts out of the fire with what looks like a pretty crap alibi, the whole world and its dog will know within the hour, the way the tabloids have got the cop shop staked out. And if there's one thing that's guaranteed to lose you any credibility you've got in this union, it isn't that you're gay. It's that you're a liar who was scared to tell people you're gay.'

His eyebrows dropped into a heavy frown. 'You're no' real, you,' he growled.

'I'm real, all right. Don't forget, Andy, I've been in the frame for this too. And I can't go home till the police have cleared all this mess up. It would be hellish easy for me to tell them that now I've had time to think, I remember Andy Spence being on the scene before anyone else. Almost as if he'd been waiting for something to happen.'

'Jesus Christ, that is all I need. Painted into a corner by the fucking gay activists. Come out or we'll fit you up for murder.' He shook his head, looking strangely vulnerable in his baffled anger.

'I always knew you printers were past masters at twisting the truth, but that takes the biscuit. Don't you understand? I'm trying to help you, not threaten you. I'm trying to show you what *could* happen, not what I'm going to make happen,' Lindsay was almost shouting in her exasperation.

Seeing that Lindsay's words were having no effect other than to make Andy look more hunted, Sophie chipped in again. 'Andy, if you can't bring yourself to do this on your own account, do it for Jed. After his performance this afternoon, the police are bound to take an interest in him. His room's only half a dozen doors away from Lindsay's. Without you telling the truth, he hasn't got an alibi either, and once the police start investigating him, it's not going to be too long before they make the link between the pair of you. No matter how discreet you've been, someone somewhere knows you're lovers. And that gives Jed a motive for killing Tom Jack.'

There was a brief silence, while Andy considered Sophie's words. 'Did you say you were a doctor?' he asked.

'That's right.'

'I bet your patients come out of the hospital

thinking it was *their* idea to have the hysterec-tomy,' he said bitterly, turning on his heel.

Sophie stepped back as if she'd been slapped.

'You bastard,' Lindsay hissed, taking a step towards him.

Andy looked back over his shoulder. 'You think I got where I am today by being *nice*? Go take a flying fuck at a bag of nails, the pair of you.' He stormed back through the swing doors in the hall, leaving the pair of them standing in shocked silence.

It was Lindsay who spoke first, moving over to Sophie and hugging her close. 'I'm sorry, my love. You didn't deserve that.'

Sophie kissed Lindsay's ear. 'I know that. But at least he might go to the police off his own bat now. I get the feeling that the only kind of fight Andy Spence understands is the dirty stuff.'

'Only happy below the belt, eh?' Lindsay chuckled.

'He's not the only one, is he,' Sophie teased, pinching Lindsay's bottom. 'Now, do you want to go back to the hotel and try this hypnosis, or do you feel the need to make someone else's day?'

'Let's go back. And if the hypno doesn't work, I'm sure you can think of something else to make me feel good.'

'Colonic irrigation, perhaps?'

'I'm not convinced, you know,' Lindsay said, lying back on the hotel room bed.

'You don't need to be. You just need to be cooperative and willing,' Sophie told her. 'Now just do what you're told, for once.'

Lindsay grinned. 'Okay, boss.'

'Now close your eyes, take a deep breath, and relax.' Lindsay let Sophie's voice wash over her. Her tone was warm, her voice even. 'Imagine you're on a tropical beach. It's just before daybreak, and you can still see the stars in the dark blue sky. You can hear the gentle sounds of the waves lapping the shore and the distant cries of the sea-gulls. Picture the scene as the sun starts to rise, turning the sky pink. The stars slowly fade, and you can see the palm trees waving in the soft breeze. You're relaxing here on the beach, as the sky turns from pink to gold, and the first rays of the sun start to warm your body.

'Now, while you're enjoying the new day, I want you to relax. Starting with your toes, let those muscles go, and relax.' Her voice fell on the final word, and she paused momentarily. 'Now your feet and ankles, release all the tension and relax.' Pause. 'Move on up into your lower leg, and let those muscles go, and relax'.

Sophie continued, working up Lindsay's body, but she was only half-way through the initial induction when a change in Lindsay's breathing pattern signalled she had already slipped over into an altered state of consciousness. Sophie continued with the relaxation, then said, 'I'm going to count backwards from five, and with

185

every number, you will go deeper and deeper, deeper and deeper. Five, four, three, two, one, zero, zero, zero.'

Lindsay's body became even more limp. Sophie did a few reflex tests to make sure Lindsay really was as deeply under as she thought, then she began to work. 'I want you to imagine you're in a video library. In this video library, there are shelves of tapes, and they're all videos of your life. What you're going to do now is choose a video to watch tonight. I want you to find the tape from last night. I want you to take down the video that has the Scots-Irish night on it. Have you got that tape in your hand?'

Lindsay grunted.

'Okay,' Sophie continued in a soft, measured monotone. 'I want you to put that tape in the video and press play. Now, I want you to tell me what you can see.'

'Can see the band playing, in front of me. I've got a bottle of White Horse.' Lindsay sounded defiantly proud of herself. Her voice was slightly blurred, as if she were half-asleep or half-drunk.

'What can you hear?'

'Can hear the band. They're playing an eight-some reel, but nobody knows how to dance it properly. Or else they're like me, they know but they'd rather be drinking. I can hear a lot of voices, talking, shouting, but I'm not listening to them, I'm listening to the music. It's not bad, though the fiddler's a wee bit slow on the key changes.'

186

'What can you smell and taste?' Sophie was checking which senses had been most important to Lindsay the night before.

Lindsay's nose wrinkled in disgust. 'Cigarette smoke. Stuffy. Sweaty bodies. The band doesn't smell nice. Somebody's got a pipe.' Then her face cleared and she gave a half-smile. 'I can taste the peat in the White Horse. 'S from Islay. Proper whisky.'

'What can you feel?'

'Hot.'

'I want you to press fast forward now, and I want you to take us forward. You're outside now, you've been talking to Desmond, the Irishman who's going to Minnesota. What can you see?'

'Fountain. 'S boring. Lots of lights gone off. Big blocks of darkness against the sky. No stars out, just black.'

'What's happening?' Sophie probed.

'I told him I've got to go, it's late and I've got stuff to do. He's standing up and saying he's going back to the ceilidh, and I laugh because I think it's funny because he can hardly stand after that last swallow of Jameson's. Don't like Jameson's, doesn't taste of anything proper. So I watch him stagger off, and I go back to Maclintock Tower. I'm *really* tired. I want to go to sleep and the room not go round and I'm sort of talking to myself and I wish Sophie was here because then I wouldn't be drunk because, 's funny, but I don't get drunk when Sophie's here, not because she makes me not, just because I don't feel the need.' Lindsay stopped.

'What's happening now?' Sophie prompted her.

'I'm waiting for the lift,' Lindsay said in the irritated tone of a child who has just been asked a question they knew how to answer when they were a year younger.

'Okay, let's move forward. The lift's come to a standstill on the tenth floor, and you're stepping out. Can you see?'

''S hard. They've only got those stupid blue nightlights, and you can hardly see to the next corner. I look to my right, then I look to my left, and I sort of see somebody moving fast round the corner.'

'Look carefully at the picture. Take it back, look at it frame by frame. What can you see?'

''S all a bit blurry. I'm a bit pissed, you know,' Lindsay said confidentially. 'Let me see. 'S not wearing shoes. 'S a leg. A leg going round the corner. The bottom bit of a leg. It's not wearing clothes. Just a leg.'

Sophie checked that Lindsay's mini-cassette recorder was still turning. 'Keep looking at that frame. Now, is it a man's leg or a woman's?'

'Don't know. Quite slim. Nice leg. Probably a woman, because I think it's nice.' Lindsay giggled.

'What can you hear?'

'The lift shutting and going down.'

'What do you feel?'

'Sweaty and tired and drunk.'

'Can you smell anything?'

Lindsay sniffed loudly. Her face changed, and she frowned. 'Perfume. Faint, but I know it. I know what it is.'

Sophie felt a thrill of excitement. This was completely new. 'What is it, Lindsay?'

'Cartier. Le Must de Cartier.'

'Are you sure?'

'Of course I'm sure.' Lindsay's voice had grown hard and cold. She no longer sounded like an amiable drunk. 'I bought it often enough. For Cordelia. Perfume for treacherous bitches. *She* wears it too.'

'Who wears it too, Lindsay?'

'Laura Craig, of course. 'Nother treacherous bitch.'

'Anybody else?'

'Nobody I know,' Lindsay said.

'I want you to carry on, frame by frame, until the moment when you open the door, then I want you to press stop. Okay?' Lindsay nodded. Sophie listened patiently for another five minutes, but there was nothing else of any significance in Lindsay's story. Gently, Sophie brought Lindsay back into full consciousness.

Lindsay sat up, stretched and yawned hugely. 'Oh God,' she sighed. 'That was wonderful.' She yawned again. 'I feel so-o-oh relaxed.' She rubbed her eyes and swung her feet on to the floor. 'Well,

I suppose it was worth a try. If nothing else, I've had a good rest.'

'I'm glad I've got my uses,' Sophie said drily. 'Don't you want to discuss what you came up with?'

Lindsay did a double take. 'What I came up with? I don't remember coming up with anything!'

Sophie smiled. 'Oh yes you did.'

Lindsay looked suspicious. 'You said I was in control. You said I'd be able to remember anything that happened under hypnosis.'

'You do, in the sense that what was in your subconscious is now part of your conscious mind. But you were very deeply under. You'll have to think quite hard about what you came up with. Luckily, I was here to listen.'

'How do I know you're not just making it up?'

'Because you'll know what I'm talking about as soon as I remind you that what was niggling at the back of your mind wasn't something you saw or heard. It was something you smelled. Le Must de Cartier.'

'As used by Cordelia Brown and Laura Craig. They should rechristen it Betrayal.' Suddenly, Lindsay sat bolt upright. '**Conference Chronicle** must have got it right about her being a Special Branch plant. No way she could afford Cartier on what the union pays her.'

'You've completely lost me, Lindsay,' Sophie complained. 'Although you do seem to have astonishing recall considering this hypnosis business doesn't really work,' she added, tongue firmly planted in her cheek.

Lindsay apologised and brought Sophie up to date on the allegations about Laura. 'And there's something else I didn't go into detail about. I don't know what bearing it has on what's happened now, but old sins cast long shadows. It was another unexpected death that looked like it could have been an accident. Let me tell you a bedtime story,' Lindsay said. She put her arms round Sophie and cast her mind back nine years to her first union conference.

Succinctly, reviving her dormant journalistic skills, Lindsay outlined the circumstances of Ian Ross's death. 'He died instantly,' she concluded. 'And all because his inhaler ran out at the wrong time.'

Sophie, who had been listening intently, frowned. 'That *can't* be right, Lindsay. It can't have happened like that.'

10

'I'm telling you, that's what happened,' Lindsay said obstinately.

Recalling in the nick of time her partner's fondness for being right, Sophie diplomatically said, 'I'm sure that's what people were saying at the time, but I find it hard to credit.'

Lindsay's chin lifted. 'What exactly is it you are taking issue with? I mean, I *was* there, and I've not exactly gone senile yet. I can still remember what happened, even if it was nine years ago.'

'I didn't say there was anything wrong with

your recollection, sweetheart. Just that whoever told you what happened might have got it wrong, that's all.'

'Wrong about what?' Lindsay persisted, only slightly mollified.

Sophie absently massaged the back of Lindsay's neck, kneading the tight muscles as she formulated the least inflammatory approach. 'How long had Ian been asthmatic?' she eventually asked.

'I don't know. Since he was a kid, I think. Certainly as long as I knew him. He didn't make any secret of it. He used his inhalers wherever he happened to be – in the middle of the office, in the car, down the pub. Mmm, that's wonderful, gimme more!' Lindsay groaned, leaning back into Sophie.

'And did he use his inhalers often?' Sophie asked, moving out across the firm trapezius muscles that Lindsay had built up on the volleyball court and in the surf.

'Mmm,' Lindsay breathed. 'Yeah, every few hours or so, I guess.'

'And did you ever see him have an acute attack?'

'Only the once. The day after we arrived at Blackpool. Laura brought her golden retriever over to our table in the bar at lunchtime. The dog was next to Ian. He took his inhalers right away, but it didn't seem to help. He was really wheezing and struggling for breath. Don't suppose I have to tell you, you'll have seen it often enough. Oh,

God, Soph, that's perfect, just there,' she added as Sophie dug her thumbs in around Lindsay's spine.

'QED,' Sophie said, trying to keep the note of triumph out of her voice.

'What is?' Lindsay groaned.

'The point I was trying to make. Any asthmatic whose condition was bad enough to require the use of inhalers every few hours and who was prone to acute attacks provoked by specific allergens would never have been caught out with one empty inhaler,' Sophie said.

'But they must run out some time,' Lindsay objected.

Sophie nodded. 'Of course they do. But asthmatics have a healthy respect for their illness. They know it can kill. When I was a student, I shared a flat with a woman who had relatively bad asthma, and she had inhalers like most people have personal jewellery. There was always at least one in her bag, usually a couple. There was one tucked down the seat of her armchair, one in the bathroom, one in the cutlery drawer and one by her bed. Whenever we were going out anywhere, she always gave her inhaler a shake to check there was enough in it to cope if she had an acute attack. It was a reflex. And she wasn't paranoid. From what I've seen of asthmatics, she was pretty typical. That's why I don't believe what you've told me about Ian's death. I find it inconceivable that he didn't have a spare inhaler either on his person or in his car.'

'So how come nobody pointed that out at the time?' Lindsay asked.

'Speaking purely as a subscriber to chaos theory, I'd assume that the coroner was a lawyer rather than a doctor and that no one involved on the official side knew much about asthma. But you're right to ask the question,' she added. 'It's curious that it didn't crop up.'

Suddenly, Lindsay jumped to her feet. 'The hot water!' she exclaimed, hitting the heel of her hand against her forehead. 'Of course, the hot water!'

Sophie sat patiently, watching Lindsay bouncing on the balls of her feet like a runner waiting for the starting-pistol. 'The hot water?' she asked.

Lindsay closed her eyes and summoned up a picture from the past. This time, she didn't need hypnotherapy to reach the information.

'Ian used to drink herbal tea, so he just used to get the waitress to bring him a pot of boiling water and he'd dunk his own bag. Anyway, on the morning he died, Laura cannoned into our table and sent his pot of water flying. It looked just like a regular bit of clumsiness, and they had a bit of a shouting match. Laura ended up marching off to the kitchen and getting him another pot. And that's how she did it,' Lindsay concluded triumphantly.

Sophie sighed. 'Did what, Lindsay?'

'D'you remember that woman who was at Paige's birthday party? The allergy specialist?'

Sophie nodded. 'The one from Sonoma?'

'That's right. Well, she was telling me how they do allergy testing. They make a concentrated extract of the allergen and put it in solution. Apparently, you have to be really careful with labelling, because the liquids are mostly colourless, odourless and tasteless. Just the sort of thing you could dump into a pot of hot water without anyone noticing, don't you think?'

Sophie shook her head, bemused. 'That's a bit of a jump, isn't it?'

'Logic, that's what it is.'

Sophie couldn't help chuckling. 'Fine. So what next, Sherlock?'

Lindsay flopped on the bed and stretched out. 'I suppose a quick bonk would be out of the question?'

'You suppose right. On the other hand, the offer of a long, slow, sensuous night of passion might just persuade me . . .'

'Blackpool,' Lindsay muttered sleepily.

'Sorry?' Sophie yawned. 'I thought you said Blackpool.'

'I did. What time is it?'

Sophie rolled over and picked up her watch. 'Ten to nine. If we're quick, we'll make breakfast. I don't know about you, but I'm ravenous. Must be all that passion last night.' She turned to cuddle Lindsay, but clutched at empty air as her partner rolled out of bed and headed for the shower. 'Hey,' Sophie yelled in protest. 'What happened to "I'll respect you in the morning"?'

Lindsay grinned. 'I can still respect you from the shower, can't I? We need to get a move on if we're going to get to Blackpool this morning.'

If she said anything more, it was drowned in the hiss of the shower. 'What did I do to deserve this?' Sophie groused amiably as she followed Lindsay into the bathroom. 'What is all this about Blackpool? Does this mean you've given up hunting for Union Jack's killer? Are we going for a ride on the big dipper? Do I get to wear a kiss-me-quick hat? Will you smother me in candy-floss and lick it off slowly?'

Lindsay tilted her head back to rinse the shampoo out of her hair. 'We're going to see a man about an inquest. Or at least, I am. You don't have to come if you don't want.'

'How could I resist?' Sophie asked, gloomily picking up her toothbrush and squeezing an inch of toothpaste on to it. 'At the risk of sounding dense, why Blackpool?'

'Because that's where Ian was murdered.'

Sophie cast her eyes heavenwards. 'Me and my big mouth,' she muttered. 'You'd think I'd know better by now.'

Lindsay lathered herself with shower gel and said, 'Well, it stands to reason, doesn't it? If what you said about asthma was right, then Ian's death obviously wasn't accidental, was it? We could have a serial killer stalking AMWU, you know.'

'Has anyone ever told you you were born at the wrong time? You'd have made a great Victorian melodrama writer. What about suicide?' Sophie said through a mouthful of foam.

'Nah,' Lindsay said definitely. 'Not Ian's speed at all. No, mark my words, it was murder. And unless my nose is mistaken, Ian's killer has struck again. What a grade A bitch!'

'Hang on a minute,' Sophie said, climbing into the shower as Lindsay swilled the last of the suds from her body. They embraced briefly, bodies slippery under the stream of water. 'I know how unlikely it is that Ian didn't have an inhaler. I also believe you saw someone – possibly Laura – leaving the scene of Tom Jack's death. But where's the evidence that either of them was murdered? And if they were, where's the link? And what's the connection to Laura?' Sophie watched her lover's jaw set stubbornly. She sighed. 'All right, Gordon, tell me what your famous nose says about the woman.'

'You mean, apart from the fact that she's a snotty, patronising, fashion-obsessed careerist who probably secretly votes Tory? Oh, and a heartless homophobe to boot? This is the woman who told me that one less dyke in the world was no great loss. That was, oh, about six weeks after Frances died.'

Sophie raised her eyebrows. 'So it's just possible you might be a tiny bit biased?'

Lindsay couldn't fight the smile. 'Never let the facts get in the way of a bit of honest prejudice, that's me. But I bet you a bottle of the Islay malt of your choice that it *is* her.' She shrugged. 'All I have to do now is prove it.'

Sophie sighed. 'So why are we delving into ancient history? Surely it's going to be a lot easier to come up with evidence of something that happened a couple of days ago rather than a nine-year-old death that everyone thinks was accidental anyway?'

Lindsay stepped out of the shower and wrapped herself in a white fluffy bath towel. 'Theoretically, you're right. But there's a signal lack of motive here. I can't think of any reason why Laura Craig would want to off Union Jack. Maybe the answer is buried in the past, along with poor old Ian. Just call it a hunch, as Quasimodo said to Esmerelda.'

Sophie's heart sank. This wasn't the time to remind Lindsay that hunches weren't her strong point.

Blackpool looked more like a ghost town than a holiday resort. A salty fog swirled patchily through the streets, adding gothic emphasis to the eerie emptiness of the pavements. Sophie followed the signs that led to the prom. 'And this is the famous Golden Mile, is it?' she remarked

199

as she pulled up on double yellow lines. The neon signs from the amusement arcades and seedy hotels barely penetrated the mist. Every few minutes, ancient trams loomed out of the gloom like strange hallucinations from the past and hurtled on towards Fleetwood or the South Shore, their clatter muffled by the fog. 'Do you mean to tell me that it's for this that thousands of Glaswegians desert their native city for a fortnight every July? Dear God!'

'Tell me about it,' Lindsay said. 'Don't forget, I once spent a week here at a JU conference. At least in Torremolinos you tend to get decent weather.'

A traffic warden materialised out of a thick patch of fog. 'Wouldn't you just know it?' Sophie complained, starting the engine of Helen's tinny Toyota.

'No, wait!' Lindsay said, opening the door and climbing out on to the pavement. 'Thank goodness you've come along!' Sophie heard as the car shook to Lindsay's resounding door slam.

A few moments later, Lindsay jumped back into the car, clutching a sheet from the traffic warden's notebook. 'Natural charm, that's all it takes. Even traffic wardens like to feel needed. Okay, straight ahead, then take the second right by the Balmoral Bar and Grill,' she said with a slight shudder.

Ten minutes later, Lindsay was forced to admit she'd chosen the one traffic warden who either hated all visitors or didn't know her left from her right. Furious, she stomped into the nearest newsagent's, where she borrowed their telephone directory then bought an A-Z. It took a further ten minutes to zigzag through the one way system to the sixties office block that housed the coroner's office.

As they stood waiting for the lift to carry them to the fifth floor, Lindsay said casually, 'I still haven't come up with a good cover story for this little exercise.'

Sophie grinned. 'I love you, Lindsay Gordon,' she said.

'Why? Because I wrecked your UK trip by getting arrested, I can't keep my nose out of other people's business and I'm not even smart enough to think up good excuses for it?'

'No, actually, it's because you've got endless bottle.'

'Some would say stupidity,' Lindsay remarked.

'Then they'd be wrong.'

'I'm not so sure. I suspect it's pretty dumb to rely on the tradition that coroner's officers are generally the nicest guys on the force. That's why they get the job – because they have to spend their time dealing with bereaved families.' The lift arrived, and they got in. 'I guess I'll think of something when I'm staring into the whites of his eyes,' Lindsay added with a nervous grimace.

'He really will be Mr Nice Guy, will he?' Sophie asked.

'Probably,' Lindsay said gloomily. 'Which will

make me feel like a real shit. Lying to the bad guys is no problem. But taking advantage of the good guys always leaves my self-respect in shreds.'

'Have you got any university ID with you?' Sophie asked. 'Something that attaches you to the university without being specific as to subject or faculty?'

Lindsay patted her shoulder bag. 'My library card and my researcher's pass for the stacks. Never leave home without it.'

The lift shuddered to a halt and the doors opened. 'Good. Just in case. For once, you follow my lead, sweetheart,' Sophie said. 'Busk it.'

'You play glockenspiel, I'll play drums,' Lindsay muttered as she followed Sophie out of the lift. At the end of the short corridor was a half-glazed door with 'Coroner's Officer' stencilled in gilt Olde Englishe lettering. Sophie tapped on the glass and they walked in. Three walls of the room were lined with filing cabinets that stretched to the ceiling. The fourth wall was a window, its view blanked out by the mist. Behind a cheap, chipped desk, a burly middle-aged man sat, flanked by precarious heaps of files. He looked up from the form he was filling in, and a broad smile lit up a creased, wind-burnt sailor's face. Lindsay suppressed a groan.

'Good morning, ladies,' he said in a gruff voice, his Lancashire accent noticeable even in those few words.

'Good morning, officer,' Sophie said, returning the smile with interest. She produced her wallet and flipped it open to the pass that revealed her to be a member of the medical staff of the Grafton Clinic, San Francisco. 'I'm Dr Sophie Hartley from California. I wrote to you about six weeks ago regarding a research study that my colleague and I are currently doing the groundwork for.'

The policeman's smile faded and a look of surprised bafflement took its place. 'I'm sorry, love,' he said, 'but I don't recall any letter like that.'

Lindsay couldn't help admiring Sophie's matching look of bewilderment. 'I don't under-stand,' she said. 'It was one of a batch that were all sent out together. The letter explained what the project was about, and asked for your coop-eration, and said I'd visit one morning this week while I was in the UK, if that was convenient.'

He got to his feet, and produced two wooden folding chairs from the narrow gap between a pair of filing cabinets. 'Well, it's not inconvenient,' he said, unfolding the chairs and waving the two women to them. 'I was just doing me paperwork, nothing that can't wait a bit. Mebbe you could tell me what it's all about?' He plonked himself back down in his own battered typist's chair.

Lindsay cringed as Sophie launched into an elaborate explanation, heavily larded with medical, statistical and sociological jargon. What it boiled down to was that she and Lindsay were allegedly researching causes of death among national newspaper journalists, to see if there were any statistically significant changes following the introduction of computer technology in the eighties. To Lindsay's ears, it sounded so outrageously silly it could only be true. Certainly, it seemed to impress the coroner's officer.

'I see,' he said slowly. 'And that would mean going back a few years, I take it?'

Sophie nodded. 'We need to go back ten years before the introduction of new technology, which, in most cases, means going back between fifteen and eighteen years.'

'You'll be after that lad that died during the union conference in 1984, then?' he asked.

Lindsay hoped her face didn't betray the shock she felt. Sophie's eyebrows rose. 'You remember the case? That's extraordinary,' she said.

'We don't get many conference delegates popping their clogs,' he said. 'You tend to remember, on account of how the tourist information lads get their bowels in a right confusion over it. If they had their way, we'd hold inquests at the bottom of a coalmine at midnight whenever they involve a holiday-maker or a conference delegate. They've never forgiven Neil Kinnock for falling in the sea before the Labour Party Conference. They said he made it look like Blackpool beach was a life-threatening place to go on holiday. I ask you!' He got to his feet. 'The lad's name?'

Sophie pretended to consult her personal organiser. 'Ian Ross,' she said.

He went straight to one of the cabinets flanking the door, and stood on a set of library steps to reach the top drawer. He pulled out a bulky file and climbed down with it. 'Here we are,' he said.

'I'm impressed,' Sophie said.

'I like to keep things methodical,' he said. 'You never know when somebody's going to need to take another look at a file. Things can take on a different perspective down the years, can't they?' he added, almost wistfully.

'You're absolutely right,' Lindsay chipped in. 'I wish all your colleagues were as organised. Now, will it be possible for us to make a copy of this file?'

He looked doubtful. 'I thought you'd just be wanting to have a look at the inquest report.'

Sophie shook her head. 'We really do need to examine the whole file, I'm afraid.'

He tapped his fingers on the edge of the file. 'I'm not right sure about that . . . I mean, whether the rest of the stuff's confidential or not.'

'The other officers we've dealt with in London and Manchester didn't have a problem with that,' Sophie said soothingly. 'I suppose they felt that enough time had elapsed to remove any possibility of an invasion of privacy. And of course, the study won't be identifying particular cases by name.'

His face brightened. 'Well, if they thought it

was okay, I suppose they'll know best, being more at the heart of things. I haven't got a photocopier in this office, but I use the one in the county council office down the hall. If you don't mind waiting, I'll pop down and do it now.'

As his footsteps receded down the hall, Lindsay leaned over and planted a kiss on Sophie's neck. 'You are a bloody genius!' she said. 'Pathology, epidemiology, epistemology: you didn't leave an ology unturned. Eat your heart out, Maureen Lipman!'

Sophie studied her fingernails in a pose of mock modesty. 'Elementary, my dear Watson. When in doubt, blind the buggers with science, that's what I always say. After all, it's been good enough for the medical profession for centuries. Why change a winning formula?'

'There's just one thing niggling me,' Lindsay said.

'What's that, sweetheart?'

'The fact that he knew right away who you were talking about. And his explanation didn't ring true to me. Methinks the laddie doth protest too much, and all that. Once you've got your mitts on our "research material", I'm going to have another go at our local friendly copper,' she said.

They had twenty minutes to argue about the likelihood of Laura having murdered Union Jack before the coroner's officer returned, carrying a large manila envelope as well as the file.

'Here we are,' he said, handing the bulky envelope to Sophie. 'I took the opportunity of having a word with Mr Entwistle, the coroner, just to make sure I wasn't doing anything out of order, and he's cleared it.'

The two women rose to their feet. 'Thanks, we really appreciate this, especially since my letter had gone astray,' Sophie said.

'We certainly do,' Lindsay echoed. 'And I still can't get over your mental filing system. Fancy being able to remember the case and the year, just like that. Nine years ago!'

The policeman shrugged. 'Well, some things do stick more than others. If you'd been asking about sudden deaths among hoteliers, I'd have had a lot more to think about!'

'Yeah, I suppose journalists are a bit more uncommon,' Lindsay said, still desperately fishing.

'They are that,' he said. 'And this chap seemed a bit out of the normal run of things for journalists, even.'

'How do you mean?' Lindsay asked, trying to sound nonchalant.

'I'd probably have forgotten all about it if it hadn't been for that business on the news the other day. You know, that union leader that got himself killed earlier in the week?' He cocked an eyebrow at Lindsay, who nodded casually. 'Well, a few months after this Ian Ross met his maker, that selfsame union boss was here, asking all sorts of questions about him.'

11

*'Some debates are more glamorous than others.
But delegates have a duty to devote as much attention to international affairs as they do to finance.
Like mother used to say, eat up your bread and
butter or you can't have any cake.'*

from *'Advice for New Delegates',*
a Standing Orders Sub-Committee booklet.

Lindsay swallowed hard. Before she could open
her mouth, Sophie said brightly, 'No wonder you
remembered! That must be pretty unusual, two
people wanting details about the same person.
Though I don't suppose the union man was after
the kind of gory details we need,' she added with
a smile.

'I don't know. He wanted to know all sorts. He
said the union were going to set up a trust fund
for training officials as a memorial to this Ian Ross,
and he was meant to write a sort of tribute to
him, though why he needed to know all about

the way he died I could never work out. Still, ours not to reason why, eh?' the friendly policeman said, diplomatically easing them towards the door. 'I hope your research goes well, ladies,' he added, opening the door for them.

By the time they got to the lift, Lindsay looked as if she was going to burst with the urgency of her desire to raid the envelope that Sophie clutched tightly to her chest. 'Wait,' she hissed at Lindsay as they joined the two men already in the lift. 'It'll still be there in five minutes.'

As they walked back to the car-park, Lindsay exploded. 'I can't believe it! Union Jack was here before us! That's wild!'

'Did the union ever actually set up a memorial fund?' Sophie asked.

'Of course they didn't,' Lindsay snorted. 'But what I've been forgetting is that long before he was ever a full-time union official, Tom Jack used to be a bloody good investigative journalist. He knew every trick in the book, and a few that never made it that far. If he was sniffing around the inquest records, then at least one other person was as unhappy about Ian's death as we are. And maybe what he found there is the reason he's lying in the morgue now.'

'It seems a bit far-fetched. He can't have had any proof, otherwise why would it take nine years for his discovery to catch up with him?'

Lindsay shrugged. 'Dunno. But I'll be a damn sight closer when I've read what's in this envelope.'

They had reached the car, and Lindsay drummed impatiently on its roof while she waited for Sophie to unlock the passenger door. As soon as she'd banged the door shut with a teeth-rattling slam, Lindsay grabbed the envelope, ripped it open and tipped the contents into her lap.

'I have a suggestion,' Sophie said. 'Why don't we go and find somewhere for lunch, then we can go through this stuff together.'

'Oh, all right,' Lindsay said resignedly. She shovelled the papers back into the envelope reluctantly. 'I know a really good fish restaurant.'

'Well, it *was* nine years ago,' Lindsay said apologetically half an hour later. 'And all these streets look the same in the fog. Try the next left.'

'We've been down there already. To hell with it, Lindsay, we'll just stop at the next pub we come to and grab something there.' Sophie drove straight on, then turned right down a street she thought would bring her to one of the main roads.

'That's it!' Lindsay suddenly shouted, waving her arm in front of Sophie, who was forced to stand on the brakes.

'*That's* it?' Sophie demanded. 'It looks just like a terraced house to me.'

'That's right. They fry in the front room and they've got half a dozen tables in the back. It's wonderful, I promise you.'

'It had better be,' Sophie said darkly as she followed Lindsay.

While they waited for one jumbo haddock and chips and one halibut steak and peas, Lindsay eagerly pulled out the coroner's reports on Ian Ross's death. She flicked through them, separating out the pathologist's report and handing it to Sophie. 'There you go, darling, your area of expertise.' Lindsay herself concentrated first on the report of the officer who had gone through Ian's car to see if there were any physical reason why he had lost control of the car and had failed to brake.

When she got to the list of the car's contents, she let out a low whistle. 'You were right, Sophie,' she said. 'Ian Ross was murdered. No question about it.'

'You sure?' Sophie said, sensibly not reminding Lindsay who had first mentioned the m-word.

Lindsay nodded. 'Look at this,' she said, waving the sheet under Sophie's nose. '"On the floor behind the passenger seat, one plaid travelling rug with large quantity of what appear to be dog hairs, white or blond in colour." He'd never have had a rug in the car covered in dog hairs – he'd never have allowed a dog in the car. He was hopelessly allergic. And let's not forget Laura's dog was a golden retriever. And here; "On the floor under driver's seat, two Magic Tree air fresheners". Ian hated air fresheners – they used to really set his chest off, yet here we have not one, but two. And the final nail in the coffin, Soph; "In offside door pocket, one Ventolin

211

inhaler, approximately half-full". That's the clincher,' she ended triumphantly.

Sophie frowned. 'I don't understand. Surely, if he had another inhaler in the car, he would have used it in so acute an attack?'

'That's what you'd expect, isn't it?' Lindsay said. 'But Ian didn't keep his spare inhaler in the door pocket. He kept it in the glove box. I know, because he used it when we were driving up to Blackpool. He had one in his jacket, of course, but he'd taken that off while he was driving, and he used one from the glove box. There were actually two in there, I noticed. But look at the list of what was actually in the glove box; "One torch, one packet tissues, one pair sunglasses, one owner's manual, half packet extra strong mints, one blue Biro, one Michelin map of the Pas de Calais, one photocopied street plan of central Blackpool". No mention of inhalers at all. When Laura set up Ian for the kill, she realised that it would be suspicious if there was no spare inhaler in the car. So she just moved it from the place where he'd expect it to be and put it somewhere it would be found afterwards.'

'That's a pretty big jump, Lindsay,' Sophie protested. 'I mean, couldn't Ian have tried to use the inhaler, lost control of the car and just dropped it, letting it fall into the door pocket?'

Lindsay scowled. 'It'd be quite a coincidence, wouldn't it?'

Sophie was saved from getting into an argument

by the arrival of their lunch. Lindsay's haddock was almost too big for the stainless steel salver it arrived on. 'Thank God you didn't order the giant one,' Sophie said. Her eyes widened further as her own massive portion of halibut swimming in a viridian sea of mushy peas was plonked unceremoniously in front of her along with a pile of white cotton wool bread and butter.

'The only question left,' Lindsay said through mouthfuls of hot haddock, 'is why. I mean, we know Laura killed Ian and then she killed Tom, but we don't know why or the reason for the nine year gap. Hey, this is really good,' she exclaimed, pointing to her haddock.

Sophie nodded agreement. Both women concentrated on their fish in respectful silence. Sophie scraped her plate clean first, and said, 'There's obviously something I'm missing here. How exactly do we *know* that Laura killed Ian and Tom?'

Lindsay shovelled the last few chips on to her fork and paused for a moment. 'She came over to our table at breakfast that day. She could easily have nicked the inhaler out of Ian's jacket pocket. She might even have been wearing a perfume he was allergic to – he once said to me he had to trot off to the cosmetic department at Selfridges every time Laura wanted to try out a new perfume, to get a whiff of it and make sure it didn't set his chest off. And then there's the water.' She polished off the chips.

'Pure conjecture,' Sophie said.

Lindsay swallowed the last mouthful of fish, pushed her plate aside and poured herself another cup of strong tea. 'Okay. But who else had access to Ian's car to plant the rug and the air fresheners? And who knew where the spare inhaler was kept, so they could allay suspicion by moving it?'

'Well, you did for one,' Sophie said.

Lindsay grinned. 'Yeah, but I didn't have a set of keys for Ian's car, whereas Laura, who had lived with him for years, almost certainly did. And she had a golden retriever, so she was in a pretty good position to get her hands on a travelling rug covered in dog hairs. And she'd already established how allergic Ian was to her precious hound.'

'All circumstantial, though. Where's the smoking gun? And what possible motive could she have had?'

Lindsay ran a hand through her hair. 'I don't know. Yet. I've been trying to remember exactly what Ian said to me about their break-up. But it's nine years ago, and even my trained reporter's memory is having a bit of a struggle.' She frowned and sipped her tea. '*He* threw *her* out. He said there were some things you can't forgive and forget. There was another bloke involved, but I never found out who. Whoever he was, he didn't stick around for long, because Laura was footloose and fancy-free just a few weeks later, I seem to remember . . .' Lindsay's voice trailed off in the effort of concentration.

'Wait a minute,' she breathed. 'Now I remember. It was *Laura* who confirmed my suspicion that there was another man. From what Ian said, it sounded to me like Laura was seeing someone else and he'd found out and given her the jaggy bunnet. Then I spoke to Laura on the beach and gave her the hard word about being unfaithful. She looked really shocked, and I took it that she was surprised because Ian had talked to anyone about it. But thinking about it now, it could just as well have been because I'd hit on the wrong thing altogether.'

'Not for the first time,' Sophie said affectionately.

Pretending to ignore her, Lindsay continued. 'Which means that the break-up might have been nothing to do with their relationship, as such.'

'Meaning what?' Sophie asked.

'I wish I knew,' Lindsay said. 'Maybe some deep dark secret from her past. Maybe he got hold of the same story as 𝕮𝖔𝖓𝖋𝖊𝖗𝖊𝖓𝖈𝖊 𝕮𝖍𝖗𝖔𝖓𝖎𝖈𝖑𝖊.'

'But you said that story was complete garbage,' Sophie reminded her.

'So maybe I was wrong. We've got to get back and see what we can dig up about this.' Lindsay pushed her chair back with a squeal. 'Do you want me to drive?'

Sophie laughed. 'No way. Helen's car wasn't designed with frustrated boy racers in mind. You'd have the gearbox burned out half-way there.'

As she followed Sophie back to the car, Lindsay found a moment to wonder what had become of her old MGB roadster, the car that had been her partner for longer than any woman to date. Eyeing up the boxy Japanese wedge that passed for a sports car in the nineties, Lindsay felt a brief stab of regret. With a sigh, she settled into the passenger seat and returned to the attack. 'I still find it hard to believe that Laura is a Special Branch plant,' Lindsay confessed. 'And I can't imagine why Tom Jack would keep quiet about it for all those years if he thought she was.'

'Personally, I find it hard to believe that she'd kill to preserve her cover even if she was a right-wing infiltrator. I mean, what was the worst that could happen to her? She'd be blown, okay, but I bet the powers that be would have found her some comfortable little niche in the Civil Service. Now, if we had some convenient money motive . . . Do we know who benefited financially by Ian's death?'

Lindsay shook her head. 'I don't remember, if I ever knew. But I could find out easily enough. Pull up at the next motorway services and I'll set the wheels in motion.'

'Okay.' Sophie slotted a k.d. Lang tape into the cassette and hummed along to it as Lindsay flicked through the rest of the coroner's records and the inquest report into Ian's death. At the service area, she waited in the car while Lindsay gave the details of her request and her credit card number to a London paralegal firm that specialised in company searches and birth, marriage and death checks at St Catherine's House.

'They'll have something for me by close of business tomorrow,' Lindsay said when she returned.

'Great. Well, you've just about made out a circumstantial case for Laura killing Ian, but that doesn't bring us any closer to tying her into Union Jack's murder. If it was murder,' Sophie said as they headed for the motorway.

Lindsay chuckled. 'Even you can't talk me out of a murder verdict on that one,' she said. 'Somebody had it in for Tom Jack, it stands to reason. You don't shove someone out of a tenth floor window if you just want to put the frighteners on them.'

'He could have fallen. It could have been an accident during a struggle.'

'So what were they doing in my room in the first place if they weren't up to something funny?' Lindsay demanded.

'Maybe that was just coincidence. Maybe they just slipped in there to be somewhere more private than the corridor.' Sophie sounded doubtful, even to her own ears. 'Anyway,' she continued more strongly, 'what's to connect Laura?'

'The smell of her. Le Must de Cartier isn't a common perfume. I've only ever known two women who wore it, and if I'm sure of one thing in this whole twisted case, it's that Cordelia didn't kill Union Jack.'

Sophie shrugged. 'So Laura was in the corridor. It proves nothing. So was Andy Spence. He had motive, especially if Tom Jack knew about his sexuality. So was Jed Thomas. He had motive too. He wanted his boyfriend to have a crack at the top job before Jack completely wrecked his union. Your old mate Dick McAndrew didn't happen to mention where he was at the crucial time, did he? And that's just the ones you've mentioned to me.'

Lindsay pouted. 'I still reckon that double-dealing Laura Craig is the best bet.'

Sophie smiled, but took pity. 'Well, maybe she did kill him. But the one thing that sticks out a mile in this whole business isn't so much the motive. It's this nine year gap between Ian's death and Union Jack's. Maybe if we explored the time span, it would bring us closer to unravelling what connects the deaths. If indeed there is any connection.'

Lindsay stared out at the dark Pennine moors through a curtain of drizzle, pondering Sophie's words. The lowering sky seemed to swallow the afternoon light, forcing drivers to switch on their headlights. 'What you're saying makes a lot of sense,' she said eventually. 'But I don't know where to start.'

'Speaking as a scientist,' Sophie said, 'if I was looking at a condition that had remained dormant for a while and then had suddenly flared up again, the first question I'd ask is, "What has changed in the immediate past to provoke this?" In other words, we should be asking not, "Why did Tom Jack keep his mouth shut all those years if he knew about or suspected murder?", but rather, "What has happened to alter the situation? What is different from last week, or last month, or even last year?"'

'Point taken, but I think there's a flaw in your argument,' Lindsay said.

'Now there's a surprise,' Sophie teased.

Lindsay poked her tongue out at her partner. 'Tom Jack may well have taken action nine years ago when he uncovered the evidence that Ian's death wasn't as simple as it appeared. Just because we can't see what he did, it doesn't mean that he sat on his hands. He could have acted in a secret, underhand way, presumably for his own ends.'

'That's not a flaw in my argument, dear heart. In fact, it reinforces the point I was making. The crucial issue is what has happened to change the circumstances and turn Tom Jack into a threat. So what's different, Lindsay? What are the new circumstances?'

'Well, there's the merger for one thing. That went through with indecent haste, according to some. It all happened so quickly that there wasn't a full audit of both union's finances before they took the irrevocable step of joining forces. Apparently, Andy Spence has been complaining that the JU was less than frank about its financial problems. And as usual, people have been muttering about hands in the till. But that's nothing new.'

Sophie swung off the motorway and headed cross-country towards Sheffield. 'Didn't I read something in **Conference Chronicle** suggesting that the finances of the former JU were riddled with corruption? And that under Tom Jack's leadership, AMWU was going the same way?'

'Yeah,' Lindsay sighed. 'And it was probably not far off the mark. The other thing that's changed, of course, is Tom Jack's role in the union. In the past, he was a lay official who could shunt the blame for any financial irregularities at the door of paid officials. This time around, there would have been no hiding place for Tom. Unless, of course, he intended to make himself the hero of the hour by pointing the finger at the person who was creaming cash out of the union accounts.'

12

'As you will have to spend long hours engaged in conference business, we recommend that you bring a selection of loose, comfortable clothing with you. Of course, T-shirts supporting a wide variety of radical causes are invariably on sale outside the conference hall for those who have failed to follow this advice.'

from *'Advice for New Delegates'*,
a Standing Orders Sub-Committee booklet.

By the time they returned to Sheffield, Lindsay felt like her head had spent the day in a tumble-drier. Although she and Sophie had continued to discuss the case, she felt they'd made no more progress. Like kittens chasing their tails, they kept coming back to the idea of money. As Sophie pulled up outside the conference headquarters, Lindsay said with a sigh, 'If we're talking money, we're not going to find the answer here in Sheffield. We need to look at head office.'

'I had a funny feeling you were going to say something like that,' Sophie said. 'Oh boy, you really do know how to show a girl a good time, don't you? Today Blackpool, tomorrow Watford.'

'Who said anything about tomorrow?' Lindsay asked sweetly, getting out of the car. She leaned on the roof and winked at Sophie as she locked it up. 'No time like the present, is there? Still love me, babe?'

'Not if you call me "babe" again today,' Sophie said. 'So what's the plan?'

'Your turn to busk it,' Lindsay said, striding off purposefully towards the conference office. To Lindsay's surprise, the clerical staff seemed as busy as they'd been the previous afternoon, although logically, there should have been little for them to do so close to the end of the conference. She spotted Pauline's flat-top above a computer terminal on the far side of the room and made her way over to her. Sophie stayed near the door, idly browsing through a copy of that afternoon's order-paper.

'Why does my heart always sink whenever I see you heaving into sight?' Pauline asked resignedly as Lindsay perched on a corner of her desk.

Lindsay grinned. 'And there's me thinking it was passion that made your heart flutter.'

'That was before you appointed me your un-official source. Walls have ears around here, you know. Some people don't like me talking to you, and they let me know. Frankly, there are times when I think I won't be sorry to leave,' Pauline replied, keeping her eyes fixed on the screen as she typed. 'Where you been hiding yourself?'

'Would you believe Blackpool?'

Pauline shook her head. 'I don't know how you can think of enjoying yourself at a time like this.'

'Put it this way. Nobody got a kiss-me-quick hat,' Lindsay said grimly. 'Let's just say we had a little ride down memory lane on the ghost train. And I'm sorry if me sticking my nose in has caused you aggravation.'

'Forget it. I've got broad shoulders. How goes the sleuthing anyway?' Pauline asked.

'Slowly. Uncertainly. A bit like British Rail. You carry on in the hope you'll eventually reach a destination. Unfortunately, the one you reach isn't always the one you wanted to arrive at. How come you're all still slaving away?' Lindsay asked. 'I expected you to be partying, with only one session left.'

'Dream on,' Pauline sighed. 'Conference has been extended for an extra day so we can complete the agenda. At least that's what the officials are saying. The real story is, the cops have asked the NEC to keep the conference in session for a bit longer so they can continue their investigations without the delegates scattering to the four winds. So we've all been told to stay on at least till Saturday, maybe even Sunday. Handy

Andy pulled this big sob-story routine on us that the poor old union can't afford to pay us overtime, on account of all the other unforeseen expenditure they're facing because of conference overrunning.'

'An appeal to your better natures, eh? I bet he was as popular as a gingham frock at a thrash metal gig. So did you all agree to work on for buttons?' Lindsay asked.

'What do you think?' Pauline said angrily. 'There's enough mugs in this clerical section to open a coffee bar. Anyway, since we're on the subject of exploitation, what can I do for you?'

Lindsay had the grace to look embarrassed. 'Yeah, right, spot the hypocrite. It's all right for me to come creeping for favours, but it's all wrong for Andy Spence to do the same. What can I say?' She shrugged and held out her hands, palms upward. 'In my defence, I've got to say I've always really admired you, Pauline!' She grinned and winked.

'Dear God! Spare me the charm!' Pauline exploded with a giggle. 'What can I do for you, light of my life, joy of my existence, fire of my lions?'

'Don't you mean loins?'

'What, and me a happily married woman? Just be grateful for the lions. What is it you're after? Come on, spit it out. Some of us have got work to do.'

'Media House,' Lindsay said.

'Yes, Lindsay, Media House. It's where I work.

It's where we all work. It's the head office of the Amalgamated Media Workers' Union. Also known as Mafia House,' Pauline said sweetly.

Lindsay pulled a mock scowl. 'Careful. I've been patronised by experts, you know.'

'You saying black people can't be experts?' Pauline counter-teased. 'Now what was it about Media House?'

Lindsay swung one foot back and forward, studying her Nike trainer as if seeing it for the first time. 'I don't suppose there are many people there this week, with you all being at conference.'

'Skeleton staff,' Pauline said. 'Switchboard, a couple of clerks in membership records and Phil Jackson from admin as the sort of goalkeeper, there to deal with emergencies. Poor sod has to stay on till eight in the evening just in case we've got any problems here with agendas and if SOS or the NEC or the officials need any information from head office records. Was that the sort of thing you wanted to know?'

'Mmm,' Lindsay said casually, still letting the Nike hypnotise her. 'I suppose only a handful of people have got keys to the building?'

'Wrong,' said Pauline. Lindsay raised one eyebrow. 'Nobody has keys to the building. Entry is controlled by security code. Most of us have codes that are only valid between 8.45 a.m. and 6.15 p.m., Monday to Friday. Only department heads, full-time officials and NEC members have codes that allow them access at other times.'

'Oh.' Lindsay tried not to sound too disappointed. The Nike stopped swinging and she got to her feet. 'Sorry to trouble you.'

'It's no trouble,' Pauline said. She tapped her keyboard. 'What do you think of this motion, by the way?' She gestured at the screen. Lindsay read, 'Gen Sec 0719/Dep Gen Sec 4719.'

She cleared her throat. 'Well, it should achieve something useful, for a change,' she said. 'Anyway, I must get on. My bloodhound awaits,' she added, gesturing with her thumb towards Sophie, who was by now completely absorbed in her reading. 'I'll let you know how we get on. Take care.'

'I suspect I should be saying that to you,' Pauline said, clearing her screen as Lindsay walked away.

Just after ten, Sophie cruised slowly past the eight-storey office building that housed the headquarters of AMWU. The union's initials trickled down the side of the building, a gash of red neon in the night. As she checked out the building for lights, Lindsay said, 'When the four unions merged, they each found it impossible to accept that any of the others possessed a building suitable for their new mega-union's headquarters, so, with traditional trade union logic and efficiency, all four put their existing head offices on the market.'

'At the bottom of the biggest property slump

since the Second World War?' Sophie asked resignedly.

'You got it. At least the lease on this building is relatively cheap, on account of it had been standing empty for eighteen months and the roof leaks. But they've got an option to buy after five years. Everyone in AMWU fervently hopes that by then the other buildings will have been sold, the union's finances will be restored to health, and the election of a Labour government will have given the whole trade union movement a new lease of life. Only about two members actually believe these hopes are going to become reality. They're the ones who also believe the tooth fairy really exists and that the cheque is in the post.'

'Yeah, right. Well, what do you think? Do we go in, or what?' Sophie asked as she swung round the corner to circle the block.

'I think so. No lights showing. Park up somewhere unobtrusive, and we'll go for it.'

They decided to enter the building via the underground car-park, rather than the more conspicuous main entrance, next door but one to a busy Burger King. At the head of the ramp, Lindsay suddenly stopped without warning, forcing Sophie to stumble into her back. 'Shit!' Lindsay said, 'Look, closed circuit video surveillance!'

'So?' Sophie said. 'We're not burglars. We're not going to steal anything, we're not about to break and enter. You are a member of AMWU, which I reckon gives you a right to be on the premises. And I'm wearing an Amnesty International sweatshirt.'

'Remind me never to call you if I need legal representation,' Lindsay muttered. 'Okay, I'll take your word for it, against my better judgement. Just keep your head down, and follow me.'

'Eat your heart out, Catwoman,' Sophie said under her breath as Lindsay set off, hugging the walls and tucking her head down into her chest.

They quickly worked their way round to the building's entrance, avoiding the arcs of the cameras as far as possible. Lindsay keyed in the combination Pauline had given her for the general secretary. No one had thought to cancel it following Tom Jack's spectacular plunge, and the door lock clicked open. The two women slipped inside, finding themselves in a dimly lit corridor. At the end was a lift. Lindsay punched the call button, and in a matter of seconds, the doors slid noiselessly open.

'Which floor?' Sophie asked, finger poised.

'Er . . . I don't actually know,' Lindsay confessed, scuffing the toe of her trainer on the carpet.

'You – don't – know?' Sophie demanded, articulating each word slowly and distinctly as the doors closed.

'Not as such,' Lindsay said. 'I couldn't really ask, could I? Not without making it really obvious in a room full of head office staff that I was about to go off and do a Watergate.'

'Fine. So we're in an eight-storey office building without a clue which office we should be looking in? Well, Lindsay, that's a lot of locks to pick before morning,' Sophie said, pulling a rueful smile to take the edge off her words.

Lindsay scowled and leaned past her lover to hit the ground floor button. When the doors opened, she marched across the foyer to a semi-circular desk marked 'Reception. All visitors must sign in here.' The light from the lift provided enough illumination for a cursory search. Sophie leaned against the lift door, her finger on the 'doors open' button, a smile in her eyes. Nothing worked better with Lindsay than a little needle, she thought to herself. Meanwhile, Lindsay pulled open the top drawer of the desk. She took out a clipboard with yesterday's brief list of visitors and gave it a quick glance. She let out a low whistle. 'Police were here yesterday,' she said. 'Let's hope there's something left for us.' Dropping the clip-board, she rootled through the drawer. 'Gotcha!' she said confidently, waving a stapled bundle of paper above her head. 'Name, title, extension number, office.'

She walked slowly back to the lift, flicking through the pages. 'Here we are. Tom Jack, general secretary, extension 8111, room 803. Safe to assume that's on the top floor?' Lindsay said.

'Good thinking, Batman,' Sophie said, pressing

the button marked eight. Moments later, they stepped out into blackness, which became impenetrable as soon as the lift door shut behind them. 'I don't suppose we remembered a torch?' Sophie asked.

Lindsay rummaged in her bag, finally finding a small pencil torch with a powerful, narrow beam. 'Give the girl a coconut?'

She shone the light on the doors as they moved along the narrow corridor. 803 was the third door on the left. Lindsay tried the handle, and to her delight and surprise, the door swung open. The torch beam revealed a small, businesslike secretary's office, complete with filing cabinets, word processor terminal and a low, three-seater sofa, presumably for Union Jack's visitors. On the right-hand wall, there was another door. Lindsay headed purposefully in that direction, while Sophie made for the computer, which she switched on as Lindsay opened the door to the inner sanctum.

'Well, Union Jack didn't stint himself,' Lindsay commented as she swung the torch beam across the room. The office was done out in top-of-the-range hi-tech black and chrome, a style that had already dated. Lindsay walked over to the two walls of windows that made it look as if the corner office extended indefinitely into the sodium-lit night streets. There was an array of buttons in the central pillar, and she pressed the one marked 'close'. A sweep of vertical blinds whispered across the windows, shutting out the town below. She moved over to the desk and switched on a black halogen lamp. On a stand to one side was a PC, but Lindsay wasn't interested in that. She knew her limitations. Besides, she could already hear the sound of Sophie's fingers on the secretary's word processor. When she'd had enough of playing with that machine, she could unravel the secrets of Union Jack's PC.

Lindsay sat on the edge of a luxurious black leather swivel-and-tilt chair and tried the drawers of the massive black ash desk. They were locked. Of course, the police would presumably have had Union Jack's keys. They wouldn't have had to bust open his expensive desk. And she didn't want to if she could avoid it. 'Sophie?' she called.

'Problems?' came the reply.

'Are the drawers in that desk open?'

There was a brief pause while Sophie experimented. 'All except the bottom one. Why?'

Lindsay returned to the outer office. 'Any keys in them? I'm looking for a key that would unlock a serious desk.'

'Help yourself,' Sophie said, returning to the menu on her screen. Lindsay searched the top drawer, with no result. Then she felt the underside of the drawer.

She let out a satisfied sigh. 'Oldest trick in the book,' she said, pulling the key away, complete with the sellotape that had held it in place. 'I don't know, some days it's just all too easy.'

Back in Tom Jack's office, she slipped the key into the lock that held all three drawers on the left-hand side shut. It turned effortlessly, and Lindsay started her search. The top drawer contained stationery, a couple of half-used pads with scribbled notes from committee meetings, pens, pencils and paperclips. The second drawer held three loose-leaf folders crammed with press clippings about Tom Jack and his role as general secretary of AMWU. There were also a few computer discs and a contacts book, which Lindsay slipped into her bag for later.

The third drawer was filled with an assortment of document wallets. The first few contained details of union-management disputes which Lindsay soon discovered involving Tom Jack himself. They had all been resolved, not exclusively to the greater good of the AMWU members, but there was nothing contentious enough in any of them to lead to threats, never mind murder.

The next said on its cover SIGS. It contained a bizarre assortment of documents. There were photostats of membership applications for the former Journalist's Union, some going back more than twenty years. There were nomination forms for JU lay officials' posts, properly filled in and signed by the appropriate branch officers. There were applications for Press passes, photocopies of motions for annual delegate conferences sent in by branches and a few meetings' attendance sheets. All the documents related to the JU, but there was no other common factor that Lindsay could discern, apart from the fact that they all seemed to be completely in order. Frustrated, she shoved the contents back into the file and continued her burrowing.

The bottom folder in the pile was unmarked. Lindsay opened it and pulled out a thick sheaf of expenses dockets. Almost all of them were JU forms, though the last few dozen were AMWU ones. Off the top of her head, Lindsay estimated there must be several hundred. A quick flick through the pile revealed they had all been stamped 'paid'.

Lindsay sat back in the seat and began to go through the dockets more carefully. Soon, she began to discern a pattern. The earliest went back almost nine years. They covered a wide range of committee and executive meetings. What was fascinating was the signatures on more than three quarters of the dockets. In an assured, sprawling hand, they read 'Laura Craig'.

13

*'If you think you're entitled to loss of earnings
expenses for attending conference, you should fill
in Form FAD21A and return it to conference office
no later than Wednesday morning. If you think
you're entitled to travelling expenses, you're
wrong. (see minutes of NEC meeting 2.3.92)'*
       from *'Advice for New Delegates'*,
    a Standing Orders Sub-Committee booklet.

Feeling slightly dazed, Lindsay walked back
through to the outer office, where Sophie had
also closed the blinds and switched on a desk
lamp. 'Find anything?' she said, with an air of
preoccupation.

'I think so. I'm just not sure exactly what it is.
How about you?' Lindsay asked, leaning over
Sophie's shoulder and peering at the screen.

'Nothing of any interest. Letters, balance
sheets, confidential reports about restructuring. I
suppose some of it must be controversial, but I

can't for the life of me imagine anyone killing Union Jack because he proposed halving the size of the Printing New Technology Steering Group,' she said drily.

'Is this machine a stand-alone or part of a network?' Lindsay asked.

'My God, Gordon, you're not finally getting to grips with modern technology, are you? Where did you learn about things like networks? Have you been reading adult magazines again?'

'Very droll. I didn't just ask for fun, you know,' Lindsay said huffily.

Sophie cast her eyes heavenwards. 'So-rree. It's part of a network.'

'Does it have committee minutes on it?' Lindsay asked.

'I don't know. Let's have a look.' Sophie left the file she was reading and made her way back to the main network menu.

Lindsay scanned the list and pointed to the seventh item. 'That'll do. Industrial Sector Councils. Can you get that for me?' Sophie hit a key and brought up a sub-menu. Lindsay consulted her dockets, then said, 'Broadcasting Technology.' Sophie selected another key, and an array of dates appeared. 'Okay. Let's try 25.2.92.' Sophie moved the cursor over the date Lindsay had chosen and hit 'enter'. On the screen, the minutes of the meeting appeared.

Lindsay ran her finger along the list of those present. Then she checked two of her dockets.

She compared them to the list again, then let out a long, slow sigh of satisfaction. 'I can see a light at the end of the tunnel, and I'd bet a month's salary that it's not an oncoming train.'

'Care to enlighten me? Or do I get treated like the typical Watson, kept in the dark till the very end?' Sophie asked.

'Sorry. I think that someone has been fiddling expenses on a scale to make your eyes water. It works like this. When you're a lay official of the union, and you come to head office for meetings, you're entitled to claim travelling and meal expenses, and sometimes overnight allowances too. If you're a freelance, you can also claim a sum of money that's supposed to go some way towards covering loss of potential earnings while you're attending meetings. What usually happens is, you get to the meeting and the full-time officer who's responsible for that sector of the union dishes out expenses forms. You fill in your form, the officer authorises them with a signature, takes them up to the accounts department and goes back in an hour or so to pick up the cash and hand it out.'

'Cash? In 1993?' Sophie said incredulously.

'The theory is that it's cheaper to the union than issuing dozens of cheques for relatively small amounts. Anyway, not everyone gets round to filling their form in on the day. For example, if you're actually chairing the meeting, it can be difficult to make the time. So in those cases, you send the form in later, an officer authorises it retrospectively, and the accounts department hang on to the dosh till the next time you're in head office for a meeting. If you specifically ask for it, they'll send you a cheque, but they don't like doing that. So what I have here is a bundle of expense dockets that have apparently gone through the system and been paid out. Only problem is, according to at least one set of minutes, people appear to have been paid money for attending meetings they weren't at. And in the vast majority of these cases, Laura Craig was the officer responsible for signing the dockets.'

Suddenly, Lindsay leapt to her feet with the look of a woman whose brain has just made a racing change from second to third gear.

She dashed back through to Tom Jack's office, shouting, 'And that's what the SIGS file is for! Union Jack was comparing the signatures on the dockets with those people's real signatures!' She came tearing back with the SIGS wallet. 'He was stitching her up! He'd signed some of those phoney dockets himself, and so had other officials, but I bet she'd actually taken them up to the finance office and grabbed the dosh. He was covering his own back by stitching her up!' Lindsay sounded like an over-excited five year old on Christmas morning. She thumbed through the documents till she found the one she was looking for.

'Here!' she shouted triumphantly. 'Look at this.

It's Peter McKellar's signature on his application for a Press card. Now look at this expenses docket that's supposed to cover his return train fare from Newcastle!' She thrust the documents under Sophie's nose. While there were similarities between the two signatures, it was clear that they were by different hands.

'The one on the expenses form is much more rounded,' Sophie said. 'I agree, they do look as if they've been written by different people. So where exactly does that take us?'

'Sophie, we're looking at thousands of pounds here over the last nine years,' Lindsay said, awe in her voice. 'Tom Jack was obviously about to expose Laura Craig. There's no way she could survive that. She'd be facing charges of fraud, maybe even prison. One thing's for sure, she'd never work in the labour movement again. What better motive could anyone have for getting rid of him?'

Sophie got to her feet, switching off the computer as she rose. 'Personally, I'd sell my soul to someone who promised me I'd never have to work in the labour movement again. Your theory does presuppose that she knew what he was doing. I suppose you want me to have a poke about in his PC to see if there's anything in there to support that?'

Lindsay nodded. 'I bet there is! He knew that he couldn't put off any longer a full-scale probe into the finances of the Journalists' Union. And he was determined to head them off at the pass before they started asking too many questions about his stewardship by giving them Laura. It's one of the great maxims of trade union politics – always have a body to trade. Once they had Laura bang to rights on the expenses fiddle, Union Jack could have laid any other swindles at her door, and he'd have come out of the whole thing smelling of roses as usual.'

'What I can't understand is why the documents are still here if Laura killed him to avoid exposure,' Sophie said as she booted up Tom Jack's PC. 'I'd have expected her to get down here faster than a speeding bullock before someone stumbled on them and put two and two together.'

Lindsay frowned, instantly comprehending the hole Sophie's throwaway remark had blown in her theory. 'Hmm,' she said. 'Good point. Maybe she was intending to, but hasn't been able to get away. Or maybe she doesn't know where the evidence is. I mean, nobody in their right mind would just leave it lying around in a drawer, would they?'

'Or maybe she didn't know yet she had a motive for killing him,' Sophie added with a cheeky grin.

Lindsay smiled back. 'I hear what you're saying,' she sighed. 'Okay, I'll take the blinkers off. Maybe it's pure coincidence that Tom has something on Laura. Maybe it's got nothing to do with his murder.'

'And maybe you should wander off and find a photocopier so you can copy the evidence and put it back where you found it. What you absolutely don't need right now is some officious copper deciding to hit you with a charge of interfering with the evidence,' Sophie said.

'You mean, would I kindly sod off and leave you in peace with your toy? Okay, will do.' Lindsay kissed the top of Sophie's head and headed off in search of a photocopier. It was almost an hour later when she returned, to find Sophie leaning back in Tom Jack's chair, feet on the desk, a sheaf of printout on her lap.

Lindsay dumped her stacks of papers on the desk and threw her arms round Sophie. 'Don't tell me! You've cracked the case! It was the butler!'

Sophie kissed her mouth, damming the flow of Lindsay's excited conversation. Lindsay closed her eyes and moaned softly, before she pulled away. 'Don't,' she groaned. 'Don't start what we can't finish. Apart from anything else, it's probably a disciplinary offence to bonk in the general secretary's office.' She pulled away, shook her head like a retriever emerging from a pond, and said, 'So what's the print-out?'

'I found the audited files of expense payments for the last nine years. Alongside the official files, Tom Jack had worked out which expenses were phoney. It looks as if Laura was creaming off an average of £200 a week. Sweetheart, would anyone kill to avoid being exposed for defrauding ten grand a year?'

Lindsay's jaw jutted stubbornly. 'There's got to be more to it than that. Is that all you found?'

Sophie shook her head. 'No, but I don't understand the rest of it. There are a few similar sets of files. One seems to relate to pensions. From the look of it, Laura, Tom and three other officials have pension arrangements which give them far better benefits than anyone else.'

'How do you mean? I thought there were legal limits on pensions? That you couldn't get more than two-thirds of your final salary?' Lindsay said.

'I don't know about that. But how does a lump sum payment of an index-linked £50,000 sound to you?' Sophie said.

Lindsay looked as shaken as she felt. 'How could they?' she gasped. 'How could they say the things they said about the "rights of working people" and then rob us blind? Shit, Soph, how long had this been going on?'

Sophie handed her the print-out, and pointed to the relevant sections as she spoke. 'See for yourself. Two of the arrangements, Laura's and Malcolm Bridgnorth's, started eight years ago, then two years later, Alan Porter joined them. Two years after that, Barney Price. Then, just after he was elected general secretary of the JU, Tom Jack enters the frame.'

Lindsay shook her head. 'I don't understand. Malcolm left the JU five years ago. But Alan and

Barney are okay guys. I mean, they're not crooks, no way. What the hell's going on here? Is that it?' she asked Sophie, apprehension in her eyes.

'Nope. There's another set of figures relating to strike pay. It looks like every time you had a strike, an extra body was added to the tally. There's no documentary evidence as to who was pocketing the cash, but it was definitely being paid out to someone.' Sophie gently took the print-out from her lover and folded it up. She stood up and held Lindsay in her arms.

'I just can't believe it,' Lindsay said. 'I feel physically sick at the thought of it all. Let's get out of here, Sophie. We're going to have to do some more digging, but not here. I can't face finding out any more of the truth.'

Sophie swam up into consciousness after only five hours sleep. She rolled over to cuddle up to Lindsay, only to find the other side of the bed cold and empty. She ungummed one eye and read the clock. 08:23. 'Oh God, Gordon. Oh no, where are you now?' she mumbled, dragging her stiff body out of bed and across the room to the bathroom. She stumbled through the door into a glare of fluorescent light and the improbably floral smell of hotel bubble bath. Lindsay lay stretched out full length, up to her chin in foam, Walkman clamped to her ears, head nodding almost imperceptibly in time to the music.

Sophie pulled one earplug out and bellowed, 'Couldn't you sleep?'

'Shit,' Lindsay yelled, almost submerging as she jumped with the shock. 'And a very good morning to you too,' she groused as she straightened up. 'No, as it happens, I couldn't. I know it might seem daft to you, but what we found out last night really shocked me. I mean, more than Union Jack being dead, in a funny kind of way.'

'You're all heart,' Sophie said. 'Seriously, I know what you mean. So what now?'

'Tom Jack's widow. If he shared what he knew with anyone, it might well have been her. And he might have stashed some more evidence back home. There's obviously some proof of the other scams to correspond to the fiddled expenses dockets we found,' Lindsay said, removing her Walkman and shoving her damp hair back from her forehead. 'Fancy joining me?'

'In the bath or visiting the grieving widow?' Sophie asked.

'Both or either,' Lindsay said.

'I'll pass on the bath. And before I commit on the widow, where are we talking about? After yesterday, I don't think I can handle any more British motorways. They've turned roadworks into performance art.'

'Don't panic. It's just down the road. Tom was a Yorkshireman, born and bred, as he never tired of telling anyone who'd sit still for long enough. And although he kept a flat in London for the week, his wife had no intention of leaving her patch. They live about twenty minutes drive from the centre of Sheffield, on the edge of the moors. Can I count you in?'

'Wouldn't miss it for the world,' Sophie lied. Before she could say more, the phone trilled like a dentist's drill. She reached out and picked up the extension. 'Hello?' she listened for a moment, then waved the receiver at Lindsay. 'It's for you. Dick McAndrew.'

Lindsay hauled herself out of the bath, grabbed a towel, and said, 'I'll get out of your way and take it in the room.' She picked up the phone by the bed and said, 'Dick? Lindsay. How did you know where to find me?'

'I'm supposed to be an investigative journalist, for fuck's sake. Jet set medics don't stay in poxy bed and breakfasts,' he said. 'Believe me, that cut the choice down dramatically.'

'So, to what do I owe the expenditure of all this effort?'

'Not to mention all the 10p pieces,' Dick responded. 'Put it on the slate of favours owed. What I rang for is, unless you want to be mobbed by the world's press, and probably South Yorkshire's finest, you'd be well-advised to give this place the body swerve for today.'

Lindsay sighed. 'Spit it out, Dick. What's happened now?'

'You're headline news again, kiddo. **Conference Chronicle** has thrust you into the white-hot glare of notoriety yet once more,' Dick said. 'Joking apart, Lindsay, you're gonnae have to keep your bunnet below the parapet on this one.'

'God, how you journos love talking up a good story,' Lindsay complained, only too aware of her own hypocrisy. 'C'mon, give it to me straight. Just read the words, Dick. I can pick the tune up for myself.'

'Okay, you asked for it. Here we go. Headline first, "See No Evil, Hear No Evil, Speak No Evil. The burning question today is why Lindsay Gordon isn't telling the whole story about Tom Jack's death, a death, incidentally, which the police are still showing a remarkable reluctance to call murder.

'"In a spectacular editorial coup, **Conference Chronicle** can reveal exclusively that Gay Gordon not only *knows* it was murder, but she also saw the only person who could have committed the horrific crime leaving the scene.

'"Everyone should be asking why Gay Gordon is protecting AMWU's Broadcasting Officer and Special Branch plant Laura Craig. Our sources tell us that Gordon saw the lovely Laura sweeping out of the murder room only moments after Union Jack had done his spectacular shuffling off of the mortal coil. Yet Gay Gordon has kept her mouth tightly clamped shut about their close encounter, even after a night's interrogation in South Yorkshire police cells.

'"Maybe the answer is simple. Maybe Gay

Gordon is the person that Laura is stripping off her expensive designer wardrobe for these days. And of course Gay Gordon's gynaecologist girlfriend isn't going to be overwhelmed to discover that the reward for her loyalty is that Gay Gordon has been bonking her brains out with someone as politically incorrect as the lovely Laura. It also explains how Union Jack and his killer got into Gay Gordon's room in the first place.

'"Or maybe it's just that Lindsay Gordon hated Union Jack and all he stood for so much that she thinks it's right to keep quiet about his murderer. After all, how could she drop a sister under the skin in deep shit for getting rid of a sexist pig like Tom Jack? Not very PC at all.

'"Either way, it's time Lindsay Gordon started telling the truth about what she really knows, instead of running round the country playing at detectives. Incidentally, is the police's reluctance to call Jack's death murder anything to do with Laura's SB connections? We think we should be told." And that, for what it's worth, is it,' Dick concluded. 'You can imagine, the place is in uproar, with Laura Craig heading the lynch mob.'

'I bet she is,' Lindsay mused. 'Dick, you're a real pal. You're right, I'd better keep a low profile today. Thanks, I owe you one. I better get off now, before the rest of the pack work out where we are.'

'Hang on,' Dick protested. 'You're not going to just –'

Lindsay gently replaced the phone in its cradle. Much as she liked and trusted Dick, there was a murderer out there. And one way or another, it began to look as if Lindsay was getting too close for comfort.

14

'The fact that conference observers have no voting rights is no reason not to treat them with civility and respect. Just because you don't like who they represent (Chamber of Commerce, Conservative Party, You've Been Framed*) is no reason to attack them, either verbally or physically.'*
                    from *'Advice for New Delegates'*,
          a Standing Orders Sub-Committee booklet.

Lindsay put her feet up on the dashboard and wriggled in the seat until she was reasonably comfortable. Her years as an on-the-road reporter had taught her that the secret of sticking out a stake-out was comfort, and although there wasn't a lot of scope for stretching out in Helen's cramped car, Lindsay was determined to make the most of it. Sophie was less fortunate; the driver's seat offered even less room for the reasonable rearrangement of limbs. She put her hands behind her head and a deep bellow filled the air, as if from an appreciative audience.

'You're sure these aren't guard cows?' Sophie asked, with an apprehensive glance out of the window.

They were parked in a gateway leading to a field of disturbingly large cattle in varying shades of dun and caramel, with horns that wouldn't have disgraced the monarch of the glen. Every few minutes, one of the huge beasts would wander across to the gate, chewing, slobbering and studying them with the utter confidence of something that knows it's bigger than the object of its curiosity.

'Nah,' Lindsay said scornfully. 'Some rare breed or other. Like Sylvester Stallone, all front and no bottle.'

'As long as you're sure. I just don't want to have to ring Helen and tell her that while we were watching Union Jack's house, some demented steer infected her camshaft with BSE.'

Lindsay shook her head. 'I keep forgetting you're a city girl,' she said. 'I tell you, we've got more to fear from Union Jack's neighbours than from that entire herd of cattle. For one thing, none of them have got a mobile phone to alert PC Plod that there are a couple of suspicious characters lurking up the lane from Union Jack's hacienda.'

'What neighbours?' Sophie asked sarcastically. 'The nearest house must be half a mile away. And

249

frankly, I can see why. I wouldn't want my expensive Pennine view to include that monstrosity.'

Both women fell silent, contemplating Mr and Mrs Jack's idea of a Yorkshire country residence. Its brilliant white stucco beamed out of the limestone landscape like a beacon. The red pantiled roof leapt out of its grey and green background like a spilt pot of paint on a Berber carpet. There were enough wrought iron features to have kept a Sheffield steelworks going for a year. Eventually, Lindsay said, 'It could have been uprooted, lock, stock and cartwheels, straight from the Costa del Sol.'

'The Spanish cultural ministry were probably so glad to see the back of it they paid the relocation costs,' Sophie replied. 'It's grosso. Having said that, though, looking at the size of it, plus the conservatory, the four-car garage, the swimming pool and the grounds, I'd say we were looking at a pretty substantial investment, even for a trade union baron.'

'Yeah,' Lindsay agreed with a sigh. 'That's what was worrying me too. If Union Jack was here right now, I'd want to grip him by the throat and ask how he'd managed to afford Dun-wheeling-and-dealing. Maybe **Conference Chronicle** ought to be asking questions about Rancho Jacko rather than slinging mud at me.'

'Run that story past me again,' Sophie asked. 'I'm not sure I took in all the implications first thing this morning.'

Lindsay obliged. Summing up, she said, 'The bottom line is that the writer of 𝕮𝖔𝖓𝖋𝖊𝖗𝖊𝖓𝖈𝖊 𝕮𝖍𝖗𝖔𝖓𝖎𝖈𝖑𝖊 knows altogether too much about the murder.'

'Which means that whoever is behind 𝕮𝖔𝖓𝖋𝖊𝖗𝖊𝖓𝖈𝖊 𝕮𝖍𝖗𝖔𝖓𝖎𝖈𝖑𝖊 is also Tom Jack's killer?' Sophie suggested.

'Either that or else he or she is pretty deeply in Laura's confidence. She may have revealed that she was in fact around at the time of the killing, though she obviously won't have confessed to her own involvement in it. That would make sense if she thought I'd seen her coming out of my room, which she may have done if she'd heard I'd gone to Blackpool to rake up the one bit of the past she can't afford to have disturbed. But whoever it was she trusted has betrayed her, either by writing the tale in 𝕮𝖔𝖓𝖋𝖊𝖗𝖊𝖓𝖈𝖊 𝕮𝖍𝖗𝖔𝖓𝖎𝖈𝖑𝖊 personally or else by passing it on, wittingly or unwittingly,' Lindsay said.

'There's a lot of ifs and buts there, Lindsay,' Sophie objected.

'I know, but I prefer ifs and buts to the thought that the killer is writing 𝕮𝖔𝖓𝖋𝖊𝖗𝖊𝖓𝖈𝖊 𝕮𝖍𝖗𝖔𝖓𝖎𝖈𝖑𝖊 and has me in their sights.' They fell silent again, both lost in their respective fears and speculations. The morning trickled slowly past, accompanied by selections from Helen's cassettes, ranging from Annie Lennox to Deacon Blue. 'If they haven't got a Scottish accent, Helen won't listen to them,' Lindsay complained, replacing The Proclaimers with Del Amitri.

'Just be grateful she's not a Geordie. Wall-to-wall Dire Straits and Jimmy Nail,' Sophie said with a shudder. She searched her backpack for diversions, and produced the Pocket Scrabble she'd bought to keep Lindsay amused on their transatlantic flight. By two o'clock, Lindsay's stomach was rumbling. At her insistence, Sophie drove off to buy sandwiches, leaving Lindsay leaning on the gate like a refugee from *The Archers*.

Their vigil was finally rewarded just before four, when a new-looking Land Rover Discovery passed them and swung between the gryphon-topped pillars of Union Jack's drive. They could see it was driven by a woman with long blonde hair, with no passengers. 'That's the grieving widow, right enough,' Lindsay said. 'I met her once at an office thrash in the good old *Daily Nation* days. Let's give her a few minutes to get the kettle on.'

'You didn't say you knew her,' Sophie complained. 'What's she like?'

'I *don't* know her. We met; I was pissed. My overwhelming impression sounds like a cultural stereo-type – she was bouncy, a bit brassy, she drank brandy and Babycham, she had terrible dress sense, her voice was too loud and her husband was mildly embarrassed by her.'

'Why?'

'The old story. When they tied the knot, he was a lowly reporter on the *Sheffield Star*. He climbed up the greasy pole, while she essentially remained a working-class lass from Sheffield who steadfastly refused to move to London when his career took him south. I was always mildly surprised that the marriage survived, but it seemed to. Union Jack was always keen to get home at the weekends. They've no kids, by the way. She breeds dogs. Yorkies, I think. Right, let's go. I can hear that kettle whistling from here.'

The Julie Jack who opened the door to the sound of distant yelps was a very different proposition from the lip-glossed loudmouth who had hung on Tom Jack's arm though not his every word. Her eyes were puffy and dark-ringed, her blotchy complexion undisguised with foundation and blusher. Her greying blonde hair was loosely tied back in a pony-tail. Instead of an evening dress which had somehow contrived to look both over the top and cheap at the same time, she wore a baggy Aran sweater over a pair of jodhpur-style leggings. She had aged more than the ten years since they had last met, Lindsay thought. And it couldn't all be laid at the door of bereavement. The disapproving lines round the mouth went too deep for that. She looked the pair of them up and down and said, 'I've got nowt more to say to the press.' She began to close the door.

'I'm not press, Julie. Not any more,' Lindsay said. 'Remember me? Lindsay Gordon? We met years ago, when Tom was still at the *Nation*.'

'I know who you are,' she replied, her Yorkshire accent as strong as her late husband's.

253

'And you should know better than to try that one on me. Once a hack, always a hack.'

'Hand on heart, Julie, I'm not here as a journo. I'm here 'cause I'm in the shit and I thought you might be able to help me,' Lindsay tried.

'Just why would I want to do that? It was your window he went through. And in my book, that means you know more about my husband's death than you're letting on.' Julie's face settled into a scowl, and one of her ankle-length riding boots began to tap softly on the marble tiled floor of the hall.

'I thought you Yorkshire women were supposed to be shrewd cookies,' Lindsay said, shaking her head sadly. 'Do you think if I was going to do anything shady with your husband I'd be daft enough to do it on my own doorstep? Come on, Julie, only the cops would go for something that obvious. You should know better. You've been around the trade union movement long enough to know just how bloody devious we all are.'

'Never mind the flannel. Tell me what you're after and why you're after it and who your oppo is and I'll mebbe think about it.' The scowl hadn't shifted, but the foot had stopped tapping.

'Sophie Hartley, Julie Jack. Sophie's my partner. She's a doctor, not a hack,' Lindsay said.

'Partner as in business or as in knocking off?' Julie demanded, folding her arms across her chest.

'Partner as in lover,' Sophie said coldly. 'That

can hardly come as a surprise if your husband shared his working life with you.'

Julie gave an unexpected smile, vividly reminding Lindsay of the woman she'd seen dancing the night away in London. 'I'm not a bigot like my Tom. I don't have a problem with that, Doctor Hartley.' Then she turned back to Lindsay and her face closed down again. 'You've still not told me what you're after or why you're after it.'

'Like I said, I'm in the shit. The police haven't arrested anyone, and I'm the only person they've given a really bad time to. Everybody thinks I had something to do with it, and I didn't. I want to clear my name, because I want to go back home to America. I've got a funny feeling that might not be too easy if the police tell US Immigration I'm a murder suspect.'

'Don't tell me, let me guess,' Julie interrupted. 'Like every hack that ever learned a line of shorthand, you think you can find out things no other bugger can. Me, I blame that Woodward and Bernstein. Life were simpler when *Deep Throat* were just a bluey.' The ghost of a smile crept across her eyes.

Lindsay shrugged. 'I have been doing a bit of poking around, I don't deny it.'

Julie looked as if someone had cracked a rotten egg under her nose. 'And you came out here because somebody told you the Jacks lived in high style'.

Lindsay was genuinely surprised. 'No, not at all,' she stammered.

Julie shook her head sceptically. 'Oh, bugger it, you might as well come in,' she said, unexpectedly swinging the door open and heading down the hall.

Lindsay and Sophie followed, not too intent on pursuing their hostess to appreciate the professional footballer/Northern comedian school of decor taken to an extreme rarely seen, even in sitcoms. Dazzled by gilt cherubs, silver photo frames, onyx and marble, they followed Julie through the spacious hall into a kitchen that could comfortably have contained the entire Sheffield United first team squad. As they entered, they were swamped with what felt like dozens of furry balls, equipped with more than the normal allotment of teeth and claws.

'Down, you buggers,' Julie roared and four black-and-tan Yorkshire terriers dropped to the floor and scuttled obediently to a large dog basket by the Aga.

Lindsay mustered what dignity she could and moved away from the wall she'd spread-eagled against during the onslaught. 'Still breeding them, then?' she asked.

'Keeps me occupied while Tom's away,' Julie said absently, spooning instant coffee into bone china beakers. Then reality crept up on her again, as it would continue to do until Tom's death became as mundane a part of her daily round as his life had been. Her head dropped, and she rubbed her eyes with one hand. 'He loved t'dogs,' she whispered. 'I sometimes thought it were t'dogs he come home for, not me.'

'I'm really sorry, Julie. I won't pretend we didn't have our differences, me and Tom, but he didn't deserve what he got,' Lindsay said.

'No, and I'll not have people blacken his name now he's dead. You want to know how we afforded all this?' She swept an arm round, embracing the gleaming kitchen with its array of state of the art appliances, mahogany units and Italian tiles. 'I'll tell you how.' She thrust a beaker of coffee at each of them. 'Betting, that's how.'

Lindsay looked at Sophie, relieved to see her partner looked as bemused as she felt. 'Betting?' she tentatively repeated.

Julie marched across the kitchen and removed the lid of a tall, glazed earthenware jar marked 'Meal'. She plunged her hand into it and brought out a small black notebook with elastic keeping it shut tight, like beat policemen use. 'It's all in here. Dates, races, horses, amounts. He had a system. It were boring as hell, but it worked. And that's what paid for this place. It were nothing crooked. See for yourself.' She thrust the notebook at Lindsay, who took it and snapped the elastic back. 'It means nowt to me,' she added to Sophie. 'It's all in short-hand. Mebbe she'll be able to translate it for me, so I can carry on working the system. Only, Tom never explained it to me in any detail.'

Lindsay frowned in concentration. Absently, she pulled a chair out and sat down at the long mahogany table that ran along one wall. She took her notebook out of her handbag and scribbled a couple of notes. The other two women stared at her, the suspense they felt obvious on both faces.

'The system's pretty simple,' Lindsay finally said, having studied the first few pages closely, then flicked through to the end, stopping here and there to translate the occasional sentence or paragraph. What she read there made her feel physically sick. Lindsay forced herself not to reveal her feelings and looked up at the expectant faces. 'Though you're right, Julie, it must be bloody boring. It's based on the principle that favourites statistically win more often than not. What you do is, you basically bet on as many races as possible, chronologically. In the first race, you put 50p on the favourite. If it loses, you put £1 on the favourite in the second race. If it loses, you put £2 on the favourite in the third. As soon as you win, you go back to the beginning, with 50p on the next favourite. And so on. You never win huge amounts, but if you do it consistently, you win a substantial amount over time. As your lovely home demonstrates so amply,' she added, managing to keep a straight face.

'It should be lovely, it cost enough,' Julie grumbled proudly. 'And I'll need that bloody system to carry on paying for it. Not that he hasn't left me well provided for. Thanks, love,' she added belatedly. 'I do appreciate that. I don't trust any of them fellas that do shorthand to tell me the truth. They'd be wanting Tom's system for themselves, selfish bastards, all of them.'

'There's more than his horse-racing stuff in here, Julie,' Lindsay said seriously.

Julie frowned. 'How d'you mean? That's all I ever saw him use it for.'

'Nevertheless, that's not all that's in here. I didn't actually get round to telling you what I was after today, did I? Well, the thing is, Julie, I came here with a theory about who killed Tom, only I wasn't sure if I had any motive for that person to kill him.' Lindsay closed the notebook and tapped it against the edge of the table. 'Now I have. The only question is, what do we do about it?'

15

Lindsay glanced over her shoulder, checking that Sophie was still on their tail. Her attempts to persuade Julie Jack to stay out of the impending confrontation had resembled water dripping on a stone; carrying on for a thousand years might have had an effect, but in the short term, there was no visible change. Now all Lindsay could hope for was damage limitation. Which was why she was sitting in the passenger seat of Julie's Land Rover, bucketing through the Yorkshire lanes, with Sophie struggling to keep up on unfamiliar roads.

When Lindsay had dropped her bombshell, Julie Jack had seized Tom Jack's notebook from her and flicked frenziedly through the pages, desperately trying to find something that would make sense of Lindsay's monstrous words. Frustrated by his neat shorthand, she'd thrown the notebook back at Lindsay, shouting, 'Show me! You just bloody show me were it says owt about getting hissen killed! Don't tell *me* he knew he were for it and he did nowt to stop it!' She raised a fist as if to strike Lindsay.

Swiftly, Sophie gripped the frantic woman by the shoulders, moving her away from Lindsay and into a chair. Julie glared at them both, then suddenly dropped her head on to her folded arms and bawled like a calf taken from its mother. Sophie patted her shoulder, making 'there, there' noises. The storm of weeping stopped as suddenly as it had begun, and Julie looked up at them both, wiping her nose on her sleeve like the defiant child she must have once been. 'Time you told me what's been going on, Lindsay Gordon. I'd rather hear it from t'horse's mouth than get it second hand on t'telly.'

'Okay,' Lindsay said. If anyone deserved the truth, it was Julie. She'd lost more than anyone, hard though it was for Lindsay to imagine Union Jack's death as any kind of loss. 'It wasn't just the geegees that put the jam on your bread, Julie. There's no easy way to say this. There isn't a polite word for what Tom was up to.' She sighed. 'Julie, Tom had been supplementing your income for the last nine years with a bit of blackmail.'

Julie shook her head confidently. 'You've got it wrong, you've not read his shorthand properly. What kind of a man did you take him for? He might have rubbed a lot of people up the wrong way, for he were never shy about speaking his mind. But blackmail? Not Tom. Blackmail's for cowards. Tom were no coward.'

'The proof's here, Julie, in his own hand,' Lindsay said. 'Nearly nine years ago, Tom discovered that one of his union officers was a murderer. Rather than hand them over to the police, he bled the killer dry. There's a list of dates and amounts, ranging from £150 a week to £500. Then, when he became general secretary of the Journalists' Union, he discovered that the officer in question was financing those payments by embezzling union funds. Tom couldn't do anything about it at the time, because he was desperately trying to paint a wonderful picture of the JU so that the merger with the inkies would go ahead without a hitch. The last thing he could afford was the scandal of an officer with a hand in the till.

'But circumstances changed. After the mergers, it became clear that AMWU's finances were far from as healthy as they should be. The pressure was on for a full-scale inquiry into the union's finances. Tom knew as soon as that happened, the truth was going to emerge, and it was going to look as if his stewardship of the JU was, at the very least, less than careful. He'd be lucky not to end up looking negligent, and his chances of surviving were pretty slim. The only way he could safeguard himself was to cash in his chips and reveal who the guilty party was. That way, he'd end up looking vigilant for making the discovery, and selfless, for not hesitating to expose someone who'd formerly been a JU official.'

Julie was still shaking her head in disbelief. 'I can't tek it in,' she said. 'He never said owt to me about any of this. I thought everything were sound as a pound now the unions had all come together. Poor Tom! What a thing to carry round with you. He must have been itching to clean the slate and let the union know who'd been stealing their money.'

Not for the first time, Lindsay marvelled at the power of love. Already Julie seemed conveniently to have forgotten that Laura Craig had only started embezzling her employer because Tom Jack had started blackmailing her. If her need to preserve good memories of her man was so strong, Lindsay was relieved she hadn't aroused Julie's wrath by revealing the other secrets of Union Jack's notebook. Just thinking about some of the things she'd read made rage rise in her like a spring tide. She swallowed and said calmly, 'It's all here, Julie, I promise you. The circumstantial evidence that pointed to murder nine years ago, the details of the blackmail payments, and his record of a confrontation last week between him and his blackmail victim. He was going to blow the lid off the embezzlement scandal, with the killer as scapegoat. Only, the killer was afraid that when the police started digging, they'd find out about the blackmail, and the reason for it. The killer was more willing to kill a second time than face charges of murder. And that's why Tom was killed.'

'So who was it?' Julie snarled. 'Which of those double-dealing bastards killed my Tom? Tell me that!'

'Only if you promise me you'll leave it to me and the police from here on in. What I propose is to take this notebook to them and tell them what I've uncovered. Then we can leave it to them to do the rest,' Lindsay said, getting to her feet.

The next thing she knew, she was flat on her back on the floor, with Julie Jack straddling her and clawing at her hand to get at the notebook. With her other hand, Julie clutched Lindsay's hair in a tight grip. 'Hand it over, you arrogant bitch,' she yelled. 'Hand it over or I'll split your head open.' Sophie moved towards Julie, but the angry widow gave Lindsay's head a threatening shake in response.

Immediately, Lindsay released the notebook, and Julie released her, letting her head crack on the tiled floor. 'You're not the only one as can read shorthand,' she panted, pushing herself back to her feet. 'I'll ask somebody as knows widows have got rights when it comes to knowing who killed their husbands.'

Desperate to retain some control over the situation, Lindsay pushed herself up on one elbow, trying to ignore the splitting pain in the back of her skull. 'It was Laura. Laura Craig, the broadcasting organiser.'

'Julie,' Sophie said softly. 'I know this has all come as a hell of a shock. But Lindsay's right. We should go to the police now. I know she didn't put it very tactfully, but they're the ones to handle this.'

Julie shook her head vehemently. 'He was my husband. I've got rights. I've got the right to see the look on her face when she realises she hasn't got away with taking my Tom's life. Anyway, you said she'd already murdered someone else and got away with it. Who's to say the police won't make a bollocks of this one as well?'

Lindsay struggled to her feet, clutching her head. 'The police weren't even involved last time. And believe me, if it comes to having axes to grind, you're not the only one. The man she killed nine years ago was one of my closest friends. If you're going to front up Laura Craig, then I'm going with you. Besides, you need my evidence. I'm the only person who can put her at the scene of the crime at the right time.'

In spite of Sophie's protests that they should go to the police, that had been the end of the argument. Now, hurtling towards the conference centre at a speed calculated to get them the worst kind of police escort, Lindsay couldn't stop herself returning to the notebook, like a child irresistibly drawn to picking the most painful scab. Her first reaction to the discovery that Union Jack had dug into the Blackpool files long before her had been chagrin. Then she'd grown puzzled, wondering what had set him off on his search, wondering what she had missed that had pointed all those years ago to Laura as a killer.

But reading the notebook had made everything clear. It was no mere chance that had taken Tom Jack to the coroner. It had been just another step in his highly organised plan to arm himself with dirt on everyone in the Journalists' Union who was potentially either a help or a hindrance in his relentless climb to the top. It was all there, all the dirt, in tiny, immaculate shorthand. Who was sleeping with whom, who had been driving while disqualified, who was having money problems, who had an illegitimate child. Most of it wasn't the sort of stuff you could use to blackmail cash out of people; but it was certainly the kind of information most of the victims wouldn't want to be public knowledge. And that had been enough to extort the favours and support Union Jack had wanted. But what had really engaged Lindsay's contempt was a section where he'd recorded snippets of information he thought he could use to undermine opponents, real and imagined. Amongst them one date had leaped out at her. It was a date she'd never forget. Against it, Tom Jack had noted, 'Frances Collier died. Use to demoralise LG if she's difficult.' It wasn't just the malice that hurt. It was the paranoia of a man who felt the need to act like that against someone as insignificant in union terms as she had been back in 1984.

Lindsay forced herself not to brood on this discovery, and tried to remember exactly what the notebook had said about Laura. After Ian's will had been probated, Union Jack had checked it out and discovered Laura was the sole beneficiary. Then he'd decided to go to Blackpool in search of something that he might be able to use as a lever against Laura. It was clear that he hadn't seriously suspected her of anything, merely thought there might be some little detail he could persuade her would interest the police. What he'd found instead had been a gold-mine.

Lindsay sighed. Poor Ian. His kindness and support had been a vital factor in her winning the battle to rediscover reasons for living after Frances' death had shattered her world. He had helped her to realise that failing to be the best she could be was a betrayal of the love that she and Frances had shared. But most of all, he had reminded her that laughter hadn't died with Frances.

It had been easy at the time to ignore the circumstances of his death. The fact had been all that had mattered. It had been the harshest year of her life, a year when death closed in on her life like a fist crushing a flower. But Lindsay couldn't help feeling guilty now that she hadn't paid more attention to Ian's death. Not that uncovering the murder would have made her feel any better. But at least Tom Jack would still be alive now, and regardless of how she felt towards him while he was alive, he had been a human being and he hadn't deserved to be murdered in cold blood by a selfish and ruthless killer. But what she desperately wanted to know was why Ian had had to die. What benefit had Laura gained from his death that made it worth killing the man she'd supposedly loved? Surely it couldn't just be the money?

Lindsay's reverie was shattered by Julie's strident voice. 'I said, we've lost your oppo,' she repeated. Lindsay swung round in her seat. The evening rush-hour had choked the main roads in and out of the city with traffic. In the clogged road behind her, Lindsay could see no sign of the sky-blue metallic roof of Helen's car. 'She fell behind at last roundabout,' Julie said. 'I thought she'd catch us up, but we've lost her, I reckon. Does she know where she's going?'

'She knows where she's headed. I'm just not sure if she knows how to get there,' Lindsay said with an indulgent smile.

Behind the wheel of the little sports car, Sophie was in no doubt about that. There was nothing wrong with her sense of direction. Besides, she'd checked out the whereabouts of police headquarters within half an hour of crossing the Sheffield city boundary only two days before.

Michael Jackson getting on down in Oxford Street at noon would have stood more chance of escaping unnoticed than Lindsay and Julie's arrival at Pennine University campus. Julie hadn't even switched off the engine before there was a knot of delegates staring at the pair of them, muttering excited identifications to each other. 'Let me handle this?' Lindsay said.

Julie unfastened her seat belt and let it snap back with a crack. 'Only as long as I like the way you do it,' she replied, opening the driver's door and climbing out. As they marched towards the main building, they accumulated a trail of followers, like a pair of Pied Pipers. Some of the pursuit tried to head them off, circling round in front of them like wasps driven demented by the smell of raspberry jam, buzzing questions at them which the two women brushed aside indifferently.

They had arrived too late to catch the delegates and officials in session. Outside the hall, there were still knots of people standing round, deep in conversation, reluctant even at this stage of conference to relinquish the wheeling and dealing that was meat and drink to them. Seeing Lindsay stopped the conversations dead, and the handful who recognised Julie immediately fell into huddles with their political sidekicks, speculating on what this strange alliance could mean.

They didn't have to wait too long for their answer. With an instinct born of long experience of trade union and academic conferences, Lindsay swung round on her heel and made straight for the main student union bar. She and Julie paused at the door, as studiedly melodramatic as Clint Eastwood. 'All that's missing is the poncho and the cigar,' Lindsay found time to say under her breath. As if they were in a spaghetti Western, the two women moved slowly forward, scanning the room for their target. Gradually, the buzz of conversation in the bar died away as the drinkers became aware that something out of the ordinary was happening.

One of the last groups to be touched by the atmosphere was centred round a woman, who ran a hand through her crest of wavy brown hair as she laughed too loudly at a remark from one of her companions. The lines of her thigh-length heavy silk shirt flowed round her in a smooth wave as she realised something in the room had changed and slowly turned to face Lindsay and Julie. Lindsay marvelled at her cool. Laura's face showed no sign of the panic their arrival must have triggered inside. Her eyebrows twitched fractionally, then she forced her lips into a smile of welcome that did nothing to defrost her ice-blue eyes.

'**Conference Chronicle** got a bit too close for comfort this morning, don't you think, Laura?' Lindsay asked in a conversational tone.

'Your idea of humour has always been idio-syncratic, dear,' Laura sneered. 'You know as well as I do that there wasn't a word of truth in that stinking heap of innuendo and lies. Apart from anything else, no one who knows the least thing about me could imagine for a moment that I'd dream of sharing anything more intimate than a conference platform with you.' There was a murmur of support from the crowd that had closed in around them.

Lindsay shook her head pityingly. 'Nice try, Laura. Pick on the one thing in the piece that genuinely was a load of crap, and try to tar the rest of the article with the same brush. Whereas, you and I both know that 𝕮𝖔𝖓𝖋𝖊𝖗𝖊𝖓𝖈𝖊 𝕮𝖍𝖗𝖔𝖓𝖎𝖈𝖑𝖊 was bang on the button when it came to your whereabouts when Union Jack was killed.'

Laura's laugh sounded forced, even to her supporters, who exchanged uneasy looks. 'You really have gone too far this time,' she snapped. 'Any more lines like that and you'll be facing a slander writ. God knows, I've got enough witnesses,' she added, waving an arm at their audience.

'If we're talking witnesses, then let's talk about me, Laura. I'm the one who can put you on the tenth floor of Maclintock House minutes after Union Jack died. And his widow can supply the motive.' Lindsay moved to one side and let Julie step in front of her.

'It's not the first time you've killed somebody,

is it?' Lindsay said softly but clearly. 'You'd already murdered one man to keep the secret that **Conference Chronicle** revealed earlier this week.'

Laura shook her head. 'You're completely mad,' she said, sounding genuinely incredulous. 'I'm not listening to another word of this,' she added, trying to push past the two women. But the crowd was too dense, and before she could wriggle through, Julie gripped her arm.

'You're stopping,' she said grimly. 'Time everybody else found out about you, madam.'

'This is an outrage!' Laura exclaimed. 'You're not going to stand there and let them get away with this, are you?' she demanded of the other officers she'd been drinking with. They shrugged, embarrassed, neither of them willing to be the first to get into a ruck with three angry women.

'The story won't take long,' Lindsay said soothingly. 'I don't know if **Conference Chronicle** got the details of your recruitment right, but what I do know is that when your lover, Ian Ross, discovered how you managed to afford your designer wardrobe, he threw you out of his bed and his house, and threatened to expose you to the colleagues you were spying on unless you ended your association with F Division of the Special Branch. You were caught between a rock and a hard place, as they say. Didn't your SB buddies come riding to the rescue like the US Cavalry?'

Lindsay saw a momentary flicker of emotion flash across Laura's cold face. She pounced. 'You just couldn't be certain, could you? Sure, they *should* have been there to protect you, but they might have decided just to throw you to the wolves. If Ian had gone ahead and blown your cover, you'd have been no further use to them. Ian was the only risk. So far, he'd let me believe he'd kicked you out because you were screwing around. But as long as he was alive, you were at risk. So you killed him. It was cleverly done, I'll grant you that. No one thought twice about it at the time. I know I didn't. Accidental death, the inquest said.'

The excited buzz of conversation that sprang up in the wake of Lindsay's accusation was stilled by Laura's voice. 'And it was right, you bitch,' she spat, the sophisticated veneer showing its first crack. 'I wouldn't have killed Ian! I loved him! I was distraught when we split up.'

'Yeah,' Lindsay said sarcastically. 'So distraught you got yourself a dog he was wildly allergic to. Why was that, Laura? To keep him firmly away from you, so that you couldn't have the kind of public row where he'd have blurted out the truth? But then, the dog hairs came in more useful than you could have imagined. You thought you'd committed the perfect murder. Until Tom Jack told you otherwise. Then you realised you had a price to pay. And you couldn't afford it. So you started your programme of embezzling union funds to meet the blackmail payments that Union Jack demanded from you. I don't imagine for a moment that Tom knew where the money was coming from,' she added to placate Julie. 'But once he became General Secretary, you knew you were living on borrowed time.'

Lindsay paused for dramatic effect, and to gauge the effect of her reasoned explanation on her audience. Most of the people she could see were beginning to look sideways at Laura, unwilling to catch her eye. Her drinking cronies had unconsciously moved away from her, distancing themselves from any taint. Laura looked around, her movements swift and staccato. 'My God!' she exclaimed contemptuously. 'Surely none of you believe a word of this poisonous rubbish? This is a woman who had to leave the country once before because the stories she was peddling were so ridiculous she could only get them published abroad.'

Unmoved, the crowd's eyes turned back to Lindsay. 'Where's your proof?' someone called out.

'My proof's the same as Tom Jack's proof. A week ago, he fronted you up, Laura, didn't he? You were going to be the sacrificial lamb so he could come out of the whole mess smelling of roses. He recorded it all in his little black book. You told him he'd never nail you, that you could destroy the evidence before he could get to it. Then he dropped his bombshell. He told you he'd already dug out all the expenses dockets you'd forged over the last nine years. You weren't going to be able to destroy the evidence, so you destroyed Tom Jack.' Pandemonium broke out. Excited voices almost drowned out the rest of what Lindsay had to say. She raised her voice to a shout. 'You thought no one else would find the evidence, or if they did, it would be meaningless. But I found it, Laura, and I know exactly what it means.'

Almost imperceptibly, the bodies began to close in on Laura and her accusers. She looked wildly around her. Seeing how the mood of the room had changed, she made a quick decision. Instead of making for the door, she ducked down and pushed between the bodies and the counter itself. As she broke free of the crowd, she ran towards the fire exit at the back of the room.

Caught off guard, Lindsay wasted valuable seconds twisting and weaving through the confused group of people. She was a good half minute behind as she threw herself through the fire door. Julie was on her heels, and the curious mob were only a few steps behind. Finding herself in a long corridor, Lindsay paused for a moment to get her bearings. Off to the left, she could hear a distant clattering of running footsteps. She took off in pursuit, her trainers squeaking on the cheap vinyl flooring.

The corridor opened out into the wide foyer outside the conference hall itself. There was no sign of Laura. Lindsay grabbed the first person she saw and gasped. 'Laura Craig? Did you see her just now?'

The man shrugged. 'I don't know her.'

His companion, however, was more help. 'She went into the admin offices,' he volunteered. 'What the hell's going on?' he added as her retinue of excited followers appeared behind her.

Lindsay didn't stop to answer. She ran to the conference office and threw the door open. Laura Craig stood facing the door, a telephone to her ear. 'I don't care if he's in a meeting,' Lindsay heard her shout angrily. 'You get Chief Superintendent Collinson down here right now. Tell him Laura Craig is about to be lynched.' She stared at Lindsay, the defiance not nearly strong enough to hide the fear.

Laura slammed the phone down, and stood her ground. The face off between the two women silenced the office staff and the crowd who were pushing into the room behind Lindsay. Then Pauline stepped away from her desk and moved between the two women. 'What the hell's going on? Lindsay? What are you playing at?' she demanded.

Her words broke the spell. Suddenly, the crowd surged forward, angry muttering rising to a crescendo. Before they could reach Laura, the picture changed again. Above the hubbub, a voice bellowed, 'That's enough! Let's all keep calm now.'

Heads turned towards the door. A stream of

uniformed policemen flowed into the room. The crowd stopped uncertainly. 'Thank God,' Laura said.

Lindsay swung round. Behind the police officers, she could see a familiar face. Sophie gave a little wave as the inspector who had shouted for calm stood uncertainly in the middle of the room. 'Which one of you ladies is Laura Craig?' he asked.

16

'While you are at conference, you are a delegate and not a journalist, printer, machine minder or whatever. The interests of the union must at all times be the paramount consideration in your mind.'

from *'Advice for New Delegates'*,
a Standing Orders Sub-Committee booklet.

The only real difference Lindsay could detect between being a witness and a suspect was that the tea came in pottery mugs rather than polystyrene cartons. The attitude of the police officers was only marginally less aggressive. And the interview room reserved for witness statements was just as charmless as the room where her previous interrogation had been recorded. Luckily, Jennifer Okido had been only too happy to sit in on the interview since her services as duty solicitor had not been required by Laura Craig. Apparently, Laura was already closeted with the city's most experienced, most expensive and least iconoclastic criminal lawyer, a man who had made his name working both sides of the fence. So, the Special Branch had turned out for their smooth operator after all.

Lindsay's statement had been lengthy and comprehensive, starting with the discoveries in London though not their means of entry into Media House, and ending with the confrontation in the bar. The two police officers continually fired questions at her, trying as hard to trip and trap her as they had when they had suspected her of the murder. At the end of the statement, Lindsay leaned back in her chair, unable to avoid a sense of satisfaction.

Neither policeman relaxed an inch. The younger one finished the sentence he was writing and looked up at her. 'Go on,' he invited her.

'I'm finished,' Lindsay said. 'That's the lot.'

'Not according to what we've been told. You've left out the one bit we wouldn't have found out ourselves by good detective work.'

Lindsay looked puzzled. 'I'm not with you.'

'You're supposedly able to put Laura Craig at the scene of the crime, something you omitted to mention when you were interviewed under caution before,' he replied, the cold edge of sarcastic anger in his voice. 'It might have helped our inquiry along a bit if you'd told us about her then, instead of deciding to go for glory yourself.'

Lindsay looked to Jennifer for guidance. They

had already agreed how Lindsay should respond, depending on who asked the question and how. Jennifer nodded twice. Lindsay took a deep breath and went for Plan B. 'I didn't realise it was Laura till afterwards,' she said, aiming as close to bimbo as she could realistically bring herself to try. 'After all, I was completely exhausted, and I really wasn't feeling great. I mean, you'd had me locked up so long I'd gone straight from drunk to sober to hung-over without a proper sleep. I did say to you that I had the vaguest impression of having seen someone. It was only after I'd slept that my head put all the pieces of the jigsaw together. Then, the next day, I saw Laura again, and I smelled her perfume really clearly. That confirmed it for me.' She almost batted her eyelids, but stopped herself in time. Over the top was the wrong place to be right now.

The policeman who hadn't been trying to get Lindsay's words down on paper leaned forward belligerently. 'So why didn't you tell us the next day, when you'd had the chance to think it over and sleep on it? You'd still have saved us a lot of time.'

Lindsay tried her best to look vulnerable. If Sophie could see me now, she thought wryly. 'I didn't think you'd believe me,' she said plaintively. 'I thought you'd think it was all amazingly convenient, that I was just trying to get myself off the hook. Besides, everyone knows I don't like Laura, and she'd have just said I was lying out of

280

spite. I thought I'd better get some more evidence before I came to you.'

Her interrogator shook his head in weary disbelief. 'Your client better take some acting lessons before this gets to court, Ms Okido,' he said.

'I hope your budget runs to bringing her back for the trial, Sergeant Timpson,' Jennifer Okido replied with a sweet smile.

He scowled. 'Perhaps your client could expand on exactly what she did see?'

Lindsay gave them a version of events that was only very slightly exaggerated, but credible. The two policemen looked slightly sceptical, but finally grudgingly accepted that a glimpse of the back of a head, a dark shape and a pair of legs, coupled with identification of the exclusive scent of Le Must de Cartier was enough to place Laura Craig firmly in the frame.

As she walked back with Jennifer Okido to her car, Lindsay said, 'What do you think? Will they charge her?'

'No doubt about it. With what you've given them, plus the evidence in Tom Jack's desk and his notebook, I'd say they've got a prima-facie case. I'm told she's denying it with the sort of vehemence that only the guilty ever seem capable of working up,' Jennifer said drily.

'I can't say that's a surprise,' Lindsay said. 'Is she claiming an alibi?'

'Not so far, according to the police officer I had an off-the-record word with. Doubtless if there's

281

anything to dredge up on that score, my colleague Mr Malone will make the most of it.' Jennifer stopped by her silver Audi. 'Can I give you a lift?'

Lindsay jumped at the chance to get back to Sophie and their hotel room. Since Sophie had decided that Lindsay's Lone Ranger days were long behind her and had decided it was time to fetch the sheriff and the posse, the two had had no chance to exchange more than a few words. Sophie's own brief witness statement had been over before the murder squad had even started on Lindsay, who had urged her to return to the hotel and unwind.

As Jennifer approached the hotel entrance, Lindsay's heart sank. If what she could see was anything to go by, Sophie's chances of unwinding had been rather less than nil. 'Oh shit,' she muttered. 'Jennifer, could you keep driving, please.'

The solicitor kept her foot on the accelerator and glided smoothly round the car-park and back into the road. 'Problems?' she asked.

'Nothing I couldn't handle normally. I just feel like I've had enough confrontation for one day,' Lindsay said wearily. 'There was a guy standing just outside the front door, under the awning. I don't suppose you noticed him, but he's the *Sunday Star*'s chief reporter. He's obviously the advance guard. The rest will be inside, staking the place out. Sophie's probably ready to kill by now, and I can't say I blame her.'

'What do you want to do?' Jennifer asked, pulling up a few hundred yards away from the entrance.

'In an ideal world, I'd like to get Sophie out of there so we can drive back to Glasgow and disappear for a few days with our friends till it's time to go home,' Lindsay said.

'Let's go for it, then,' Jennifer said calmly. She picked up her car phone and called Directory Enquiries for the hotel's number. Then she keyed in the number and passed the phone to Lindsay.

'Sheffield Metro Towers Hotel, Kimberley speaking, how may I help you?'

'Room 603, please,' Lindsay said.

'May I ask who's calling?' Kimberley's artificially bright voice twittered.

'Lindsay Gordon.'

'One moment please.' The electronic bleeps of the Cuckoo Waltz assaulted Lindsay's ears for the best part of a minute. Then, abruptly, Kimberley was back. 'Sorry to keep you,' she breezed with no trace of regret. 'Ms Gordon, room 603 is not accepting any calls at this point in time, unless the caller is able to supply us with the name of room 603's pet Labrador.'

'I'm sorry?' Lindsay exploded with a giggle. 'Her pet Labrador?'

'That is correct. Are you in a position to supply us with the name in question?' Kimberley asked.

'Her black, two-year-old Labrador is called Mutton, as in Cockney rhyming slang, because when he was a puppy, you could scream your-self hoarse telling him not to do something and he wouldn't take a blind bit of notice. Is that enough, Kimberley?' Lindsay said condescend-ingly.

'Thank you,' Kimberley said with a descending intonation. 'Putting you through now.'

There was a click, a buzz, then Sophie's wary voice. 'Hello?'

'Taking a poor dumb animal's name in vain,' Lindsay said. 'I like it. Has it worked?'

'Like a charm. I haven't had to speak to a single hack till now. Fortunately, the reception desk thought it was a great game. They've been wonderful. Where are you, sweetheart?'

'I'm about half a mile down the road from the hotel, with Jennifer Okido. Listen, how do you feel about going back to Glasgow tonight? If the hotel have been this accommodating about keeping the vultures at bay, they'd probably smuggle you out the back door and you could just slip into the car and we could shoot off.'

'That sounds like the best idea you've had this week,' Sophie said.

Twenty minutes later, Lindsay and Sophie waved their goodbyes to Jennifer Okido. Sophie started the car and said, 'Before we go, we need to eat. At least, I do. I was waiting for you to get back before I hit room service.'

'There's an Italian about half a mile down the

hill. I noticed it the other morning. We should be far enough off the beaten track to avoid the other delegates.'

'What about the world's press?' Sophie asked.

'Are you kidding? They're staked out in a place with a bar and sandwich service. You won't get them shifting till tomorrow lunchtime,' Lindsay snorted.

As they tucked into a tomato and mozzarella salad, Sophie said, 'By the way, there was a message for you back at the hotel. The people you got to do the search for Ian's will? They've got a copy of it, and they want to know where to fax it or send it.'

'That's it?' Lindsay asked in dismay. 'No details?'

'Oh yes. Simple will, one beneficiary. Laura Margaret Craig.'

Lindsay smiled grimly. 'I'm glad I was right. But even with that, they'll never nail her for Ian's murder. Too much time's gone by, and the evidence was never more than circumstantial at best.' Lindsay paused while their lasagne was placed in front of them.

'At least she can't wriggle out from under with Union Jack,' Sophie consoled her. 'You did a great job there.'

Lindsay shrugged. 'I had some pretty serious help,' she said through a mouthful of green salad.

'What I'm still not clear about is how so many details came to be published in **Conference**

285

Chronicle. It can't have been Laura herself behind it, or that story about her being a Special Branch plant would never have seen the light of day.'

Lindsay frowned. 'That's true. So how did they know I'd spotted her in the corridor? Who else had the remotest notion that I was interested in Laura?'

There was silence while they both chewed that over with their pasta. 'Do you suppose . . .' Sophie started, then trailed off. Lindsay gave her an inquiring look. Sophie sighed. 'It's just a thought. But loads of people knew you were nosing around into Union Jack's death. And anyone who's been around the union long enough to remember there was a curious death at the Blackpool conference would also probably remember that it was Laura Craig's ex-lover who died. When you said you'd been to Blackpool smack-bang in the middle of the conference office where anyone could have heard, then mentioned it in passing to dozens of other people . . . Well, anyone could have jumped to the conclusion that the link between the two deaths was Laura and guessed that she was your number one suspect. Don't forget, you and your doings were hot gossip round the conference hall. It's not surprising it made it to the **Conference Chronicle**.'

Lindsay sighed. 'You're right, I had forgotten.' She ate another mouthful, her face screwed up in distaste.

'Something wrong with your food?' Sophie asked.

Lindsay shook her head. 'No. It's you. Sometimes you really piss me off.'

Sophie knew her lover too well to be offended. 'Oh yeah? Just because I remembered you'd been shooting your big mouth off?'

'No. Because I'm sitting here, congratulating myself on a job well done and you have to remind me that there's still a hulking great mystery floating around in the atmosphere. I still don't know who's behind **Conference Chronicle**, and now you've reminded me, it's going to bug the hell out of me.'

Sophie grinned. 'It'll just have to remain one of the mysteries of the universe, won't it?'

Lindsay scowled. 'Not necessarily.' Then her eyes twinkled in an evil grin. 'After all, we've not left town yet.'

Sophie put her head in her hands and groaned. 'Me and my big mouth. Why couldn't I have held my tongue till we were safely back in Glasgow?'

'Look at it this way. It's saved you having to drive all the way back. Let's go through this logically,' Lindsay said. 'After the dramatic events of tonight, there's bound to be a **Conference Chronicle** tomorrow morning. So whoever is behind it has to be writing it and distributing it tonight. Okay so far?'

'Can't argue with that.'

'Thinking about it logically, they must be using a photocopier somewhere within the campus,' Lindsay went on slowly, thinking out loud.

'How do you work that one out?' Sophie asked.

'Elementary, my dear Hartley. At least one of the morning issues has featured events that didn't take place till late the night before. In other words, it happened way too late for any commercial operation to have done the copying. Which only leaves the conference centre.'

'Unless someone's got one of those portable desktop computers.'

Lindsay shook her head obstinately. 'The quality's too good. Besides, they cost more than your average conference delegate would be willing to spend just to make life a misery for a handful of union activists. There's also the sheer volume of paper the writer has gone through. Best place to hide a needle is a sewing-box, not a haystack. I'd still put my money on the conference centre.'

'Surely if it was that easy, someone would have discovered who's responsible before now?' Sophie asked.

Lindsay shrugged. 'Well, who would actually have bothered? Only the victims – everybody else was enjoying it too much. Besides, they wouldn't waste good drinking and bonking time in the pursuit of idle curiosity. And it was too late for the victims anyway.'

'So?'

'So get that lasagne down your neck. We've got an appointment with a photocopier.'

*   *   *

'I told you you're crazy,' Sophie muttered as she stumbled over another small shrub. The soft Yorkshire rain was inching down the inside of her jacket collar and she'd already stripped a layer of skin off her knuckles. She was closer than she'd ever been to falling out with Lindsay.

'There's got to be a way in,' Lindsay repeated, oblivious to Sophie's hostility, thrusting her way through the undergrowth that covered the steep slope behind the hexagonal building.

'Why? The place is all locked up. Everyone with any sense has gone home. The entire building is in darkness. It's ten o'clock at night. The editor of **Conference Chronicle** is almost certainly getting legless in a bar somewhere. Oh shit!' Sophie cannoned into Lindsay's back as she stumbled on the slope.

'There!' Lindsay exclaimed triumphantly. 'An open window.' She pointed at a small frosted-glass window that was cracked open an inch.

'Oh whoopee,' Sophie groaned. 'It's too high,' she added, giving the window a second look.

'Not if I climb on your shoulders,' Lindsay enthused. 'Come on, over here.'

'You shouldn't go in by yourself,' Sophie protested uselessly as Lindsay dragged Sophie over to the wall and started to scramble up her body, depositing sticky yellow mud on her clothes as she went.

Lindsay prised the window open and gripped the sill. 'Why the hell not?' she gasped as she pulled herself up, nearly kicking Sophie in the head as she struggled for leverage. 'We're only talking one maverick journo here, not the Boston Strangler.'

As Lindsay hauled her upper body over the sill, Sophie recovered her breath and said, 'Not necessarily. There is one other way 𝕮𝖔𝖓𝖋𝖊𝖗𝖊𝖓𝖈𝖊 𝕮𝖍𝖗𝖔𝖓𝖎𝖈𝖑𝖊 could have known that Laura was in the right place at the right time to have been spotted by you and translated into prime suspect for Union Jack's murder.' Lindsay's legs suddenly stopped thrashing. 'That's right, sweetheart. Whoever writes 𝕮𝖔𝖓𝖋𝖊𝖗𝖊𝖓𝖈𝖊 𝕮𝖍𝖗𝖔𝖓𝖎𝖈𝖑𝖊 might just be Union Jack's real killer.'

Lindsay's voice, muffled by her position, floated back to Sophie. 'We just passed a fire exit. About twenty feet back. I'll open it from the inside, okay?' She gave a final heave and pulled herself over the sill. There was an ominous crash, followed by, 'Don't worry, I'm all right, I just knocked some chairs over.'

Lindsay groped round in the dark till she found a door and emerged into the gloom of a corridor dimly lit by emergency lighting. Cautiously, she headed in the direction of the fire door she'd spotted from the outside. Praying it wasn't alarmed, she pushed down on the bar and felt the door give. Sophie grabbed the edge and hauled it towards her, slipped inside then grabbed Lindsay in a tight hug. 'I didn't mean to scare you,' she said.

'I know, I know, you just didn't want to miss the fun,' Lindsay mock-grumbled.

'I just like to keep you on your toes. What's the plan of action?'

Lindsay shrugged. 'I guess we just wander round till we find our rogue photocopier.'

Sophie ran a hand through Lindsay's tousled hair. 'That's what I love about you, Gordon,' she said fondly. 'Always first on the block with a clear strategy.'

They moved down the silent corridors, trying to keep quiet. On the ground floor, the conference hall occupied the central area of the building, surrounded by a corridor. The opposite side of the corridor was lined with different sized offices, like a motley ring of covered wagons. It was easy to eliminate them simply by walking the corridors; there were no strips of light showing under doors, no telltale humming and paper-shunting of photocopiers to be heard. It took less than fifteen minutes for Sophie and Lindsay to be certain that wherever **Conference Chronicle** was being produced, it wasn't on the ground floor.

At the head of one of the flights of stairs to the basement floor, Sophie paused. 'Sure this is wise?' she asked. 'Maybe there was a silent alarm on that door. We could be living on borrowed time.'

'That's a chance I'm prepared to take,' Lindsay said. 'I've come this far, I'm not bottling out now.'

The implication that her bottle had gone, clearly meant to sting Sophie into action, merely amused her. But the thought of Lindsay charging headlong and alone into a potentially explosive situation did persuade her to stick by her lover's side as she plunged down the stairs. 'Into the valley of wossname,' she muttered under her breath as she followed.

The basement was home to medium-sized committee rooms and more small offices. As they turned the first corner at the foot of the stairs, both women stopped dead in their tracks. A slender shaft of light spilled on to the floor at their feet. And they could both hear the fast shuffle and hum of a state-of-the-art photocopier.

17

'And don't forget. Although conference is about serious business, there's no reason why you can't have fun.'

from *'Advice for New Delegates'*,
a Standing Orders Sub-Committee booklet.

Lindsay was poised to indulge her taste for drama by flinging the door wide and leaping through it like the SAS when Sophie calmly gripped the handle and silently opened the door a crack. She peered through, then moved to one side to let an impatient Lindsay see beyond her. For a seemingly endless thirty seconds, Lindsay just stood and stared. Then she pushed the door open and stood silhouetted in the gap. 'I don't believe I'm seeing this,' she said wonderingly.

The small office looked like a miniature business centre. It contained a few desks, one with a PC, another with an Amstrad PCW, a third with an electronic typewriter, all firmly chained to the floor. A fax machine sat on a small side table, and against the far wall stood a photocopier, which was spitting out sheets of paper at an impressive speed. Standing by the photocopier, transfixed with shock, was a tall black woman with an immaculate Grace Jones flattop.

'I just don't believe it,' Lindsay repeated, moving across the room like a sleep-walker. She picked up one of the sheets from the photocopier and saw the familiar masthead of **Conference Chronicle**. Pauline was still motionless, her brown eyes wide with shock and fear. She licked her lips, a tiny movement magnified out of all proportion by her frozen stillness.

Lindsay screwed the sheet into a ball and stepped another few paces forward till she was only inches away from Pauline. 'Are you satisfied? Now Tom Jack's dead and Laura's in jail, are you satisfied? Does that justify all the lies?' she ranted.

Sophie moved closer, partly because she was baffled by the line Lindsay was taking, partly to prevent things getting out of hand. She picked up a copy of **Conference Chronicle** and glanced down at a strangely anodyne story about Laura's arrest. Her movement more than Lindsay's bitter words seemed to shake Pauline out of her rigid immobility. 'What do you know about it?' she snapped scornfully. 'They got what they deserved.'

'And me? Did I get what I deserved too? I thought we were friends, for fuck's sake. Why the hell did you print all those lies about me? You of all people!' Lindsay said angrily.

Pauline shrugged her straight shoulders. Her face was as expressionless as an Easter Island statue. 'I had to say something. With your track record, you were the best bet. Then Laura.'

Lindsay shook her head, unable at first to make sense of what she was hearing. Then she saw a faint glimmer of light. In a hard, clipped voice that Sophie had never heard before, she said 'This is complete crap.' She tossed the crumpled ball of **Conference Chronicle** straight at Pauline's face. Pauline scarcely blinked as it bounced off her left cheek. 'You know it is. Don't you think it's time for the truth?' she challenged. 'Haven't you had enough of the lies? Come on, Pauline, you've proved you can get your audience hooked with the fairy-tales. What about giving them the truth? What really happened? Because, damn it, if you don't tell them, I'm going to.'

Pauline shook her head, like a boxer trying to clear his vision. But Lindsay continued relentlessly. 'You think because you knew enough to peddle the lies that you're the only one who knows the truth? That's bullshit. But if you don't start to tell the truth now, then you're going to be stuck forever with somebody else's version, just like Laura is right now. Come on Pauline,' she goaded her. 'What are you so fucking scared of? After all, we're friends, aren't we?' She gripped Pauline by the arm, and shook her angrily.

Pauline pulled free. 'You've got no idea, have you?' she said bitterly, turning away.

'Let's cut the crap and get right to the heart of this. Let's talk about the night Union Jack died. Let's talk about how you knew Laura Craig was there at the same time as me. The truth, Pauline! I want the truth!' Lindsay yelled.

Suddenly Pauline's legs seemed to fold under her. She stumbled, but Sophie caught her and steered her into a chair. Pauline's body seemed to collapse into itself, her wide shoulders stooped and hunched, her chin tucked into her chest, her arms tightly folded round her. Almost at once, two fat tears splashed on to the desk in front of her. Then her body began to shudder convulsively. Lindsay mimed a shrug of uncertainty at Sophie, who waved her back before crouching down beside Pauline and placing a hand on her knee.

'It's going to be okay, Pauline,' she said gently.

Pauline shook her head, and her body, held rigid, shook with her. 'N-n-no it's n-n-not,' she stuttered through chattering teeth. Her body began to sway from side to side.

Sophie looked up at Lindsay. 'A hot drink?' she asked softly.

'I think there's a machine upstairs,' Lindsay said, heading straight for the door. By the time she returned with two cardboard cups of what was alleged to be drinking chocolate, Pauline was clinging to Sophie and weeping quietly. Lindsay handed one of the drinks to Sophie, who shifted Pauline's head and held the cup to her lips. She drank greedily, then found the strength to take the cup from Sophie and finish it on her own. She sniffed, then rubbed her eyes with the backs of her hands.

Pauline looked up at Lindsay, her eyes both wary and beseeching. 'I'm sorry,' she said at last. Lindsay said nothing, merely handing her the second hot chocolate. Pauline drank half of it, then shook her head wonderingly. 'I don't know where to begin.'

'Try the early hours of Wednesday morning,' Lindsay said, a hard edge still noticeable in her voice.

'You really think that's where the story begins?' Pauline asked, anger and contempt in her voice.

'So begin at the beginning,' Lindsay said.

'Why should I?'

'Because if you don't, I'm going to produce a special edition of **Conference Chronicle** telling the whole world how you killed Union Jack to get back at him for his plans to make you and your colleagues redundant,' Lindsay answered coldly.

'For God's sake, Lindsay!' Sophie protested. 'The pair of you are behaving like five year olds. Will you both remember you're supposed to be friends!'

'Friends?' Lindsay scoffed. 'The things she printed about me my enemies would have been hard pressed to come out with.'

'I told you, I had to say something,' Pauline said. 'You think I wanted to slag you off? You think I don't feel guilty about it? Look, do you want to hear this or not?'

Lindsay shrugged. 'You've proved how good you are at fiction with **Conference Chronicle**. Let's see how you get out of murdering Union Jack. Don't tell me, let me guess – it was an accident.'

Pauline drew herself erect, finding some reserves of inner strength to combat Lindsay. 'You're damn right it was an accident. Now, are you going to listen, or are you just going to interrupt with smartass remarks every other sentence?'

Lindsay held her hands up. 'Okay. I'll listen. But I reserve the right to disbelieve every word.'

'Feel free. Just before he was elected general secretary of the JU, Tom Jack sexually harassed me,' Pauline said in a curiously empty voice. 'Not once, but a few times. A couple of times it was just verbal, but on two occasions, it got physical. The second time, if another member of staff hadn't come in, I think it might have got out of hand. Anyway, after that second occasion, I told him that if he ever laid a finger on me again or made a sexual innuendo in my hearing, I would take out a formal complaint against him. He couldn't afford the risk of that, so he backed off. It ended the hassle, but it left me feeling like shit. Every time I saw him, I got the taste of bile in my mouth. That's how I started with this stuff.'

She rummaged in the pocket of her jacket and pulled out a packet of chewing gum. She unwrapped a piece and slipped it into her mouth. 'When the redundancies were announced, it brought all the anger back to me. It was like I'd been turned into an object all over again, something him and his cronies could throw on the scrap-heap. I felt like I'd got nothing left to lose, so I decided to get my own back on the lot of them. One day, a couple of weeks before conference, I was photocopying a whole pile of amendments to motions and I came up with the idea of **Conference Chronicle**. I thought at least I could make Union Jack and his sleazy sidekicks look like the bunch of wankers they really are.'

'You certainly succeeded,' Lindsay said drily. 'Pity you had to take me with them.'

Pauline pulled a face. 'It was just bad luck that it was your room it happened in.'

'So what did happen?'

'Tuesday was my birthday. A bunch of us from head office and a few of the Equality Committee people got together and went out for dinner, then on to a club in Sheffield. I was going to ask you, but you were going to the Scots/Irish night. Afterwards, we went back to Mandy Martin's room in Maclintock Tower for a drink. When I left and got into the lift, it must have gone up instead of down, but I was a bit drunk, so I didn't pay attention. When the lift stopped, I stepped out, and that's when I realised I wasn't where I should have been. Before I could do anything about it, the doors closed and the lift went down without me. I pressed the button, but before it came back, that slimeball Tom Jack came lurching round the corner. I was wearing a red sequinned off-the-shoulder cocktail dress, so I suppose when the *News of the World* get hold of the tale, it'll all be my fault!' Pauline gave a bitter laugh.

'Tell me about it,' Sophie said with feeling. 'Surgeons get so used to thinking about people as pieces of meat, they forget women have the right to say no.'

'Anyway, he leered at me, then jumped me. I know I look pretty big and strong, but just because I work out doesn't mean I know how to fight. And like I said, I was a bit pissed. He started smacking me about the head, giving me all the stuff about how I was just a black slag, a whore . . .' She tailed off and sighed deeply.

'I'm sure we can fill in the blanks,' Sophie said reassuringly.

'Don't be so sure of that,' Pauline snapped back. 'Believe me, being working class and black gives you access to a whole new range of insults. Shit, just remembering it makes me boil up inside.' It took a visible effort for her to regain a grip on herself, but she managed it.

'He grabbed me by my hair, and dragged me away from the lift. Do you know, I didn't even think about screaming? Isn't that crazy?'

'It happens more often that you'd think,'

Sophie said. 'I've had patients who were raped who have said exactly the same thing.'

'He tried the first couple of doors, but they were locked. Then a door opened and he dragged me into the room. All the time, he was kicking at me, slapping me with his free hand and pouring out all this foul abuse. It was like hate was flowing out of him all over me.' Pauline's hands clenched and the muscles in her jaw bunched tightly at the memory.

'He threw me on the bed and then he was on top of me, forcing my dress up, ripping my knickers. I managed to get a grip of myself and I screamed that I'd tell everyone what he'd done to me. Can you believe it, he just laughed and said no one would believe a black whore who'd just been made redundant. I guess I just snapped then and I used the muscles I spent all that fucking time building up. I pushed him off me and he staggered back. I jumped off the bed and followed him, pushing him and telling him what I thought of him. I wasn't shouting or anything, just letting him have it.

'He was staggering away from me, and he tripped over the chair and crashed into the window. It just gave way behind him, and he tipped right out.' Pauline paused, her eyes on the middle distance, seeing yet again that slo-mo topple that had sent Union Jack into oblivion.

Lindsay reached out for Pauline's hand. Her friend gripped it tightly and took a deep, shuddering breath that seemed to go on forever. 'I'm so sorry,' Lindsay said uselessly. 'I had no idea.'

'It was an accident,' Pauline said bleakly. 'It was an accident. I keep telling myself it was an accident. But it won't go away.'

For a long time, the three women were silent, each reflecting on the chain of circumstance that had brought them all to this point of decision. Typically, it was Lindsay who broke the silence. 'So, having started **Conference Chronicle** for revenge, you continued it for self-defence?'

'That's right. I never really cast any serious suspicion at you, you know. I wouldn't have stood by and let them arrest you. But Laura was different. After the way she betrayed all of us over the years, she deserved all she got.'

'Not to mention what she did to Ian. Incidentally, how did you find out about Laura being a Special Branch plant?' Lindsay asked.

Pauline giggled. 'You won't believe me.'

'Try me.'

'You know my little boy Sam? Well, about a year ago, I had some time owing, so I took him for some days out in London. We went to the zoo. And there, by the penguin pool, like some crap spy movie, was Laura with a man I vaguely recognised. At first, I couldn't think where I'd seen him. Then I remembered. He used to drink occasionally in a pub that I go to once a month or so with my bro and my sister-in-law in Lewisham. So the next time I saw them, I asked them about this bloke, and my bro Arthur laughs and says this guy lives near the pub, but he's Special Branch, everybody knows that. So I found out his name and I asked one of my tame paranoid leftie journos if he could find out what the guy did, and it came back that he specialises in labour subversion. It didn't take much to work out what he was doing with Laura.'

'So it must have been a godsend to you when you spotted Laura just after Tom Jack fell through the window. By the way, when did you see her? And where, exactly?' Lindsay asked.

'I didn't,' Pauline said. 'The stuff that was in **Conference Chronicle** was pure *Fantasy Island*. I just put two and two together when you said you'd been to Blackpool. I thought it could have been something to do with Ian Ross' death, and the only person who could have possibly wanted Ian dead was Laura. So I figured you had something tying Laura to the crime scene, or else a bloody strong motive. So I write the story about you and her to get the cops interested in pursuing her. And then it turned out that you saw her there after all, which was amazing, since I thought you'd seen me.'

'What? Surely you were long gone by then?'

'No. I had to check your room to see if there were any obvious traces of me. I wiped down everything I'd touched, then I legged it. The lift door was opening just as I turned the corner of the corridor.'

Lindsay looked confused. But it was Sophie who asked the key question. 'Can you remember what perfume you were wearing?' she asked.

It was Pauline's turn to look puzzled. 'Sure. The women in membership records clubbed together to buy it for my birthday. Real class. Le Must de Cartier. Marion got it in the duty free at Paris Airport,' she said proudly.

Lindsay looked horrified. Then the irony hit her. She threw her head back and roared with laughter.

EPILOGUE

The cabin steward bent towards Lindsay and said, 'Would you like a drink, madam?'

Lindsay looked questioningly at Sophie. 'Champagne?'

Sophie grinned. 'Oh, I think so.'

'Make it a bottle, please. Oh, and have you got any freshly squeezed orange juice?'

The steward smiled. 'I'll check, madam.' Out of the corner of her eye, she caught sight of Sophie doubling up with silent laughter. She looked slightly bemused as she walked away.

'California, here I come,' Sophie snorted.

'Just because I like some things about the place doesn't make me a California girl,' Lindsay said with a scowl.

'Something to celebrate, ladies?' the returning steward asked, making conversation as she placed a half bottle in front of each of them. 'And your juice,' she added, handing Lindsay a small pitcher.

Lindsay grinned. 'Thanks,' she said. 'Thank

305

God we're flying back with an American airline.' The steward moved away, leaving them to fill their glasses. Lindsay tipped a little orange juice into each glass and made a silent toast.

'I feel like we have something to celebrate,' Sophie said. 'We made a good decision in Sheffield.'

Lindsay sipped her champagne thoughtfully. 'My heart agrees with you, totally. But part of me feels like maybe I'm making too much of a habit of letting people walk away from murder.'

'But you don't walk away from murder,' Sophie objected. 'If indeed what happened to Union Jack *was* murder. That's the whole point. There won't be a day when Pauline doesn't remember him going through that window, and her responsibility for it.'

Lindsay nodded. 'I know all that. And I keep telling myself that justice wouldn't be served by taking her away from her kid and locking her up in Holloway. Like you said, her punishment's in her head. And it *was* an accident, probably. I just get this little nag at the back of my conscience, that's all. And I start to worry a little about my judgement too.'

'What do you mean?'

Lindsay gave an embarrassed cough. 'I know rather too many women who kill, don't you think? It's getting a bit beyond a joke.'

Sophie could think of nothing reassuring to say to that, so she took a step backwards in conversation. 'Well, if your conscience is bothering you, console yourself with the thought that at least one of them is going to jail for a long time, even if it's for a murder she didn't commit.'

Lindsay gave a wicked grin. 'Ironic, isn't it? We couldn't find enough evidence to nail her for the murder she *did*.'

'By the way, you owe me a bottle of Caol Ila.'

'You what?' Lindsay protested.

'You bet me a bottle of Islay malt of my choice that Laura was directly involved in Tom Jack's death. And she wasn't.' Sophie smirked irritatingly.

'But thanks to my mistaking Pauline for Laura, they've got more than enough evidence to put her away for Tom Jack's murder, even if she didn't do it. So she *has* become directly involved. So you owe me,' Lindsay said triumphantly.

'Tell you what. We'll write to Laura in prison and ask her to adjudicate.'

'I wish I could believe Laura's going to end up in prison,' Lindsay sighed.

'What do you mean?'

Lindsay downed the rest of her glass and burped discreetly. 'Come on, Soph. Do you really think that's ever going to come to trial?'

'Why won't it?' Sophie demanded. 'They've arrested her, charged her, and with your evidence, they've got enough to convict her at a trial. Bang to rights, I'd have thought. And not just for the murder. They've also got her for fiddling the union's expenses, embezzling the strike pay and fraudulently manipulating the pension fund. All to keep her in blackmail cash and designer clothes. None of which is calculated to endear her to a jury.'

'I'm not disputing any of that. Nor do I think it's anything other than disgusting. But I'm not holding my breath waiting for a trip back to the UK at the taxpayers' expense.'

'But why not?' Sophie persisted.

'A Special Branch undercover operative in the witness box? You'll be telling me Britain's a democracy next!'

Sophie smiled wryly. Lindsay adjusted her seat and stretched out her legs. 'Well, at least we got everything neatly tied up.' She grinned. 'I'd have hated never knowing who the phantom Chronicler was. You know how I hate loose ends.'

'Hmmm.'

Lindsay jerked upright. She looked sharply at Sophie. 'What do you mean, "hmmm"?'

'Nothing.'

'What d'you mean, nothing?' Lindsay demanded frantically.

'Well . . .' Sophie drawled. 'I was just wondering . . .'

'Wondering what?' Through clenched teeth.

'At the ceilidh, Union Jack arranged a meeting with you for the following morning.'

'That's right,' Lindsay said impatiently. 'So?'

'So what did he want to talk to you about?'

Lindsay looked thunderstruck. Her mouth fell open and her eyes widened in panic. 'I've no idea,' she gasped.

'I just wondered,' Sophie said, the picture of innocence. 'Now I suppose we'll never know.'

Lindsay stared at Sophie, frustration incarnate. Then she saw the hint of the smile Sophie was trying to suppress, and she couldn't keep a rueful smile from her own lips. She shook her head. 'I may have mentioned this before, Sophie, but sometimes you really piss me off.'

Hostage to Murder

V.L. McDermid

Spraining an ankle is rarely a stroke of luck, but for Lindsay Gordon, jobless in Glasgow, the injury is her introduction to young freelance journalist Rory McLaren and the opening of a new chapter in her life. Rory's invitation to team up with her is irresistible. From there it is just a short step to political corruption and other juicy stories – all welcome distractions from Lindsay's problems at home. But when a local car-dealer's stepson is kidnapped, Lindsay and Rory trade journalism for detection. The trail leads them to St Petersburg and a dangerous snatch-back operation that will test Lindsay to her absolute limits.

'A well-pitched and topical mystery'   *Sunday Times*

'McDermid's snappy, often comic, prose keeps the story humming'   *Publishers Weekly*

ISBN: 0-00-717349-0

Final Edition

V.L. McDermid

When Alison Maxwell, a well-known Glaswegian journalist with an irresistible sexual attraction to both sexes, is found murdered the police look no further than the owner of the scarf used to strangle her. Lindsay Gordon, however, has other ideas. Maxwell was a serial seductress who kept a secret record of her encounters – including one with Lindsay herself. Recalling the threats that followed the end of the relationship, Lindsay knows all too well the feelings of rage, fear and passion that Alison Maxwell could invoke.

Soon Lindsay is embroiled in an investigation involving blackmail, stolen government documents and the vested interests of a group of people determined to keep her from finding the truth.

'Witty and corrosively unsentimental'   *She*

'A treat . . . gripping until the very last page'   *Pink Paper*

ISBN: 0-00-719176-6